Evolving Elizah: Initiatum

C.J. Hall

DEDICATION

For April—

Because truth is stranger than fiction, and reality harder than make believe, let's meet where the dragons fly and warriors cry, where the goddesses await to welcome us to the party. Adventure first, and then tea. Thank you for believing in me.

PROLOGUE

"Push me, Jackson, push me!" the little girl squeals as she wiggles on the swing that hangs from the sturdy branch of the old, dying cottonwood tree.

Her older brother studies her with a somber expression that will never do justice to how much he adores her.

"Okay, Lizzie," he agrees. "I'll push you this time, but you're getting too big for this. You'll be four years old soon, and you need to learn how to swing yourself."

The girl considers this, delicate brow furrowing over blue eyes as her wispy blond hair catches a hint of a breeze around her face. She bats it away as a strand tickles the corner of her mouth.

"But I like it when you push me," she says.

"You know what I like?" he asks, casting her a clever smile that instantly makes her giggle. She knows he will have something very smart to say—he always does when he smiles like that. Maybe when she's 10, like he is, she will have clever things to say too.

"What?" she asks, pressing a balled fist to her mouth to suppress her giggle. She puts both hands back on the rope as he approaches and begins to push her from behind.

"I like knowing that my little sister is so smart and strong that she can learn how to swing herself even though she isn't even four yet! Now, stretch your legs out and lean back when you're going up."

Lizzie does what her older brother tells her. She trusts him implicitly. She swings higher and higher on the wooden bench, feeling a rush of excitement as she realizes she's doing it on her own.

"Jackson!" she cries in glee. "I can see the creek!"

"I'm so proud of you, Lizzie," he calls, the sound of his voice wobbling as she swings through space.

"And look, there's the mountains!" The swing is rising high above the ground, to its highest point, as she suddenly thrusts one hand forward, pointing off into the distance. There is no time for Jackson to warn her as the momentum of the swing, which has reached the top of its arc and is now descending to the earth, unbalances her and she flies out, limbs flailing. She lands on the ground with a thump, rolling through dead remnants of grass.

Jackson runs to her as he hears a woof, and sees her mouth open in a perfect circle, soundless. Her face turns red. He scoops her up and rubs her back.

"Breathe, Lizzie, breathe," he whispers in her ear. Air rushes into her lungs, carrying a frightened cry when it comes back out.

"Don't cry," he says fiercely in her ear. "You have to be stronger than that."

He examines the bloody scrapes on her arms and legs. When her knees stop shaking and she can stand on her own feet, he walks with her down to the creek. The water is ashy, like everything else in their world, but it makes a nice gurgling sound and is as clean as any other water they have. It's clean enough to wash the blood away, which seems to boost her spirits.

"All better, right?" Jackson waits expectantly for a response.

"It still hurts," she whimpers, and he gives her a stern look. "Yes," she decides reluctantly, "it's all better."

They walk through the ashy dead grass, away from the stream, and Lizzie looks at the swing dubiously as they approach.

"Do you want to try again?" he asks.

She knows there is only one answer. She offers a reluctant nod and climbs back onto the wooden seat. Starting to swing, she pumps her legs and holds tightly to the rope with both hands.

"Look at you!" Her brother's approving voice fills her with pride. Confidence bolstered, she goes a little higher. Eventually the fear in her belly is overtaken by exhilaration, although she still clutches the scratchy rope fiercely in each hand.

"Let's go back now," Jackson says. "It's starting to get dark."

Did it ever get light? her child-mind wonders. She thinks she can remember days from before, when the sun was bright enough to beat down hot on her skin and make shadows under the cottonwood tree. She doesn't think she imagined that. But the days now are ashy and clouded, and the boundary that separates light from dark is thin.

"Is Dad coming home today?" Lizzy asks as she scuffs her feet into the ground to stop the swing.

"I doubt it." Jackson looks troubled.

"He's been gone so long. When will he come back?"

"I don't know, Lizzie."

"Will he ever come back?"

"It doesn't matter," Jackson says, his tone decisive. "We can take care of ourselves."

Lizzie considers this behind her furrowed brow. "But what about Mom?" she asks. "Who will take care of Mom if he doesn't come back?"

Jackson seems to think about this.

"She has us."

Lizzie takes his hand, satisfied with his answer. They amble back toward their small farmhouse, pausing for a moment to admire the rose bush still growing in front of the living room window. Nearly everything else has died, including the garden they need to feed themselves, but somehow their mother continues to coax life out of this particular thorny bush, this bush that feeds their eyes but not their bellies.

"What else can you teach me, Jackson?" the little girl asks, scrutinizing a small green bud that offers the promise of a brilliant pink flower.

"I can teach you how to read," he replies.

"But Mom is already teaching me that," she says, disappointed.

"I can teach you faster," he whispers.

"Oh," she says, as a knowing look spreads across her face. It's true—she learns things faster when Jackson teaches her.

"You want to learn as fast as you can," he assures her. "Reading will take you to whole different worlds."

"Different worlds?" She is apprehensive. "Do I want to go to different worlds?"

"Oh yes," Jackson assures her. "You want to see and know and explore so much more than we have here."

"Will you go with me?" She is afraid. "I don't want to go by myself."

Jackson studies her for a moment. "I'll always go where you are, Lizzie. We're family, and we take care of each other."

"Promise?" she asks, but she doesn't wait for him to answer. She already knows he will keep his word, that he will do anything for her. Instead, she turns away from the rose bush toward the kitchen door to see if any dinner awaits. Jackson follows, closing the door behind them, shutting out the world for the rest of the night.

CHAPTER 1

THE COUNCIL

***

AUGUST 14, 2059 – THURSDAY

Inside the Green Grow 3, a young woman stands in furry slippers, watching the earth ascend through a large round window that separates her from the vast emptiness of space. Her mother named her Elizah Faye Goeff, although no one here knows her full name. Well, almost no one. She goes by Liz. Liz stands silent and still, her thoughts her own. After a few minutes, with the earth in full view, she turns away and pads toward the dining hall.

From the outside, she looks pretty much like everyone else, which is how she likes it. The slippers set her apart, ragged furry things she found somewhere on the surface years ago. She forgot to take them off when she left her quarters, to exchange them for the light boots everyone else was wearing. She was too consumed with thoughts about today's mission, her mind running through endless scenarios and contingencies. Nothing can go wrong today, not after her last mission—six days ago—went completely off the rails.

Foul mother of hell, how does the smallest package I've ever been asked to retrieve turn into such a cluster? Liz wonders, eye twitching as she thinks about it for the millionth time. She was tasked to retrieve antimatter, the most important component of the new propulsion drive they are building for the ship. The antimatter itself is so small it could fit in the palm of her hand. Add some atomic batteries to keep it stable, plus impact-resistant casing to keep it safe, and the whole thing ends up being the size of a small suitcase.

She found the antimatter and brought it back to the ship. But two people died in the process, people she'd known for years. Sam Wyndham died when Ellen Ryan betrayed them; Ellen died by Liz's hands.

Liz ambles into the cafeteria, heart aching as she thinks about Sam. They worked together for years. They shared meals and jokes with each other. She remembers his short, stocky build and his easy, lopsided smile. They trusted each other with their lives, a gamble Sam lost. Now he was dead, the remains of his body littering the floor of a warehouse way too far from home.

Sam's brother Albert didn't take the news well. Liz insisted on telling him herself, as soon as she got back to the ship. She'd barely washed the blood off her body and changed her blood-soaked clothes before she was knocking at Albert's quarters, breaking the news that his brother had died on what Albert thought was a routine training mission. She can still see the incomprehension on his face, how he sat down hard on his bunk as if his legs had given out. She can still hear his keening, as he wailed the unanswerable question between sobs—*Why?*

She wasn't allowed to tell him why, because the details of the mission were secret. She couldn't tell him that Ellen Ryan, the third person on the three-man team, betrayed them. Liz shudders in disgust thinking about it now— disgust at Ellen for betraying them, but also at herself for not seeing that Ellen had switched sides. *When did I lose her?* Liz wonders. *Or was it always a lie?*

Why would someone like Ellen possibly join the New Generation? Sure, it might have made sense in the beginning, when the New Generation started. Plenty of people supported them. The world was in crisis, and the Green Grow Corporation had just announced an ambitious plan to feed the hungry planet with food grown on space farms. It seemed grandiose and outlandish. And what was more, no one really knew how the first space farm, the Green Grow 1, began operating so quickly. Not even the Green Grow Corporation could have pulled something like that off overnight.

Stakes were high. People were dying everywhere. The wealthiest of Americans fled to places like India and China, where life was rustic but safe. But, the price of admission was steep—only the richest of the rich could afford to go. The rich who remained tried to ingratiate themselves with Green Grow, or the government, at the expense of everyone else.

The New Generation formed to make sure that food and medicine from the space farms was distributed equitably, not just to the wealthy who remained living in posh underground bunkers. It was a sensible cause then, back when Liz's older brother Jackson left home to join. Liz might've even joined herself if she'd been older, and if there had been anyone else to take care of her mom.

But, it didn't take long for the sanity to unravel. Every disenfranchised person with a grudge and a hot temper began to affiliate themselves with the New Generation. Activism became terrorism, and people like Jackson, good people who wanted to save lives, disappeared.

He's dead, she tells herself for the millionth time, thinking about her brother, who has been missing since he left home all those years ago. *It's the only explanation. Otherwise, he would have come back for me, just like he promised when he left.*

The thought of him being dead is a bittersweet blade to Liz's heart, but as far as she's concerned, he's better off dead than knowing what the New Generation has become. Instead of protecting the multitudes they formed to serve, New Generation hordes began hijacking food supplies and raiding depots, killing Green Grow employees and anyone else who happened to be in the vicinity. Raiding parties washed over towns and camps, burning everything and brutalizing everyone they encountered. The New Generation terror laid to waste any chance of success the Green Grow project might have had.

Ellen told Liz plenty of bitter, angry stories about the New Generation. They'd pillaged and burned her town. They'd killed her grandparents and hung their dead bodies from a tree. Ellen herself had nearly starved when they cut off all the transports bringing food from the depot. Liz remembers listening to Ellen's stories, filled with bitterness and tears, as they both lay awake at night, unable to sleep in the dorm-style room they shared with two other women— Willow Brown and Ashley Smith. Willow, who slept on a bottom bunk across from Liz, seemed untroubled, snoring slightly until she would inevitably wake up hungry in the middle of the night. Ashley, who slept above Willow, was quiet by day, but at night she tossed and turned and cried out words that Liz couldn't decipher but was sure she understood. Of her three roommates, Ellen was her kindred spirit. Liz was sure she could sense when Ellen was lying there awake, staring into the darkness, unsure if she wanted sleep to come. It was Ellen who kept her company on many dark nights, sharing whispers and low murmurs about their lives. Ellen talked mostly about the family she'd lost, and Liz mostly about the brother she couldn't find.

Could she really have made all that up? Liz wonders, still baffled. *No, there were too many stories, told too many times. She hated them, almost as much as I do.* Liz thought Ellen was incorruptible. That was why she chose her for the three-man team to get the antimatter from Minneapolis. She's gone over it countless times in her head, looking for any signs she might have missed. But she always ends up back in the same place, fighting Ellen for her life.

It was a hard fight, and there were moments when Liz wasn't sure she'd be the one walking away alive. Ellen was bigger and stronger than Liz, and equally fierce. But Liz was stealthy, and masterful with her knife. In the end, Liz's skill won out. She killed the traitor—her friend—but not before Sam was dead.

She forces herself back to the present, back to the neatly organized breakfast buffet, which she navigates mindlessly before shuffling to an empty table. There, she sits heavily in the chair. Her eyes take mechanical stock of her surroundings, smoothly scanning the room until they lurch to a stop on a head of shiny black hair, flawlessly tied into a knot. Liz's heart skips a beat. *Is it Willow?* she wonders, only exhaling after the head turns and Liz can see that, in fact, it's not her former roommate. They aren't close, she and Willow. They never were, but nonetheless, since Ashley left the Green Grow 3 to find her family on the surface and Ellen is now dead, Willow is the only person left from that small bunk room two years ago.

Liz can't face her. Not yet, and maybe not ever. Not after what happened to Ellen. She looks back at her small bowl of oatmeal, a lonely island in the vast sea of the tray.

It's in the past, she thinks, as two familiar hands splay on the table in front of her tray. She knows those long fingers, those square nail beds with short-trimmed nails. She knows that x-shaped scar between the thumb and first finger of his left hand.

"Z."

One corner of her mouth turns up. Even her worst moods seem to lighten a little when he calls her that.

"Seth," she replies.

"You jake?" His head dips, blue eyes inquisitively seeking hers.

"Right as rain, Captain." She thrusts a large spoonful of oatmeal into her mouth. People are starving on the surface. She used to be one of those people, so she is not keen on wasting food.

"Good." Seth exhales deeply and slumps into the chair across from her. His face is rugged and handsome, framed by straight, sleek dark hair. "We have a Council meeting in thirty minutes. No doubt, there will be a lot of questions."

Liz groans, weary of the daily meetings that the Minneapolis mission has transformed into inquisitions.

"I need to change my shoes," she says. Seth glances at her feet, a corner of his mouth peeking up.

"I like those shoes," he says playfully.

"They're too small for you," she shoots back, meeting his smile.

"Perhaps," he says with a mock frown, "but couldn't we at least try?"

Liz grins, rising to return her tray.

"Haven't you heard that trying is conceding to failure before we even begin?" she whispers as she walks behind him. He clears his throat, a flush rising on his neck. They walk out of the cafeteria casually, leaving behind the chatter of the other crew still eating.

Liz's mind relaxes as she walks next to Seth. He's a full head taller than her, but it isn't his size that makes her feel safe in his presence. It's his energy. He stands straight and walks with purpose, radiating an electricity that booms like a broken sound barrier. It makes her feel small, but she doesn't mind. In fact, she likes it— she only needs to be as big as her enemies.

"Z," he says, brushing her forearm with his warm hand as she presses the button to call the lift, "everybody is on edge. Are you sure you're ready for this?"

"Ready for what, Seth? The Council meeting, or the mission?" She winks at him.

"Either? Both?" he replies, looking concerned.

"I'm jake." She smiles, but he doesn't look reassured. "I'll take it as it comes. What else can I do?"

The lift doors open, and four crew members exit. Liz presses the button for Level 2, and after Seth gives her an appraising glance, he presses the button for Level 1.

"See you there," she states simply as she exits to go to her quarters. The doors close behind her, leaving Seth to ride alone to the top of the ship—Level 1.

Liz appraises her modest quarters as she sheds the furry slippers, placing them neatly next to the bed. Hers aren't lavish like Level 1 quarters, but they are private, which is an upgrade from Level 3 where most of the crew bunk. She even has a private bathroom, which is about as lavish as she ever hoped for. She looks in the mirror, tying her wavy blond hair into a low knot. Beneath bright blue eyes, her nose is still sprinkled with freckles, although not as many as when she was little. Is this the face of the killer? *Yes,* she thinks as Sam and Ellen once again fill her mind. She quickly looks away.

She sits on the bed next to her folded pajamas and ties the laces on her boots, sparing one final glance to make sure everything is in order. She'll most likely change back into these pajamas tonight. But just in case anything unexpected happens, everything will be neat and tidy for whoever comes to clean out her few belongings.

***

Liz doesn't look back again as she walks out of her quarters, striding purposefully to the stairwell. The lift will take too long, so she bounds up the stairs to the captain's conference room, entering quietly to find a seat at the large round table.

Seth spares her a glance, but it reveals nothing. If she's lucky, she won't have to speak. Liz doesn't like talking at these meetings. She doesn't feel entirely welcome, and she is seriously outranked. Everyone else is a department head—except Seth, of course, who is the captain. Liz is simply a shuttle pilot, albeit the most proficient one who remains.

And then there's the age difference. The department heads are middle-aged and full of experience, with years and careers behind them. Liz isn't quite yet twenty-five, and while she knows the crew and the surface operations better than anyone else on the Council, the only accolade she has is surviving life on the surface and all her encounters with the New Generation.

She surveys the room. To her right sits Harry Goodworth, Head of Land Management and long-time mentor. *He looks tired,* she thinks, craving the broad smile that so often graces his craggy face. Of all the department heads, she knows Harry best. She met him the first day she arrived on the Green Grow 3.

To her left sits Jarrod Peck, Head of Engineering, and next to him, Mathilda Greenberg, Head of Astrophysics. They work together so closely that they almost seem like two halves of one person. If it has moving parts or emits any kind of signal or radiation, the two of them can conquer it. Both of them sit quietly. Jarrod's face is drawn, and Mathilda appears to be cowering in her chair. *Oh Mathilda,* Liz thinks ruefully. *If it were possible to evaporate into nothing, I would have done it at yesterday's meeting.*

The last Council member, sitting directly across from Liz, happens to be Seth's mom. The formidable Dr. Claire Harris is not only the ship's Chief Medical Officer but also the Head of Bioengineering. Liz has never known someone so brilliant. Just as easily as she can patch up scrapes and bruises, Claire can genetically enhance plants and animals, or even create new ones. Like Seth, she has dark, lustrous hair, but hers is paired with deep olive skin and chocolate eyes. Most days they sparkle, but today they are fire and fury.

"We need to be ferreting out the spies, not planning more ill-advised missions to the surface," she demands. "If the New Generation gains a foothold on this ship, they will kill all of us. We haven't come this far to be tortured and executed by those cretins. How badly do we actually need the hydrogen? And you, Seth! Why are you letting her go alone?"

Liz doesn't envy the tight rope Seth has to walk with his mother, and with the rest of the Council. Technically he is the captain, left in charge by the prior captain—Captain MacAbee—who left to attend a peace summit with the New Generation and never returned. But Seth is barely thirty, and while he is legitimately the captain, everyone in the room knows it was only intended to be a temporary appointment.

Seth is smart enough to realize people have doubts about his qualifications, and he knows those doubts could be his undoing. This is why he convened the department heads into the Council as soon as it became evident that Captain MacAbee was unlikely to return. His strategy seems to work—the department heads seem to be content with his leadership as long as they are included in decision-making.

It also helps that Seth is charming, and good at building consensus. But he has to strike a balance between charm and authority, and there are occasions—which seem to be growing in number—where he has to command respect, especially from his mother. It seems that now is just such an occasion.

"Mind your tone, Dr. Harris," he says in a low, even voice. Liz knows what's coming next—the same explanation he gives every time he is questioned about building the antimatter propulsion drive. "We're building this drive to get away from the New Generation. We don't know what capabilities they have, nor do we know their intentions. We could defend ourselves against invasion, but how do we know they didn't blow up the Green Grow 1 with a missile or laser strike just to make a point? We wouldn't even see that coming, much less be able to do anything about it. We can turn our full attention to cleaning house after we leave orbit. Regardless, we aren't here to talk about today's surface mission. We're here to figure out when and how Ellen Ryan turned against us."

Claire glares at him but says nothing. Seth continues.

"Jarrod. Mathilda. Let's go over the intel again. What do we know about Ellen Ryan? What did we miss?"

Mathilda replies. "To recap what we know, she was based out of the Atlanta depot. Since Captain MacAbee suspended the routine surface runs two years ago, she was approved to go on a total of fourteen non-routine runs. Nine of those were food runs to Atlanta before the depot closed. She co-piloted two food runs to Denver with Liz, and she was on three operations with Liz to retrieve supplies. We couldn't find evidence of any special communication devices in her quarters. It appears she simply reprogrammed her radio to an open New Generation channel when she got to Minneapolis. Based on Liz's report, we believe she was trying to notify local New Generation of the whereabouts of the shuttle, but it's not clear that she had any local contacts there."

"So either we're missing something big, or she's been a sleeper for two or more years," Seth observes. "Liz, take us through the day one more time."

Liz nods. "The antimatter was stored in a hidden Green Grow lab, underneath an abandoned railroad yard sixteen miles from the Minneapolis depot. Planned departure time was 1200 Greenwich Mean Time. I asked Sam and Ellen to report to the dock at 1000 for a day-long security drill. Both confirmed they were fit for the drill. We arrived at the Minneapolis depot just after nightfall, which is where I briefed them on the mission."

"A bit reckless, don't you think?" Claire spits. Liz doesn't intend to take the bait again. She's been down that road before, and she doesn't intend to give Claire another opportunity to systematically berate her like she's done at every Council meeting since Minneapolis. She glances over to Seth, who nods for her to continue.

"When darkness fell, we rode three personal transporters the sixteen miles to the railroad yard," Liz continues.

Claire interrupts again. "You seriously thought Segways were the best way to get there?"

Liz briefly considers pretending not to hear, but decides to respond.

"Yes, the Segways were the best option. They had range and speed, can be operated in the dark, were designed for off-road usage, and allowed us to preserve our strength for any unanticipated obstacles."

"Like killing each other?" Claire growls.

"Claire, enough!" Harry interjects loudly. "Liz, you've been over this several times. Skip to the relevant part, please."

Liz nods curtly, continuing the report.

"There were three levels of security at the lab. The first level was physical security—a locked door in the warehouse. We blew the lock, and Sam was responsible for standing watch. The second level required an electronic access card, which Jarrod provided. We gained entry, and Ellen was responsible for standing watch at that point. The vault in the lab required retinal and fingerprint biometrics, which I accessed using the glove and contact lens Jarrod provided. I retrieved the case.

"I couldn't raise Sam or Ellen on comms, so I hid the case in the lab and made my way to Ellen's station, which was abandoned. I found her in the warehouse, conversing with someone on her earpiece. I saw Sam lying nearby. Ellen had tuned her earpiece to an unknown frequency. I overheard her say, 'I'm going dark until the pilot is dead. Hold any attack. She can blow the shuttle remotely.'"

Liz pauses, remembering the other thing Ellen said. *It's Liz Goeff. You know who she is, right?* Liz doesn't know what response Ellen received, but the fact that Ellen felt the need to raise the question inspires a hint of a smile on Liz's lips. *I must have a reputation with the New Generation,* she thinks, feeling primal satisfaction at the idea of notoriety among her enemies. But as quickly as it comes, she brushes the thought away, masking her face with placid indifference as she continues.

"She became aware of my presence, and we fought. I killed her. By the time I reached Sam, he was dead. I had no way to transport the bodies, so I retrieved the case, returned to the shuttle, and took off. I saw no sign of New Generation at the depot."

"You didn't even think to make contact with us? To tell us what was happening, or ask for direction?" Claire demands, incredulous.

"No, Dr. Harris," Liz replies calmly. She doesn't usually refer to her as Dr. Harris. She usually calls her

Claire, but she doesn't want to seem disrespectful, even if her respect is diminishing. This isn't the first time Claire has grilled her like this, but it is getting wearisome. And Claire is getting more insistent, more hostile and accusatory. "Since we didn't know who might be listening, the Council agreed I would only communicate with the ship in an emergency."

"And in your mind, this didn't qualify as an emergency?" Claire is shouting now.

"No, Dr. Harris," Liz replies evenly. "The only emergency would be to request for you to detonate the shuttle remotely from the ship."

"Claire," Harry interjects sharply. "It's apparent to me that Ellen was a deep operative, a sleeper. We don't know how she was communicating with her New Generation handler, but all the evidence we have indicates that she simply tried to make the most of an unforeseen opportunity to help the New Generation hijack the shuttle. We need to focus on how Ellen was communicating with the New Generation from the ship, and we need to understand why she blew her cover on this mission instead of prior ones."

"No," Claire replies forcefully, "we need to focus on why Liz is going back to the surface today, alone, when there are so many unanswered questions about the Minneapolis mission. I don't doubt her loyalty, but clearly her judgment is impaired."

"What are you suggesting?" Seth demands, blue eyes flickering.

"She's dangerous, Seth!" Claire retorts, standing and leaning over the table. "She's a rogue operative with no respect for the chain of command. Plus, she's paranoid! What exactly are you hiding, Liz? What are you afraid we'll find?" Liz remains seated, appraising Claire coolly and knowing that any response will be a mistake.

Harry jumps to her defense, rising furiously from his seat.

"Are you finished, Claire?" They lock eyes. "Why are you so intent on blaming Liz? How about we focus on figuring out how many of the crew are spying for the New Generation, and how they're communicating with them right under our noses? If Liz wanted to betray us, we'd be dead four times over."

"I'm not blaming her." Claire sounds indignant. "But I fail to see how it's a good idea to send her to the surface again—alone—with so many unanswered questions. She has no respect for authority, nor is she a team player. She's completely unpredictable. A wild card."

Liz tries to stay calm but can't stop the surge of anger that forces her to her feet. "Yes, Dr. Harris. *Unpredictable* is a fair descriptor of any surface mission. Things don't always go as planned, which is why the guiding principles of these missions have been to trust no one, strike fast, and be gone before anyone knows we're there. Surface missions require flexibility. What you refer to as rogue paranoia has not only kept myself and others alive, it has allowed us to get all the supplies we need to stock the ship and build the antimatter drive to take us out of the killing range of the New Generation. Captain, may I be excused to execute this mission?"

"Don't condescend to me," Claire growls. "You are not excused!"

Liz turns to face her. "With all due respect, Dr. Harris, I don't report to you. I report to the captain. Ellen's betrayal is just as unsettling to me as it is to you. I thought we could trust her, and now she and Sam are both dead.

Clearly none of us know who is trustworthy, but we still need the hydrogen and the carbon fiber panels I'm going to retrieve today. Denver is my home depot. I know it like the back of my hand. Jarrod and Mathilda confirmed that it's secure and unoccupied. The details of this mission do not require a team."

"There's no need to be defensive," Harry cautions.

"Really, Harry?" Liz retorts, fury barely concealed. "Defending seems to be exactly what I require. Isn't that generally what people need when they are labeled rogue, dangerous, and incompetent? As you accuse me of these things, be reminded that I'm the only person here who has been to the surface in several years. I know the Denver depot. I know how to operate on the surface. I am experienced at evading the New Generation, and engaging with them when necessary. We each have our fields of expertise, and this is mine. Captain?" Liz met Seth's gaze, pleading with him. *Get me out of here now.*

"You're dismissed," Seth barks, waving to the door. "Today's mission is approved. Make it happen. Jarrod and Mathilda, set up comms from the bridge."

CHAPTER 2

THE FIFTY-TWO

***

Liz walks out of the conference room with her chin up and shoulders square. The moment she's out, she leans heavily against a wall, closing her eyes and trying to exhale the anger roiling inside her. She knows Mathilda and Jarrod are there as well, waiting for her to pull herself together.

"I'm sorry," Mathilda says softly, warm brown eyes inquisitive behind the dramatically rimmed glasses she always wears. Liz responds with a wave of her hand, seeing no point in talking about what just happened. Mathilda will try to find words to make everything okay, and she will defend Claire. Mathilda has a way of seeing everyone's perspective, and helping others see different perspectives, especially when they feel attacked. She's soft that way—soft in temperament, speech, and movement.

But Liz doesn't need her words of comfort. Sure, Claire's attacks are nothing short of scathing, but Liz knows she's simply afraid. Claire likes to control things. It makes her a brilliant bioengineer and doctor, but the current situation, with the New Generation spies, is out of her control. So, she's afraid, not just for herself but for her family. Liz knows this is the most insidious kind of fear. Fearing for those you love.

"The dock will require Seth's approval," Liz states, opening her eyes and straightening herself.

"We'll send it from the bridge, and handle comms from there as usual," Jarrod replies.

In no other situation, Liz muses, *would the Head of Engineering and the Head of Astrophysics be sitting on an empty bridge manning comms with a pilot making a surface run.* But the bridge is the most secure place on this ship, and until they know how deeply they have been infiltrated, every precaution has to be taken.

"Let's get this done." Liz is anxious to get to the lift before the rest of Council finishes meeting.

She descends alone to Level 5, feeling a small measure of relief as the doors open to the familiar sounds of the dock, a world apart from the heated Council meeting she just left. She breathes in deeply, taking in the smell of excitement and freedom, the smell that Seth calls rocket fuel and grease. She recognizes Charlie, the chief mechanic, walking down the loading ramp of the shuttle closest to her, filling out an electronic check sheet on a tablet. He looks up and smiles, acknowledging her with a nod.

"Here for your daily check-up?" he asks cheerfully. He never seems to have any reservations about her standing order that every shuttle be fueled, serviced, and stocked with munitions at all times. He never seems to mind her daily inspections. She likes him for that.

"Nope, I'm taking one out. Just a short mission— solo."

Charlie's smile freezes. "I'm going to need the captain's approval for that one, Liz. Sorry."

"Of course. Jarrod and Mathilda are handling comms, and they should have called already with the order."

Charlie glances nervously toward a terminal, where another mechanic is on a phone. The mechanic nods in return. Charlie exhales audibly. Liz knows he doesn't want trouble with her, but he will follow protocols, regardless of who it offends.

"Sounds like you're good to go! Need anything special?"

"Just the usual," she replies simply, heading to an adjacent locker room to find a flight suit and pilot gear.

***

Liz's chaotic mind settles as soon as the shuttle ejects from the ship. Now she is at peace and in her element, flying this magnificent machine where she can control everything and, at least for the moment, has to account to no one. Liz loves everything about flying.

She breaks left toward Earth and spares an admiring glance at the Green Grow 3, the huge metal sphere designed to orbit the planet. It looks like a manmade moon, but it doesn't function like the earth or a moon at all.

Direction in space is relative, of course—there is no true up or down or top or bottom. But inside the Green Grow 3, direction is pretty clear. Level 1 is at the top. Level 37 is at the bottom. The other layers press between in horizontal slices. When she approaches in her shuttle to dock, she might be coming from any direction. But inside, the cylindrical gravity field is linear and goes one direction, from Level 1 to Level 37.

The ship is equipped with small thrusters, which is all it needs to function in orbit, but they aren't visible from the outside. They are housed in a tubular channel that runs through the center of the ship, perpendicular to the levels. From the outside, the Green Grow 3 is sleek, unblemished.

She can see the large bridge window on Level 1. Most of the security is centralized in the first six levels of the ship, where the crew lives, although the bridge is the most secure area. Referred to as the Survival Saucer, Levels 1-6 can completely eject from the growing levels and function as an independent vessel. Levels 7-37 are designed exclusively for growing food, comprising over 1,500 acres of arable land that can be cultivated efficiently enough to feed thousands of people.

That's what we're supposed to be doing, she thinks. *Feeding people and making things better. But the only people we're saving are ourselves. Shitbiscuits, what a cluster ...* She knows the ship has the potential to make life dramatically better for so many people, but she also knows it's called "potential" because it isn't happening now. The Green Grow Corporation *could* use the 1,500 acres on thirty growing levels on the ship to feed the world, but they aren't. Only ten of the levels are active now, and those aren't even the biggest ones. And the crew is diminishing along with the rest of the operation. Liz remembers hearing there were over two thousand souls working on the ship when she first came. Now they are down to just over six hundred people on the crew. It's enough to manage the ever-withering operation as they wait for the Green Grow Executive Board to establish peace with the New Generation, but should they still be waiting? Liz doesn't want to consider the question.

Liz checks her gauges and turns her attention to the gray, hazy mass of North America. She drops into the reentry window, feeling the friction of the atmosphere push and pull against the sturdy hull that protects her from the heat and certain death of reentry. She can see nothing through the veil of ashy gas that covers the continent. Technically, it envelopes the entire planet, but it's especially thick here. She's close to ground zero, the site of the supervolcano eruption that drove the final nail into the coffin of a civilization she barely remembers—the extinction event. She holds the stick firmly, feeling for any excess vibration or pulling but finding none.

Once she drops below the haze, she doesn't have far to fly – just a few minutes. The shuttle is sluggish in the atmosphere, heavy and lethargic. She checks her coordinates and then spots the abandoned depot. All of the Green Grow depots started off as airports, so they are easy enough to find from the air. She lands and taxies toward the main warehouse, a cloud of dusty ash swirling around her. Liz clicks the talk button on her communication headset. "Green Grow Command, this is Shuttle Alpha. I have landed. Proceeding to the depot."

"Roger that, Shuttle Alpha," comes Mathilda's distant and tinny reply. "Emergency comms only until you depart. Over."

"Roger that. Shuttle Alpha, out."

Liz prepares herself, booting up the thermal imager and loading the two pistols Charlie issued for the mission. The depot, which used to buzz with people and activity, is lifeless. It's early afternoon—the sun shines, the dust blows, and when the wind picks up, it howls through the large abandoned buildings. She slides tinted goggles over her eyes, secures a breathing mask, and quickly checks the thermal imager before lowering the loading ramp and walking off. She lets herself into the security office of the warehouse, mindlessly entering a code on a keypad, a series of numbers she's come to know better than her own birthday.

Green Grow depots used to run on a combination of solar, wind, and atomic power. After the Denver depot closed, the solar and wind systems were largely dismantled and stolen, but the atomic power still feeds the security systems and provides basic power to the warehouse. She scans the security monitors, punching keys and typing access codes, looking for the pallets of carbon fiber panels and the metal racks of tall composite tanks that stored the hydrogen. Outside the security office, a loose metal panel rattles in the wind.

The part of the warehouse that most people can see— the part above ground—is empty. It used to serve as a staging area, a hub to manage and store everything coming from and going to the space farms. It used to be full of people and movement, of sights, sounds, and smells. It used to be full of hope. When the New Generation attacked the depot, this was the part they wanted—the bountiful cache of sustenance that flowed in and out of this warehouse. But the part of the warehouse that stores the maintenance supplies for the shuttles and the space ships is underground, hidden with layers of security.

"Gotcha," she says quietly as the pallets and cannisters come into view, making a note of their location. She leaves the security office and starts the long walk across the empty warehouse floor. A hidden panel on the other side will give her access to the underground, down to the treasure that waits silently for her to come.

If she closes her eyes, she can almost see it as it was. She can see her younger self running a forklift or taking inventory, at least when she could get a depot assignment on her off-ship week. She wouldn't live on the Green Grow 3 permanently for several more years, not until she worked her way up to shuttle pilot. Back then, she was a picker, and pickers worked three weeks on the ship and then came back to the surface for a week off. Sometimes you could get a week-long rotation at the depot, but there was competition for those assignments. Although people with families tended to go home when they were off-ship for a week, plenty of people had no families. Plenty of people, like Liz, had no home to go to at all. But she managed to get by.

Even when she couldn't get a warehouse assignment, or an assignment at the depot store where the public could buy directly, she still spent a lot of time at the depot. It wasn't just a hub for goods; it was a hub for information. Everybody was looking for somebody then, and she was looking for her older brother Jackson. She'd check the message boards for anything he might have pinned up, and she'd post notes and fliers, pleading for information. She had to find him—he was the only family she had left, and she had no idea what had become of him. She needed him, and she needed to tell him their mom died.

Jackson was everything to Liz, and she remembers every aching second of his leaving. By then, Liz was eight, and Jackson was fourteen. He gave her an appraising look and told her he was going away for a while, to join the New Generation. He assured her he would come back— promised, even—and told her to take care of their mother in the meantime. She knew it would be pointless to ask him to stay. So instead, she asked how long he'd be gone. He only smiled and told her he'd be back as soon as he found a safe place for her and their mother to join him. He told her not to cry. He told her that so very many times, and then one final time more. Then he walked out the door and down the road, never looking back.

Liz was sad he left, but she never doubted him. If he said he'd come back, she knew he would—he'd promised, after all. If he thought she could take care of their mother in the meantime, she knew she could, even though she was only eight. Jackson was the smartest, most capable person she knew, and she couldn't conceive of anything not going according to his plan. So, she watched and waited for him and passed the time as best she could. She tried to take care of their mom, although she failed in the end. And then she went to the Green Grow depot, determined to find a job and her brother.

She got tips from the message boards, although most of them led nowhere. It wasn't easy to get information on a person whose last known status was "joined the New Generation." Too many of the depot visitors had been victimized by them. Liz never stopped using the message boards, but her best tips came from other sources. They came from the boys who worked full-time at the depot, the boys who knew not just about survivors but about the New Generation bands in the area. They weren't forthcoming about what they knew—it was dangerous to talk about the New Generation or be associated with them in any way, but Liz usually found them quite talkative after a rendezvous in some hidden corner of the warehouse, her half-dressed body pressed to theirs, groaning and aching to be pleased. Sometimes she'd meet up with them just because she could, to feel alive. But usually she did it for information.

Of course, now there's no information to be had, and she doesn't meet up with men anymore—not on the surface and not on the ship. An image of Seth fills her mind, and she wonders what he's doing now on the ship. Whatever he's into, she hopes it's easier than the Council meeting this morning.

***

The service lift behind the hidden panel groans as it descends slowly underground. Liz finds a forklift at the mouth of the storage room and begins the work of moving the racks and pallets to the shuttle. Two hours later, she assesses the shrinking cargo bay of the shuttle.

The alarm on her thermal imager sounds, a high-pitched beep that cuts through the silence. She pulls it off her belt, wiping her dusty goggles as she stares at the screen. There's a heat anomaly, a big one, behind the warehouse, just outside the fence that runs along the old storefront. The amorphous red blob can mean only one thing—people.

Did I stay too long?

She sprints back to the security office, pressing buttons and entering codes to view the camera feeds around the depot's perimeter. The inner fence is clear—it's electrified, so that's the most important one. But a group of people stands huddled together just beyond the outer fence, by the old pedestrian entrance.

New Generation? No. They're too … peaceful.

She zooms in as far as the camera will allow but can't see them clearly. They don't appear to have any weapons, although she can't be sure. Everyone is looking at the old storefront. The group appears to include both men and women, and several have scarves wrapped around their heads. Their clothes look shabby, but not ragged or crude like a New Generation band. Some of them are taller than others, but right next to the fence she notices a very short, small person.

Is that a child?

Did they see the shuttle? Do they think there's food today? She is sickened by the thought that these might be survivors, abandoned to die by the Green Grow Corporation when the depot closed. Could she, too, leave them behind if they really are survivors?

It could be a trap, she thinks, *but no one knew I was coming.* Besides, a band of New Generation wouldn't waste time standing peacefully outside the fence trying to lure her in. If they saw her—if they thought she was here with a shuttle— they'd be ramming through or digging under the fence.

Her mind processes multiple scenarios. She could take off now, leave what's left of the cargo and go back to the ship. She could break radio silence and ask Mathilda for Seth's orders. A litany of Claire's searing insults echoes in her mind. *Rogue. Not a team player. No respect. Wild card.*

"You don't report to Claire," Liz hisses. She reminds herself that this is not an emergency. Both fences are intact. No one is attempting to breach. Liz still has the ability to blow the shuttle, if it comes to that.

She quickly exits the security office and draws one of her pistols, making her way down the length of the warehouse to the corner of the old storefront. *This could be the last thing I ever do,* she thinks, cautiously appraising the group as she walks toward the fence.

"There's no food today," she states loudly when she thinks she's close enough for them to hear her. The mass of people shift closer, some of the pressing against the outer fence. "There's no food today," she says again.

"Please help us," a woman replies, her voice clear and cutting.

"Help you?" Liz searches for the face that matches the voice. "Help you how?"

"We have nothing left, and there's nowhere to go. Please let us in."

"I can't let you in. I'm sorry." Liz's voice sounds strong as she says the words, but a churning grows in her stomach and spreads to her knees.

"Please," the woman replies, "we know you're not here to bring food. But please help us." Liz's eyes find the woman's face. She looks old, weathered.

"I'm sorry, I can't help you." Liz knows the words are untrue even as she speaks them. Her feet carry her closer to the fence. Where is the small person she saw on the camera?

"Are you New Generation?" she asks, knowing the answer even as her lips ask the question.

"No," the woman replies, "but there's a group of them tracking us. We were living in a cave about thirty miles from here, but they found us. We had to leave. This is all we have left now. There's nowhere else to go."

"I'm sorry," Liz replies firmly. "I can't risk helping you. It's not about me. If something happened to the shuttle … If the New Generation got the shuttle, well, there are other people involved." Her voice sounds strong, although she feels anything but. *These people are survivors,* she thinks as her feet carry her closer to the pedestrian gate. The pistol feels heavy in her hand, drooping at her side. She holsters it before her fingers let go of it altogether.

She sees the old woman more clearly now, her tan face varnished with layers of wrinkles. Her eyes are the color of pine bark, with a ring of bluish haze encircling the brown. They seem knowing and weary as they lock with Liz's—unafraid. The woman wears a plain cotton dress that might have flowers on it beneath all the dust, and a cotton shawl wrapped around her head. *Is she someone's wife?* Liz wonders. *Someone's mother?* Liz had a mother once.

"Please," the woman speaks again, "at least take the child. Look how little he is! Don't you have room in your heart for one little baby?"

She gently pushes a young boy in front of her, her fingers wrinkled and knobby. He presses his curly blonde hair into the fabric of her dress, clinging to the woman as he looks sidelong at Liz with terrified eyes. Is this the little person she saw on the camera? He's a willowy thing, barely reaching the old woman's waist. How old is he? Liz can't tell. The surface is deadly, not a place where children grow tall or big. It's a miracle he's alive at all. Liz looks away from the boy, hoping she isn't the reason he is afraid.

She studies the rest of the group, still standing silently. Some of them cling to the fence—others cling to each other. There must be at least forty of them. How are they here? People survive alone or in small groups, not a large group like this. Liz notices the smaller, youngest people silently being shepherded through the crowd toward the fence. More children?

The wind picks up again, blowing dusty ash against the storefront behind her. The old woman stands silent, and Liz hears a muffled sob. Her eyes instinctively track the sound, and she notices a woman in the back of the crowd, huddled under a man's arm with her face buried in his chest. Wispy blonde curls escape the confines of the scarf wrapped around her head. Is the young boy hers? How hard must that be? *But that's the stuff mothers are made of,* Liz thinks, as the memory of her own mother floods her mind.

"Please, please! At least take the children."

The desperation in the old woman's voice snaps Liz back to the present, eyes scanning the horizon. The band of New Generation is on foot. They break into a run across the ragged desert terrain, eager to close the distance between them and the survivors, who cling to one another as if they can somehow keep each other safe.

The band wear ragged scraps of fabric and leather hides, some with metal plates bound to their chests and arms. Their hair falls in long, ragged braids, interlaced with bones and feathers. They shriek and howl, brandishing homemade weapons with blades and spikes.

Liz's eyes register everything going around her—the running, screaming mass of crazed New Generation thugs, the placid group of people huddled by the fence, the old woman's gnarled fingers wrapped around the links. Her eyes register everything, but the part of her that still feels is filled with the image of her mother, her clean blonde hair, her smile. Liz can smell the rose bush outside the living room window, hear her mom humming as she combs Liz's wet hair into a braid. Her mother is patient and loving— kind.

Liz's fingers punch a series of numbers onto a keypad. The electric circuit pulsing through the inner fence breaks, and the first gate swings open. Her legs bridge the distance to the outer fence, and she punches the code into the second gate. It swings open with a click and a buzz.

The old woman grabs the boy's frayed shirt and starts to push him inside. "Thank you," she says wildly, as she tries to shake off the boy's clinging embrace. "Go!" she says, her voice fierce. He starts to cry as she pushes him farther. "Go," she insists again.

Liz hears her own voice, even though she is unaware of speaking. "Get everyone inside." She counts ten New Generation thugs. They are so close now that she can nearly make out their faces. "Now!" she snaps at the old woman.

The gate is narrow. The old woman stands outside, pushing them through one by one. There isn't enough time. They can't get in fast enough. She can't save them. Liz knows she should close the gate. The old woman pushes the people through faster. A tall man trips and falls as he comes through the gate. Two women ahead of him grab his elbows and pull him up.

Liz knows she can't wait any longer. Before the next person can pass through, she steps outside the gate. She is no longer within the depot, within the safe perimeter. There is nothing separating her from any of these people anymore.

One of the New Generation is nearly upon her. He yips and shrieks, raising a metal club over his head. Liz notices he is missing a tooth as she grabs her pistol out of its holster, raises it level with her shoulder, and pulls the trigger twice. The shrieking abruptly stops, and the man falls to the ground without ceremony.

She shifts her body slightly and squeezes the trigger again. Another one of them falls. And then another. A swell of anger grows inside her. The remaining New Generation stop, as if deciding what to do next. Are they shocked? Surprised? Unsure what to do? Are they capable of such human emotions?

"Not today, you disgusting filth," she screams. She turns to look toward the gate. The old woman is shuffling the last of them through.

Liz sees movement out of the corner of her eye and snaps her head around, squeezing the trigger again. Another one of them falls, this time with a scream. She retreats carefully behind the safety of the outer fence, pulling the gate and watching it click closed. Then she turns her back to what is left of the New Generation and strides through the inner gate, pulling it shut behind her. She punches the numbers into the keypad again. The gate clicks, and she can hear the faint hum of the electricity now surging through the inner fence. She directs the crowd of people toward the storefront, saying little and feeling very heavy. Liz wants to go back to those memories of her mother, to the faint smell of roses somewhere in her mind, but the images are gone now, like a distant dream.

***

Liz walks absently into the old storefront. The group follows, eyes wild as they huddle together, murmuring. The hazy light filters through the front wall of windows, revealing rows of empty bins with colorful signs hanging over them. It's been a long time since those bins were filled with fruits and vegetables, nuts and grain. She looks out past the fence. The living remnant of the New Generation band is gone. Liz's mind races, trying to process all the possible scenarios. What will she do about these people? Take them? Leave them? No. Take them? Stay here? Can they survive if she doesn't take them? Are they dangerous?

Can I trust them? she wonders.

She spots the little tow-headed boy, wrapped in the arms of the woman with the blonde curls sticking out of her scarf. He clutches her tightly, tearstained eyes wide and wondering. A man stands beside them. The top half of his face is shaded by a large hat, but something about him seems familiar.

"*Zzzz* …" she hears the little boy say, staring intently at a nearby sign. "What does it say, Momma?"

"Zesty," Liz hears the woman respond quietly. She glances over and sees the sign—*Zesty Tomatoes*, it reads, next to a drawing of a plump and overly red tomato.

"What's a zesty?" the boy asks, curious but pulling only slightly away from the woman to get a better look.

"It's a flavor," she says, "a description of how something tastes."

"Like sour?"

"Kind of."

The boy seems satisfied and snuggles his head back under her chin. The man with the hat turns his face slightly, smiling at the child. Liz studies him carefully.

"I know you, don't I?" Liz's voice booms in the still dusty air. "Didn't we used to work on the same growing level?" She peels off her goggles and mask, walking toward the man through a parting crowd to get a closer look.

"Liz?" he asks, incredulously. "Liz Goeff?"

"Will Dabato!" She recognizes him now, astounded at how much older he looks. "Holy hell, what happened to you? I thought you were dead!"

"At this point I'm not quite sure how any of us are still alive." His voice is weak.

"Why didn't you come back from your surface leave?" Liz asks.

"I couldn't leave them."

"Who?"

"My … my family."

"You found your mother?" Liz remembers how hard he searched for his family, and how devastated he was as he learned one by one that they were dead. His mother had been his last remaining hope.

"Yes, I followed a lead I got off the depot's message board. When I found my mom, I found this group. And I met Melissa." He motions to the young woman with the curly blonde hair, holding the little boy fiercely to her chest. Liz's eyes widen.

"Is he your boy?" she asks.

Will nods, a slight smile dancing across his worn face.

"You know the policy," he continues, turning somber. "Workers aren't allowed to bring unemployed family members to the ship, so I stayed with them on the surface."

"Where's your mom?" Liz asks breathlessly.

His brow falls.

"She didn't make it—died right after Zachary was born. We couldn't save her. But you should have seen her face when she held her grandson!"

Liz stands silent, unsure what to say to Will. She has the ability to help these people. She *needs* to help them, but she knows the Council might not understand. Can she explain this to Seth? Sure. Will he understand? She doesn't know. She does know that Will worked by her side on the growing team. They were both Denver-based, so they shared stories and news, hopes of finding missing friends and family. Liz knows him—or at least she used to, but so much time has passed.

Can I trust them? she wonders again. The question feels different to her now as she paces toward the glass storefront, gaze piercing the hazy air as she studies the barren landscape. The four lifeless New Generation bodies litter the ground, scraps of fabric and feathers wafting in the wind.

I don't know if they'll come back for their dead, Liz thinks, *but they will come back for these survivors. There is no choice to be made here.* She's taken so many lives. Sam's face flashes in her mind again, and her ears once more hear the gurgling sound of Ellen dying. Shouldn't she be allowed to save a few?

"Will," she hisses, turning around, looking for the man she knew. He stands on the edge of the group with the young woman and child. "You have to come with me. The New Generation will be back."

"I won't leave them, Liz," he says firmly.

"I know! You *all* have to come."

His brow shoots up in surprise. "But the policy—Captain MacAbee …"

"Will, Captain MacAbee has been missing for two years. He's presumed dead. Seth Harris is the captain now."

"Seth?" he exclaims. "Isn't he the captain's assistant?"

"Not anymore," she replies in a hushed whisper. "Look, it's a long story. But things have changed since you left—a lot. The surface runs are suspended, except for a few specially approved supply runs. I don't know when anyone will be coming back to this station. If you don't come … Well, I think it's pretty clear what's going to happen to everyone."

Will opens his mouth to speak, but a clear calm voice speaks over him.

"We'll go." It's the old woman. "All fifty-two of us."

Liz looks toward Will, whose eyes drop to the ground. It seems the matter is settled.

***

"Where we going, Momma?" the little boy asks as the last of the group shuffles up the loading ramp.

"Away from here," the reply comes.

"But where?"

"I don't know," she says. "It's a surprise, for all of us."

Yes, Liz thinks, watching from the top of the ramp, *everyone will be surprised, especially Seth.*

She casts a final glance at the Denver depot as she raises the loading ramp. She has so many memories of this place, but they feel strangely empty now. Did she expect to feel differently? She doesn't know. The things that made this place home are gone: the life, the trees, her mother. The blue skies and snow on the mountains that she barely remembers. Rocks and rivers and all those wonders made by someone else—God perhaps, or whatever force breathed life into this hunk of molten rock before mankind ever existed. All that remains of value now is fifty-odd people, and they are coming with her.

The engines whir as she finishes the pre-flight check she's done so many times before. She tells herself this time isn't any different, and yet, it is. Will she ever see this place again? Does she want to?

No, she thinks, *I don't care. The depot itself was never more than a means to an end.*

She knows the emptiness she feels is nothing more than the space she left for Jackson to fill. She never imagined not finding her brother, even though fifteen years is much too long to expect a happy ending. Even still, she can't accept that he's gone—not without proof. But, she also can't deny that she'll probably never know what happened to him.

Liz steers toward the runway, hoping the ride isn't too bumpy. The shuttle is meant for cargo, not passengers, so there aren't any seats, just a few straps and each other to hold on to as they sit on the floor. She presses the shuttle forward, summoning the power to defy the earth's gravity. As it wrenches free of the ground and begins to rise, Liz notices the New Generation returning, gathering outside the fence.

"Burn in hell," she whispers, as she reaches to click the talk button on her communication headset. "Green Grow Command, this is Shuttle Alpha. Come in." There is a moment of static, then silence. "Green Grown Command, this is Shuttle Alpha. Come in."

Mathilda's distant and tinny voice fills the air. "Roger that, Shuttle Alpha, this is Green Grow Command. Good to hear from you. Over."

"Roger that. I've cleared the station. Returning to base. Over."

"Roger that, Shuttle Alpha. We'll prepare for your arrival. Over."

"I need to talk to Seth. Now. Over."

"Um, roger that. You want me to get him now? Over."

"Yes, now. Over."

"Okay."

Liz waits, counting her breaths. Five. Six. Ten. Where is he? With each breath, her body quivers a little more.

"Shuttle Alpha, this is Seth. What's going on? Over."

"I have the cargo. But, umm—" Every possible combination of relevant words enters her mind at the same time.

"Shuttle Alpha, are you there? Over." Seth sounds a little impatient. Is it her imagination?

"I have a band of refugees with me, Seth."

"What?"

"People. Survivors."

"You're kidding, right?"

"No, I'm not kidding. They're friendly. Not New Generation."

"You can't possibly know that!"

"Yes, I can. Have a medical team standing by. And food. They're starving. There are children in the group."

Liz hears something like a roar begin to come through her communication set. She clicks the talk button again. "Shuttle Alpha, out." She clicks it off, and there is nothing more.

CHAPTER 3

THE SCIENTIST

***

The scientist sits alone in his makeshift lab, venom surging through his veins as he utters the name of his enemy. It rolls off his tongue like a serpent's hiss—"Seth Harris."

The makeshift lab isn't far from his real lab, but in that lab, people ask questions. They ask what he's doing, as if they would understand. They offer their opinions, as if he cares. They try to help, as if they are capable. He knows they aren't, and he doesn't have the time or patience to feed their admirable but pathetic curiosity. And so, he sits alone in his secret makeshift lab contemplating his mission, because there is so much to do and so little time to do it.

It's been a long day, and he's tired. He has many responsibilities, and they only seem to grow by the day. It seems that merely transforming impossibility into possibility isn't enough to earn one's keep anymore. Indeed, it never has been. And so, he does what is required, even when it takes him off course. Because in the end, he can always come back to his secret lab to work on *his* project, the project that no one knows about. No one needs to know about it—not yet. Plans must be laid and resources organized. Support must be gained and power transitioned seamlessly. Timing must align.

He closes his eyes and remembers the photo burned into his memory—the stunningly symmetrical face of the woman, the innocent glee of the baby. It's a momentary respite, a brief reminder of the things in life that matter, and then he sweeps the image out of his mind. Time is too precious to reminisce or dream.

It would be easy to give up, to simply flow with the current and live his life like everyone else does. But what would be the point of that? If he's going to simply succumb to the fate the world hands him, why even bother to go on at all? He might be better off dead. Sometimes he thinks it's the dead who are the lucky ones, but he knows better than this. He knows that death brings no relief, because no one ever really dies. Life is energy, and energy never ends. It simply transforms, becomes something else. And so, life is valuable. *This* life is valuable, because at least it has momentum. And he has more momentum than most— thoughts and dreams, curiosity and intelligence that dwarf the average person's intellect.

Science affords him knowledge, and with that knowledge comes great responsibility. But sometimes, even he forgets—until he remembers that life is the journey and the destination, the means and the end. And where does it go? Onward, of course. Over the next hill and down the road, each step closer in turn to happily ever after. Scientists, too, are only human.

This scientist is especially human, his heart as bruised as any. But he keeps going. He knows that just as energy never dies, the journey never ends. It's eternal, and the only constant is change—some good, some bad, but none permanent. And it is toward a purpose. He knows with every subatomic particle of his being that the journey, especially his journey, is for a purpose. He's going to save the world—*his* world—and the Green Grow 3 is the fulcrum upon which this endeavor rests.

Mind you, he has no illusions of grandeur. Life will continue no matter what he does. Even if all of humanity fails, life itself will continue (perhaps on Earth, perhaps somewhere else), but what value would that hold for him?

Besides, the fate of humanity isn't at stake here. He knows this. Even as he sits here, some version of human civilization is surviving and rebuilding on the planet. He could join them if he wanted. He is a scientist, after all, and scientists are needed everywhere.

But could he leave behind the promise of the space farms? Clearly, he couldn't—because he hasn't. He'd rather be here, standing on the shoulders of all the Green Grow scientists who came before him, moving humanity forward in a way that won't be possible on the surface for at least a thousand years. He belongs here. And so, he will find a way, not to save *the* world but to save *his* world. He won't allow a pesky brat like Seth Harris to stand in his way.

For now, he sits and he plans. He sketches and doodles as his mind churns. He defines the problem. It's a problem of both time and space—for they are intertwined in ways he doesn't fully understand yet. Time, space, and matter. How can he control one without impacting the others? Can matter move through space without moving through time?

What is time, anyway? Maybe a ninety-seven-year life isn't ninety-seven years at all. Maybe it's really four billion heartbeats, or eight million breaths. Maybe it's nothing more than an exponentially greater number of cells dividing a finite number of times. How can these things be untangled? This is what he needs to know. Or is it?

In truth, the problem is quite simple. He needs to transport the right matter to the right place at the right time. A shuttle transfers matter through time and space, but a shuttle doesn't solve all of his problems. He needs more control and precision than any conventional method will allow. He has to think bigger, or perhaps he has to think smaller.

He knows there is a solution to his problem. Because there are many ways to solve problems, and if one solution exists, infinite others must exist as well. He just needs to find the best one. It's daunting, of course, but if he's honest with himself—and he always tries to be—he admits that the challenge of it thrills him.

Everything he knows and everything he has become has led him to this moment. He will rise to this challenge, and he will conquer that pompous, spoiled imposter who calls himself the captain of the Green Grow 3. He will undo the damage Seth Harris has done.

The scientist turns his attention to the books stacked on his desk—Albert Einstein's quantum theory, and several by Stephen Hawking. Hardcopy books, especially the ones he needs, are nearly impossible to acquire, although he finds them worthy of every hardship. He considers them lovingly, wondering where he should start. Then he sighs, because he already knows. The tomes are precious, but they do not have the information he needs tonight.

He turns to a large monitor on the other side of his desk, booting up his system. He scans through the directory, through all his old NASA and Green Grow files, until he reaches the newest part of his collection. He must start by decrypting these records.

Anyone else might be overwhelmed, but the scientist sets to work, his focus singular. He's come too far to turn back now. He only hopes the new information is worth the cost of getting it. The better portion of New Mexico is still covered with a flood basalt, so activating the closed servers in the underground bunker of Area 51 was no small feat. And yet, he knows he is on the cusp of a breakthrough as the files yield and information begins to flow across his screen. It's as he suspected. He needs anti-mass. He needs rubidium.

CHAPTER 4

LIZ

****

Liz stands apoplectic on the dock, stunned by the scene she is still taking in. She worried about this moment the entire flight back from the depot, steeling herself for whatever would come. She thought she might have to immediately brief the Council. She thought they might be angry—chastising or reprimanding her like they did this morning. A small part of her hoped she'd simply be greeted by the medical team she requested. She thought Seth might come, angry or relieved or maybe just curious about the people she brought back. But she isn't prepared for this.

Seth isn't here, nor is anyone else from the Council. She receives no messages or orders, no communication at all. Instead, she is greeted by a cadre of people in biohazard suits, and they are carrying shotguns.

"Charlie, I know that's you! What is going on here?" she demands as soon as she recognizes the head mechanic behind the mask of the biohazard suit.

"I'm sorry, Liz." His voice is nasally through the filter. "It seems the dock crew has just been conscripted for security. I've been ordered to search everyone on the shuttle for security threats."

"What's with the biohazard suits?" she asks, hands on her hips.

Charlie's voice lowers. "Quarantine."

Liz's chin falls slightly. "You're going to quarantine these people? For how long?"

Charlie clears his throat. "You're *all* quarantined. You'll have to take it up with Dr. Singh. But I need your weapons—the ones I issued before you left and any other ones you might have on your person."

Liz stands silently, her fierce gaze reflecting off Charlie's mask. She can hear the breath going in and out of her body, fury tempered only by her humiliation. Realizing there is no point prolonging this, she pulls both side arms out of their holsters. She hands him the weapons, saying, "One is a few rounds short. You know where the rest is. It's all accounted for." Charlie takes the pistols tentatively.

"That's it?" he asks.

"That's it," she says, defiant. "Can I get out of this flight suit?"

"Sure, you can take it off. But I can't let you out of our custody. You'll have to do it here."

"Maybe I'm not wearing anything underneath it," she growls. She is, of course, but the pistols are all she will concede now without a fight.

"Then leave it on," he says. "I'm sorry, we don't have any females on the security team. I only got the news a couple hours ago, so we'll have to ramp up. I'm assigning Greg to stay with you until you're in the medical unit. It's been closed off for the quarantine."

Liz doesn't speak, choking on her anger. Besides, Charlie doesn't deserve her wrath. He shuffles off, leaving her with Greg, an awkward-looking fellow holding his shotgun as if it might bite him.

She unbuckles the utility belt with the empty pistol holsters, thermal scanner, and a few other gadgets, tossing it to Greg, who reflexively tries to catch it with one hand. The shotgun clatters to the floor, and he yelps. A tall and imposing man, faceless in his biohazard suit, quickly makes his way over to bark harsh words to Greg, who picks up his shotgun and resumes his awkward stance.

The man points at the utility belt. "Is that everything?" he asks. Liz nods, the anger inside her begging to be let out. "Okay then," he says, "I'm going to have to frisk you."

"Bushwa!" she barks through gritted teeth. "If you lay a finger on me, I will pull you out of that suit and tear you apart limb from limb."

"I'm sorry, ma'am," he says calmly. "Everyone has to get frisked."

"Try me," Liz growls, squaring her body and ready for a fight. He looks at her for a moment, presumably considering her offer, but shuffles away muttering under his breath.

Liz notices a small, slender form exchanging a few words with Charlie. Charlie nods, and the smaller form turns to walk up the loading ramp. *Dr. Singh,* she thinks as the woman moves away, recognizing her smooth dark skin through the plastic mask. Liz advances quickly toward Charlie while he's still alone, Greg trailing close behind like toilet paper stuck to her shoe.

"Charlie, I need to speak to the captain. Does he know I'm back? Can you raise him?

"No, I'm sorry," Charlie says, nodding his approval to a group of men setting up security tables.

"What about Jarrod?" Surely Jarrod will help her, and all of the mechanics ultimately report to him.

"No, Liz," he says, exasperated, "I can't. Maybe Dr. Singh can help you."

But Dr. Singh is clearly enmeshed with the survivors still waiting in the cargo bay of the shuttle. Besides, Dr. Singh reports to Claire, and Claire is the last Council member Liz wants to speak to right now. She makes her way over to a tug parked nearby and hoists herself onto the edge, swinging her feet. Greg approaches, waddling like a duck as he pulls his shotgun close to his body.

"Ma'am," he says, voice cracking, "I'm going to need you to step away from the equipment."

Liz responds with a guttural growl, baring her teeth and hissing like a feral animal.

"Ma'am," he starts again.

Liz cuts him off.

"Greg, I'll tell you what you *need*. You *need* to stand there quietly, practicing how to hold a shotgun. Stay in your lane. If you step into mine, we're going to collide. Are we jake?" She casts him a look that leaves room for only one answer.

"We're jake," he mumbles, shifting from foot to foot.

Liz turns her focus to Dr. Singh, who is addressing the group in the cargo hold. "We'll have to pat you down and examine any belongings you have," she explains in an even tone. "Then when everyone is done, we'll all go to the medical unit, which has been sealed off for the moment to accommodate you, and we'll get everyone fed and settled."

The old woman walks off first, unwrapping her head scarf and laying it on the table. "Hello, my name is Ruth," she says in her calm, cutting voice. Not waiting for a response, she slides two fabric straps off her shoulders, pulling off a makeshift backpack Liz didn't notice before. She carefully sets it on the table and produces three worn books, a pair of reading glasses, one metal dish, two serving spoons, and what appears to be a stack of photos. A faceless man in a biohazard suit nods as another one approaches to pat her down.

"I'm sorry, ma'am, I need you to remove your shoes," he says kindly.

"Oh dear," Ruth responds with a laugh. "Do you have a chair I can sit in?" The man motions for someone to bring one.

Liz's heart falls as Ruth removes her worn and dusty shoes, revealing strips of bloody fabric that might have once passed for socks. The man gingerly picks up her shoes, examining them. Liz can see light shining through the soles.

He hands them carefully back to her. "Are you able to put them back on, ma'am?" he asks, sounding concerned. "Dr. Singh?" he calls out, motioning her over.

"I'll manage," Ruth protests, slipping the worn shoes back onto her bloody feet with a grace Liz hasn't seen since before her mother died. "But Dr. Singh, may I have a word?" Ruth rises from the chair, speaking quietly to Dr. Singh, whose swaying gait and bulky yellow biohazard suit remind Liz of a large stuffed teddy bear she saw one time at the depot.

More people file off as Ruth and Dr. Singh walk up the ramp, returning a few minutes later with a young woman wrapped in a large swathe of what once may have been a blanket. Ruth carefully guides the woman to a table, laying an old leather bag beside her.

"I'll pat this woman down," Dr. Singh directs the men at the table. One of the men starts to object.

"She needs to remove the blanket," he states, his faceless suit towering over the trembling woman. Liz perches on the edge of the tug, ready to launch herself into the fray and handle this if needed. These people are here because she brought them, and she won't allow them to be traumatized any further.

"She has a medical condition and needs to keep the blanket on," comes Dr. Singh's cutting voice. "I'm aware of the security guidelines we've been issued, and I'm qualified to pat her down." Dr. Singh leads the young woman a few feet away, entertaining no further discussion. Liz relaxes back onto the tug.

The security screening seems to go on forever. Bodies are patted, shoes removed and inspected, possessions examined. Liz is intrigued by the array of items her passengers carry with them. They produce books, loose papers, photos, cups, and plates. Blankets have been fashioned into backpacks to carry extra clothes and odds and ends. Several people carry metal or plastic canteens around their necks or waists, but only one still contains any water. A middle-aged woman produces a silver hair brush, which she caresses before setting it on the table with care. An older man produces a guitar that is strapped to his back under his head scarf, and another produces a worn harmonica from a pocket. Other than a small burlap bag with a few dried beans, they have no food.

Liz counts eleven children, some clutching the hands of adults and others defiantly alone, and even they carry items on their backs or in pockets—books, dolls, playing cards, and one set of jacks with a small rubber ball.

Most of the items are returned, but the security team confiscates the remains of a medical kit, eight knives, and one can opener. Each time an item is confiscated, a man in a biohazard suit provides a small paper ticket to the owner, explaining how and when the item can be claimed.

One by one, the people pass through security and then gather around Ruth, squatting or sitting on the floor or in wheelchairs ordered by Dr. Singh. Liz monitors everything, quiet and motionless, mind racing with all the possible explanations for why Seth has not come to talk to her.

"Thank you for your cooperation," Dr. Singh announces in her patient, calming voice after the last person is done. "We're ready to go to the medical unit." Liz hops off the tug and joins the group, Greg dutifully behind her.

I'm really being quarantined, she thinks, realizing at last how deeply she believed that someone from the Council would have come for her by now. Her insides begin to burn. *They've cast me out, like garbage. It has to be Claire. She's already decided that I'm to blame. She's punishing me. They're all punishing me.* Her heart begins to tumble in empty circles of hurt, abandonment, and rage.

They think they have power because they sit on a Council? They think that they can send a few dock mechanics to bend me to their will? These guys wouldn't last five minutes against the New Generation. It isn't just infuriating—it's insulting.

Liz looks down at her dusty boots and tries to clear her mind, focusing on one step after another. She knows this ship. She knows all of these corridors, but she has never seen them so empty before. It seems that even the crew has forsaken her, and every door that doesn't lead to the medical unit is sealed.

How can Seth keep me in the dark like this? A vision of his blue eyes and dark hair flash in her mind, washing her with fresh waves of hurt and confusion. The tiny sliver of her mind that isn't furious whispers a reply, *Fresh hell, what did you expect him to do? He could have simply blown you to smithereens instead.* He must surely have a reason for all of this. She will go to the quarantine and try not to jump to conclusions. What else can she do?

***

Liz settles into a folding chair in the reception-area-turned-common-room of the quarantined medical unit, legs splayed out in front of her. She picks at a loose thread on the thigh of her flight suit. Her layers of clothes are stifling now—sticky and dirty. She longs for a shower, clean clothes, and a bed. No doubt, she could have those things for the taking, but she continues to sit listlessly in the chair. Flickers of anger still dance around the edges of her awareness, but the fiercest anger already burned itself out, leaving a tired, empty ash in its wake.

She watches dispassionately as Dr. Singh and other faceless medical staff in biohazard suits help the group settle in, showing them where they will sleep and eat and bathe. Ruth sits at a makeshift intake area, chatting with one of the staff about the names and ages of people in the group. If it weren't for the biohazard suit, they might pass as old friends.

Liz hears the sealed doors hiss, and she glances at a clock on the wall. Dinner. She watches a large rack of covered trays roll into the common area. No one announces that it's mealtime, or that the group should form a line to each take a tray. It seems no one needs to. The group of tired, disheveled people seem to discern what is going on and morph into an orderly line on their own. Liz watches as each person takes a tray and finds a place to sit at the clusters of folding tables set up for this purpose.

Liz feels no urgency to eat, even though she should be hungry. She continues to sit, slouched in her chair as Dr. Singh stops in front of her, wordlessly handing her an electronic tablet. Liz smiles in appreciation. *Seth hasn't forgotten me after all,* she thinks as she sees two more of the survivors take trays and sit quietly at a table. They don't touch their food. *Strange,* Liz thinks as she glances around the room and see that everyone's tray is still covered. *What are they waiting for?*

"Can I bring you anything from the kitchen?" Dr. Singh offers. "The trays are basic—vegetable soup with chicken, bread, and a bit of pudding. I'm not sure their bodies can tolerate more tonight."

Liz doesn't care what's on the trays, so she replies that the soup is fine. *Why isn't anyone eating?* She boots up the tablet and logs on to the network. No messages.

"It's a mystery to me how they've survived this long," Dr. Singh muses. "Especially the children." Liz nods in acknowledgment, noticing that the line is beginning to dwindle. The survivors continue to sit patiently at the tables, trays covered. Liz rises from the folding chair to assume her place at the end of the line.

"If it's any consolation, you're famous." Dr. Singh calls after her. "I didn't realize news could spread so fast, but it seems the entire ship knows you found survivors. Everyone wants to know who's in the group—'Liz's Fifty-Two,' they're calling them." Liz pauses, realizing that she's too tired to find words that won't sound bitter or sarcastic. *The whole ship knows, and still no communication from Seth.*

None of this is Dr. Singh's fault, and so Liz forces a smile, as if this newfound notoriety is some kind of good news—or at least humorous. Then she turns away, taking the last tray from the dinner cart. She's looking for the closest empty seat when she sees Ruth, standing and beckoning her from across the room. Everyone sits quietly, covered trays untouched as Liz makes her way to Ruth. *Aren't they hungry?* she wonders again, sitting down next to the old woman just as she begins to speak.

"Today we are blessed," she starts, all eyes focused on her. "Thanks to this young woman, we are here together in this place. I know we're all filled with gratitude. Does anyone have anything to offer before we eat?"

Offerings? Fresh hell, I hope this isn't a cult. Liz tries to keep her face slack as she waits for someone to speak.

Silence.

"Let's eat, then," Ruth pronounces with a smile, sitting down as trays open and plates and utensils begin to clink. The group that seemed so civilized begins to attack the food before them like the starving animals they are.

This woman—she's got gravity, just like the sun, Liz thinks. *They all orbit around her.* She knows this could be a dangerous thing, but she doesn't have any reason to believe that Ruth is a threat. Yet. She watches the woman sidelong as she tears a piece of bread, placing it in her mouth as she closes her eyes, savoring it. Liz fumbles with her own tray, increasingly aware that her body is tired and sore.

"We haven't been properly introduced." Ruth's voice beckons her attention. "I heard the doctor call you Liz. Is that short for Elizabeth?" she asks, patting her mouth with a napkin.

"Elizah, actually."

"I see. Is that a family name?"

"I don't know."

The woman nods somberly. "I'm Ruth," she continues, "but I suspect you know that already. I couldn't be more pleased to meet you."

"What do you usually … offer?" Liz asks tentatively, gesturing to the food. Ruth laughs.

"Oh, just little bits of gratitude—thoughts or feelings people want to share with the group. It helps keep everyone positive." Liz observes the people around her, scraping their bowls and licking spoons. Several children rise from their chairs, quietly passing by each table to collect empty trays. She can see that these people are different. Different than who, though? The New Generation? The crew? Herself?

***

The small meal feels heavy in Liz's stomach, and her mind toys with tantalizing thoughts about a shower and a cot. But before she can make her way out of the common room, Will approaches her urgently.

"We need to talk," he says.

"Where's your family?" Liz asks, seeing no sign of the woman or child.

"Melissa is getting Zachary settled. What is going on here? Why were there people with shotguns at the dock? And what's with the biohazard suits?"

"I told you, a lot of things have changed," Liz whispers. "I need you to tell me everything you know about these people."

"Why?"

"Because if anyone has any affiliation with the New Generation, we're all going to be in trouble."

"New Generation? We were hiding from them! How could any of us be affiliated? Everyone here has lost homes and families to them." There was a time when Liz would have thought his answer sufficient, but that was before Minneapolis—before she bled the life out of a woman she trusted.

"Look," Liz starts, "after you went to the surface, the New Generation got ahold of a shuttle and hijacked the Green Grow 1. The captain sent a distress call, and then the whole ship blew. All the routine surface runs were suspended."

Will gasps.

"Is that why food stopped coming to the depot?" he asks, wide-eyed.

"Yes, in part, although the New Generation attacks on the depots were becoming so brutal that many of them simply couldn't stay open. Denver would have closed anyway."

"Captain MacAbee was worried about being hijacked," Will whispers, piecing things together in his head.

Liz continues. "He told the crew it was too dangerous to continue routine surface runs until a peace was reached. He gave everyone a choice to stay on the ship and cut off all contact with Earth or return to the surface."

"Did anyone leave?"

"Several people left. I assume they had families. Then a couple of weeks later, he left for a peace summit in Detroit and never returned."

"What happened to him?"

"We don't know. We assume the summit was sabotaged. Everyone who attended disappeared."

"So, who's in charge at headquarters then?"

No one, Liz thinks, before she perpetuates the lie she's helped the Council tell the crew. "I don't know who Captain Harris gets his orders from. It's above my pay grade." She gives Will a moment to process the information.

"Is there anything I can do to help?" he asks, eyes still wide.

"The Council is going to have a lot of questions about these people. Security is the prime directive. If anyone has any ties to the New Generation, I need to know."

"The Council?" Will looks confused.

"Yes," Liz says, starting to get impatient. "Seth—I mean Captain Harris—convened the department heads into an advisory council after Captain MacAbee disappeared." Will seems to sense her irritation.

"As far as I know, no one here has any relevant ties to the New Generation," he says. "These people are terrified of them. Everything we did centered around hiding from the group."

"What do you mean *relevant* ties?" Liz asks, eyes narrowing.

"Come on, Liz. We're all connected to the New Generation in some way. Didn't you tell me once that your brother joined?" Liz feels a flush creep up her neck, embarrassed and angry. *It's not the same thing,* she tells herself. *No one knew what they'd become when Jackson left home to join.*

"I'll tell you this," Will continues, "although it shouldn't be a surprise. You know how the raiding parties pillage towns and destroy everything. You know what they do to people. That horde has fathered a lot of children, including some of the ones here." Liz feels sick. How many of these women have been brutalized?

"What about the old woman? Do you trust her?"

"Ruth?" Will's eyebrow cocks. "I trust her with my life. We all do. She's an honest woman. I'm sure she'll answer any questions you have."

He nods, then heads off to find his family, leaving Liz alone with her thoughts. She needs to talk to Ruth, to find out more about this group of people, but she doesn't have the energy—not tonight.

Can I trust them? she wonders. *Can I trust the old woman?*

She turns the questions over in her mind. She wants to believe these people are honest. She needs to believe it, because otherwise, bringing them to the Green Grow 3 will be the biggest mistake of her life. Will says he trusts Ruth, and Liz believes he does. Is that enough?

She leaves the common room with her tablet under her arm, quietly wandering the repurposed space until she happens upon an unoccupied cot with bedding and clean clothes folded on top. She carefully sets aside the clean clothes and her tablet and spreads the bedding across the cot. Then she hears Zachary's increasingly familiar voice echoing down the hallway, "Momma, I'm gonna drown!" Melissa hums low, trying to soothe him.

Liz sits on the cot and checks her tablet again. Still no messages from Seth. She pulls up a chat window and searches his name. He isn't logged in. On a whim she types in Harry's name and sees that he is logged into the system. She clicks a button to start a video call and waits. He doesn't answer. She waits a minute and tries again. Still, no answer. Liz tries a third time, fresh anger growing in her belly. She furiously types a message and punches send.

I NEED TO TALK TO YOU.

She tries another video call. No answer. She types again.

I KNOW YOU'RE THERE.

No answer.

HAVE YOU TURNED YOUR BACK ON ME TOO?

She waits, hot tears blurring her vision. Then her tablet begins to vibrate. Harry is calling. She wipes her eyes, accepting the call as she glances around to make sure she's alone. She exhales deeply, calmed by the sight of his familiar face.

"Liz, are you okay?" he asks, looking concerned.

"What's going on, Harry?" she pleads. "Why can't I talk to Seth? Why am I quarantined?"

Harry's face is pensive. She waits for his reply.

"Are you alone?" he asks. She responds with a vigorous nod. "Liz, you're a good kid. You know I've always thought so. But, bringing those people back from the surface? Your timing couldn't be worse."

"I didn't choose for them to be there, Harry!" she cries. "Why haven't I been able to brief the Council?"

He doesn't reply right away, appearing deep in thought. "The Council … has confidential business to resolve. Seth will debrief you."

Confidential? An appalling realization descends upon her.

"Is my loyalty in question?" she demands. Harry lets out a heavy sigh, a response that speaks for itself.

Shitbiscuits, my loyalty is *in question!*

"No one thinks you're *against* us," he says slowly. "But not everyone is confident you're *with* us."

What's the difference? Liz's mind is reeling. *There's no difference!*

"Harry," she begins frantically. "Please don't let Claire condemn me before I even get a chance to say what happened!"

"Liz." His voice is stern. "Calm down. Look, we shouldn't be having this conversation. Seth will debrief you. You can't afford a meltdown now. Do what he tells you to do. This will all work out."

Liz nods, trying to maintain the little composure she has left.

"Okay," she agrees, voice ragged. "But Harry, I had to save those people. They would have been slaughtered. I couldn't watch that happen."

"I'm sure that's true, Liz," he says, rushed. "I have to go. Keep it together. Seth will debrief you." He ends the call.

It all comes down to Seth. *How long is he going to leave me in limbo?* Liz wonders, feeling a surge of panic. She wants to scream into the small pillow on her cot. Whatever happens next is totally out of her hands. There's nothing she can do except wait. She needs to think about something else, even more desperately than she needs to breathe.

She stretches out on her cot, arm over her face, and exhales deeply to clear her mind. She thinks again about her mother, humming next to the window with the rose bush. Her mother is laughing. She is combing Liz's hair. She is tucking her into bed. She is pushing her in a cart as they walk the long road to the depot. Soon, washed in exhaustion, Liz begins to doze.

***

"Miss." Liz jolts into consciousness, struggling to focus blurry eyes on the unassuming man standing over her. "Sorry to disturb you. We're going to gather in the dining room, if you feel like coming." Liz sits up, swinging her legs onto the floor and stretching her arms over her head, wanting to go back to sleep but curious about what is happening.

The chairs in the common room have been arranged in concentric circles, tables pushed against the walls. Ruth stands in the middle of the circle, still wearing her dusty, faded dress. The rest of the group is mostly showered and changed. They begin to find seats. Whispers and murmurs ripple across the room as they wait. Ruth waves at Liz, beckoning her to join the inner circle. *Fresh hell, more offerings?* Wary, Liz squares her shoulders and walks deliberately toward the old woman. As if on cue, the room quiets.

"We have a tradition in this group," Ruth begins, "of telling a story every night. Stories of the past so we don't forget the way the world used to be, before it fell apart, and so that the young among us can have a chance to know of a time that was far different than this one. We tell the stories to remember. And yet tonight, here we are, and the future seems so much more exciting than the past."

Ruth smiles, acknowledging the nods and murmurs around her.

"The situation seemed hopeless, but now there's hope aplenty. We thought we were at the end, and now we've only just begun. I hope we can still have our story time each night in this new place. Do we want to continue tonight with a story?"

After a breath of silence comes a raucous response of cheering, yipping, and clapping. Ruth nods, smiling. "Okay," she says. "But before we do, there is something I'd like to say."

She gathers her words as the group waits quietly.

"This young lady next to me is Elizah. She made an important decision today. She decided to save and transform our lives, and we can never repay her. At least for now, she's staying here with us." Ruth looks over at her. "Elizah, is there anything you want to say to the group?" Liz feels the blood rush to her face. She looks out across the collection of strange faces.

"Please call me Liz," she begins. "I know it's been a very long day. I haven't been debriefed yet, so I don't have much information to offer. But I'm glad you are all here. I know Captain Harris is glad you're here, too. I'm sure this is all a lot to process—it is for me as well—but if there's anything I can do to help you, please let me know. I … I'm not sure what else to say. Ruth?"

The woman smiles affectionately, reaching out to pat her shoulder. "That's just fine," she whispers, as murmurs from the group grow into applause that soon surges in waves, washing Liz in emotion until she feels like she's almost drowning. Ruth raises her hands in the air, and the room quiets. Liz spots Will, holding his boy tightly as he weeps into his hair. The boy wriggles and squirms until Will sets him down, clean curly locks now mussed.

"Who's gonna tell the story?" he cries out, looking at Ruth. "Is *she* gonna tell the story tonight?" The boy points straight at Liz.

Ruth replies, "Liz might not be ready to tell a story, Zachary. It's been a big day, and she doesn't know us very well. Why don't you ask her another time?"

"Okay," he says, brows knitted together as he climbs into his mother's lap. "Can we hear the story about the beach? I like that one."

"Oh, yes. The beach. Who wants to remember the beach tonight?" There is a general murmur accompanied by nods of approval. Liz takes the seat that was left vacant for her, the unreadable expression on her face a product of years of practice. Ruth starts the story, and then other people add their own memories. Sand, water, waves. Seagulls, seashells. *This sounds like heaven,* Liz thinks, mesmerized by this thing called a beach—a thing she has never known. She looks over and sees Zachary's eyelids drooping as he sits cuddled in his mother's lap.

Liz's worry and anxiety begin to melt into a small glow of happiness. No matter what Seth or anyone else thinks, this is worth saving, and these people are worth trusting—at least a little.

CHAPTER 5

SETH

***

Seth sits in his quarters, staring at the camera feed from the medical unit as his fingers drum the surface of his desk. Liz is curled up on a cot, blanket pulled around her chin. She looks peaceful now, very different from the angry woman who returned from Earth. On the dock she was a feral beast on the verge of destroying its cage, but now, sleeping on the narrow cot, she exudes an endearing, child-like innocence. Nothing about this surprises Seth—it's who she is.

Seth was seventeen when he met Liz on the surface, a skinny girl with freckles and pretty blonde hair. As a young man, he was eager to transgress the stifling bounds of his sheltered life, a quest that led him to a week-long internship at the Denver depot. He was bursting to see for himself what it was like to live on Earth, and his parents begrudgingly approved—they had been summoned to an extended board meeting at that very depot.

He was glad for the change of scenery, but the internship fell far short of what he'd expected. He spent the time cooped up in an office, entering data into a computer and creating mindless reports. He barely got to see the depot, much less anything outside it, and then it was time to go back to the Green Grow 3.

He sat waiting for his parents in the secure shuttle preboard area, sulking as a steady flow of workers—pickers, mechanics, and maintenance crew—scanned their identifications to board the shuttle. Everything was running smoothly, at least until a gangly, underfed teenager in a Green Grow uniform claimed she'd lost her identification—Liz. The entire operation ground to a halt as she stood unyielding, steadfastly blocking the line, debating with the security officers.

Seth watched as they tried and failed to look her up in the employee database, pulling her out of line so others could pass through. She stayed calm and cool, telling them again and again that there must have been a mistake. They were on the verge of escorting her to the security office, and Seth knew that wouldn't end well for her. It was her shoes that gave her away—worn, patched, and filthy. No legitimate Green Grow employee with a uniform would have shoes like that.

Why did he help her? He had no reason to intervene. Yet, as a security officer took her by the arm and turned to go to the main office, her eyes found Seth's. The glance they shared couldn't have lasted more than a couple of seconds, but it was long enough for him to see her strength and fire, her innocence and pain. It was all there in her eyes, all of her contradictions that attracted him like a bee to a flower.

He remembers quickly walking up to the security officers, placing a firm grip on Liz's free arm before they could take her away.

"There you are!" he said loudly, attracting everyone's attention. "Did you get lost again? This isn't a good way to start your new job!" He remembers Liz crying the realest tears he'd ever seen. After a few words with the security officers, Seth signed her into a paper log.

"What's your full name again?" he asked her. "I'm terrible with names."

"Elizah Goeff," she responded. "G-O-E-F-F, but it sounds like Jeff. I go by Liz."

"Well, no wonder," Seth replied, trying to appear flustered and indignant. "Somebody probably misspelled it or something. She's my mom's new lab assistant."

Seth remembers the security guard's burning stare, how he kept reading the log over and over, trying to find a reason to deny her entrance. Seth flashed Liz a smile, hoping he seemed confident and in control even though his palms were sweating, his heart thumping and mind racing through the myriad problems he'd have to solve if this farce actually worked. It did work, and they let her pass.

"Are you crazy?" he asked her quietly, pulling her onto the employee shuttle and ushering her toward two empty seats in the back.

"No," she replied tersely, refusing to meet his eyes. "Why did you help me?"

"Would you rather I hadn't?" he shot back, instantly regretting the words as her bright blue eyes gleamed with fresh tears.

"What do you want?" she asked. "For helping me, I mean."

What did he want? He told her he didn't want anything, and her eyes instantly narrowed, unbelieving. Truthfully, he didn't know then what he wanted. He didn't understand until later that he wanted to jump into the sea of her mystery, to have an adventure and maybe a friend.

He certainly got what he wanted. Knowing Liz turned out to be the biggest adventure of his life. Seth smiles, thinking that his younger self would be thrilled to know just how dramatic life would become. And so much of the chaos is wrapped up in that girl.

Earlier, when Mathilda urgently called him to the bridge, he was so afraid something had happened to Liz that he wasn't sure his legs would carry him. Somehow, they did, moving quickly and efficiently as his heart thumped in his ears. He was relieved to learn that she was on the other end of the radio, not dead somewhere after self-destructing the shuttle. He was even more relieved to hear her voice, but then suddenly angry and bewildered to learn that she was bringing back strange people. He felt like his heart had been ripped out of his chest.

No doubt, for Liz, it was a simple decision. In her framework of good and evil, she found these people good, and that was all there was to it. It wasn't as straightforward for Seth, and he knew the Council would be even less understanding. In fact, they were furious.

He convened them immediately, and his mother railed with a fury he didn't know she possessed. Even Harry, who typically supported Liz's views, was agitated about the implications of bringing fifty-two unknown people to the ship. Jarrod and Mathilda didn't seem as emotional, but they had no desire to allow the refugees on board.

It wasn't until Claire suggested that Jarrod blow the shuttle in space that Seth joined the fray. He called for order, and when his mother dismissed him with a wave and continued to talk, he lost his composure, slamming his fists down on the table and roaring for silence. He doesn't yet know what consequences these refugees will bring with them, but he knows this much—he needs Liz more than the air he breathes. He won't allow her to be villainized, and he certainly won't see her blown up in space.

He takes a deep breath as he tries to dismiss the Council meeting from his mind, willing his anger to pass. Instead, he thinks about what his life would be like if he hadn't met Liz at the depot that day. It's hard to imagine— a dull existence, small and stifling. Would he still have become Captain? Maybe. Or maybe he would have continued his studies in biology and chemistry, to work in his mother's department. He dismisses thoughts of his mother as a fresh wave of resentment threatens to wash over him. He can't live his life for her—the life she wants for him is not worth living.

No, Seth requires more, and Liz opened his eyes to more, or at least to her version of the world. He never could have imagined the sheer brutality of it on his own—the loss, grief, suffering, and hunger that Liz blames completely on the New Generation. It's simple and yet it's complex, involving people and places beyond his imagination, roaming far beyond the ship and the depots he barely got to know. Her world is so much bigger than his own that it scares him, even while it intrigues and inspires him to learn more, do more, and be more.

And yet, he can never fully live in Liz's world. He is only a visitor, a tourist, and he can never be anything beyond that. No, he now travels between two worlds, belonging to neither—the sheltered and simplistic world of the Green Grow elite, and the brutal and simplistic world of everyone else.

Seth tries to use his perspective to his advantage, to see the bigger picture, but it's harder than he ever could have imagined. He needs to think three moves ahead while battling a full complement of players, and he doesn't think he's been doing a very good job so far. The Council is in turmoil. The crew has not only been infiltrated by New Generation spies but is now demanding answers to questions about the refugees. And most importantly, the deep space propulsion drive is still days away from being operational.

Seth knows they need to get out of Earth's orbit—not in several days, but now. The New Generation knows they have the antimatter drive, and Seth has no doubt they will use whatever means at their disposal to keep him from using it. If his mother is right about anything, it's that the New Generation will kill them if they overtake the ship. Leaving should be the Council's top priority, and it infuriates him that they are so easily distracted by problems that are relatively inconsequential, including fifty-two starving refugees who were easily quarantined in the medical unit.

Tensions are high, and Seth knows they will not abate as long as the Green Grow 3 sits in its predictable orbit, only a shuttle ride away from the enemy. They need distance between the ship and whatever attack the New Generation might be planning. Then, once they are safe, he can focus on the real problem—figuring out how to negotiate peace with the New Generation. For now, though, he can't think about that. His mind is over-whelmed with the problems at hand, no matter how pesky they may seem.

Seth glances at Liz one more time, sound asleep and motionless. No doubt she is wondering what's going on, but she will have to wait. He turns to the report Mathilda delivered an hour ago, the first batch of background checks completed on the refugees. He is disheartened to see how sparse it is. Sighing deeply, Seth settles in to read what little there is to know.

CHAPTER 6

QUARANTINE

****

AUGUST 15, 2059 – FRIDAY

Liz opens her eyes and sits up, stiff and disoriented. *I'm not in my quarters,* she realizes, as unfamiliar bodies shuffle around her. She hears laughter and murmuring conversations about breakfast. *The quarantine,* she remembers, fresh dismay washing over her at being confined with fifty-two people she doesn't know. *Knowing people is overrated,* she chides herself. *At least these ones like you.* Her mind flashes back to Claire and to her conversation with Harry, opening a new pit of anxiety in her stomach.

She stretches her arms and back as she eyes her tablet warily. Her body is stiff but surprisingly well rested. She doesn't remember dreaming, a welcome respite from the nightmares she's had about Sam and Ellen every time she's slept since Minneapolis.

Curiosity growing, she powers on the tablet and checks her messages. She sees that Seth has announced an all-hands meeting tomorrow. The notice, which went to the entire crew, contains very little information. *No doubt the culmination of whatever the Council was doing yesterday without me,* she thinks wryly. The anxiety in her stomach mushrooms as she sees a second message in her inbox.

> BE DRESSED IN A BIOHAZARD SUIT AND IN THE DECONTAMINATION CHAMBER AT 1400 HOURS. YOU WILL BE ESCORTED TO MY OFFICE FOR DEBRIEFING. SETH

Liz tries to blink away her unease, closing the tablet and rising from her cot. She hears lively, cheerful sounds coming from the common room, and she allows the noise to draw her in like a warm embrace. She sees a simple breakfast buffet waiting and chooses a small bowl of grits. She garnishes them sparingly with butter and milk before sitting alone at a table to take in the scene.

Others are eating, sitting at tables in pairs or small groups. They smile and laugh, sharing buzzing whispers between relished bites. At the table closest to Liz, a young woman sits with two boys, boys who might be ten or eleven. A book lies open on the table in front of them—one of the battered volumes Liz remembers from the security scan. The smaller boy points to a word, trying to sound it out.

"Skkkk … Skyyyyyy …"

"The 'c' is silent, Bobby," the woman patiently hints. Bobby's face flushes as he squeezes his fists into tight balls. She smiles at him. "You're doing great. This isn't an easy word. Keep trying."

His mouth forms the word silently. "Science!" he blurts out. The young woman nods, smiling in approval. Bobby's face beams. Liz remembers her mother teaching her to read, or was it Jackson? She digs deep into her memories, realizing they both helped her learn. And what a gift reading was—it opened new worlds for her and helped fill the hungry days, back when she still had a mother and her biggest concern was not having enough food. She turns her attention away from the lesson, away from the familiar pang of regret that stabs her heart.

At a table farther away, three older children play with the jacks and rubber ball Liz remembers from the security scan. The ball thumps as it bounces on the table. Liz watches the children, who look to be in their early teens, as they study the ball and the jacks, scooping them up between bounces. *They made up their own rules*, she observes, trying to remember how the game works.

Liz returns her attention to her bowl, carefully scooping out the last of the grits. She checks the time as she rises to return her dish to the collection bin. It is 816. In six hours, she will be sitting in Seth's office. It sounds far away, but she knows six hours isn't much time. She needs to learn everything she can about these people—her people—before then. It's time to talk to the old woman.

***

Liz finds Ruth in one of the converted exam rooms, sitting at a small table, staring at a monitor. She appears deeply engrossed in whatever she is watching, oblivious to the three children behind her who cluster around a stack of playing cards on a cot. Liz peeks over the old woman's shoulder, recognizing the first in a series of Green Grow orientation videos. She watches as a well-groomed, extremely healthy narrator who stands before a large map of North America.

"The date is February 23, 2037," his voice booms dramatically. "The United States of America is thriving as it sits oblivious atop the North American Plate, a tectonic plate covering most of North America, Greenland, Cuba, the Bahamas, and parts of Asia and Iceland. America's position in the world economy is strong. Determined to preserve their superpower status at any cost, they dominate the world economically, linguistically, and militarily.

"Then, at 9:37 a.m. Central Standard Time, a magnitude 5.9 earthquake hits the Midwest, in the middle of the New Madrid seismic zone. Tremors were felt in 24 states. Across Missouri and Illinois, the topology twisted and deformed. For the first time since 1811, the Mississippi River appeared to run backward." The screen fills with devastation, crumbled remains of buildings and piles of debris, as the narrator continues.

"Illinois, Missouri, Kentucky, Tennessee, and Arkansas were immediately declared disaster zones, and FEMA was deployed to assist millions of displaced and injured people …" Liz knows he'll talk about the second Midwest quake next, the magnitude 7.8 that destroyed cities as far south as Jackson, Mississippi. Liz was only two years old when it happened, too young to have her own memories of it. She knows the history well enough, but to her it's just a sequence of facts to be memorized, facts to explain the demise of a world she doesn't remember.

"… The country thinks things are at their worst. But, in fact, the New Madrid seismic zone isn't the most dangerous part of the North American Plate right now. It's just a small fracture in the middle of the plate that never managed to fully split."

It seems almost silly to Liz now, the melodramatic troubles of a tectonic plate that can't manage to split. Of course, she knows it's not silly, but she feels her throat creating a noise nonetheless. She doesn't know if it will be a snicker or a groan, and so she tries to suppress it. But the sound escapes her like a guttural hiccup, causing Ruth to jump and whirl in her chair.

"Dr. Singh said it would be okay to start watching the orientation videos," she says quickly.

"Of course," Liz replies, hoping to pass the noise off as a cough. "The series is quite good, especially the later ones that talk about the space farms. I was hoping we could chat, but I can wait if you'd like to finish this segment."

Ruth shakes her head. "I know well enough what happened next—the magnitude 8 California quake. The food shortages, contaminated water. The riots. The power outages."

"The videos don't say much about the California quake," Liz says thoughtfully. "The narrator spends the most time talking about the extinction event."

Extinction event—the name suggests that such an event would have killed all the life on the planet, but that clearly wasn't the case. It didn't even make humans go extinct; it only had the potential to do that. *Has*, Liz reminds herself. *It has the potential to make humans go extinct. We aren't exactly out of danger yet.* Most accounts agree that civilization could have recovered from the earthquakes. But it's less clear still whether civilization will survive the extinction event—the supervolcano that erupted outside of Las Cruces, New Mexico, on April 25, 2037.

The devastation from the supervolcano dwarfed anything anyone could have imagined. The earth exploded, sending tons of ash into the atmosphere. Some if it settled back to the ground, smothering plants and contaminating soil. Some of it remained in the atmosphere, blocking the sun. The ruptured earth belched sulphur dioxide into the air, further compounding the devastation, suffocating people and animals for hundreds of miles, killing sea algae, and causing erratic weather and volcanic winters. Lava spewed from the volcano in unimaginable proportions, burying New Mexico and most of Texas in a flood basalt over twenty feet deep.

Liz thinks that humans will survive. But civilization? If the New Generation is what remains of civilization, then it's already dead as far as she's concerned. She looks back at the old woman, whose face is drawn as if she's still trying to decide whether to finish the video now or later.

"Let's talk now," Ruth says. "I'm sure we have a lot to discuss." She turns to the children playing cards behind them. "Axle," she begins softly, "will you take Logan and Sophia into the common room?" The oldest boy, presumably Axle, smiles and nods, directing them out as the girl quickly gathers the cards. *They so desperately want to please her,* Liz observes as the children softly pad out of the room.

"Tell me about your group," Liz says as she settles onto the edge of a nearby chair, unsure how to open the conversation. Ruth takes the cue and resumes her seat as well, hands folded neatly in her lap.

"Most of us were from a small town called Oxford, between Denver and Colorado Springs."

Liz waits for her to continue, but Ruth seems to have turned inward, eyes soft.

"Are you from Oxford?" Liz prompts.

"Oh yes, I lived there all my life. I had a husband—Bill was his name—and three children. But they were grown by the time the quakes hit. I … I lost them all that first year." Ruth's eyes glimmer with a hint of moisture, but Liz knows the old woman will not cry. She radiates weariness, suggesting that all her tears have long since been spent.

"You said you were living in a cave. Why?" Of course, what Liz really means is, *Tell me how the New Generation destroyed your town and forced you into hiding.* She assumes Ruth knows this, and indeed, Ruth does. It's only a question of details, and in this case the details involve Ruth's former neighbor Steve—a Green Grow biochemist working out of the Denver depot.

"He drove to the Denver depot each day in a little electric company car," Ruth explains. "He tried to use it to help people in the town, bringing loads of food and taking people to the depot to see the doctor, but the car made him a target. It made all of us targets."

Liz cannot mask her incredulity, and so she looks away. She knows that the New Generation's arrival was inevitable. It would be wrong to blame a hapless fool like Steve. All he did was help them find Oxford faster than they might have otherwise, and yet how could he not have known the danger? Liz gets the feeling that Ruth's group lived in the cave for a long time, but were things so different, even many years ago? Was it reasonable for anyone to think they could drive an electric Green Grow car in plain sight back and forth to their home and not suffer the consequences of the New Generation? Was there ever a time that was a good idea?

Ruth continues to explain, "The first time they just rode through on their motorcycles, looking like beasts with painted faces and leather clothes. The next time, they took his car. And—they killed him. They stabbed him and set him on fire, in his front yard."

Ruth pauses for a moment, breathing deeply and wiping her palms on her legs. *She's still terrified of them,* Liz muses, knowing how frightful the raiding parties could seem. They looked like monsters—savages adorned in bones and metal and war paint who breathed death and drank pain. *They used to scare me, too,* she remembers. Until she began stalking them. Back then, Liz was determined to find out where they went, where they lived. She thought they might lead her to Jackson, or at least to news of him. But they never did. *He wouldn't have stuck around with those feebleminded barbarians, anyway,* she thinks, feeling her chest tighten. *He either died in the New Generation or left it.*

When Liz started following the raiding parties, she realized just how pathetic they really were. She'd lag behind them during the day, skulking on foot behind their roaring motorcycles. It wasn't hard because they seemed to stop every few miles, and they didn't go fast even when they were riding. They usually made camp as soon as it started to get dark. It didn't take long to catch up, to settle into a hiding place, ready to watch and listen.

The best hiding spots were high in dead pine trees. It never seemed to occur to them to look up. But she could also hide in the wreckage of burned-out cars or even old drainage ditches. She heard them argue and whine like children over the stupidest things, like who got to ride the lead motorcycle and who decided how often they stopped. She watched them fight over food and women. She saw them kill each other over insults and insinuations. Some of them seemed crafty, but none of them overly smart. *Just like the animals they are,* she thinks. *Disgusting.* She doesn't need to know the details of her brother's fate to know that she will never forgive the New Generation—whatever they did to him.

"Is that when you went to the cave?" Liz prompts, pulling herself and Ruth back into the conversation.

"I knew we needed to leave," the woman replies. "I remembered the cave from when I was a girl. My father used to take me there. I think he found it one day hunting deer. The entrance was small and hidden in a gully next to an old nature preserve that hardly anyone visited. It was quite large inside and stretched into the mountains. The ceiling had collapsed in a few places, enough to let some light filter in. And there was an underground stream that pooled in one of the caverns."

"So, you had shelter and water," Liz recaps.

Ruth nods, then her voice turns bitter. "We started moving people and supplies, but we didn't get out in time. The New Generation came again and razed the town. They took everything they wanted and burned the rest. Those of us who made it barely escaped with our lives. But, we got to the cave and settled into a new way of living."

She went on to explain how survivors joined the group as they were discovered, and a few people left to search for family members. They grew some food in the cave, but it wasn't enough to keep them from starving. Like so many other people, they relied on the depot. Pairs or groups of three would make supply runs to the depot on bicycles, pulling carts behind. They scavenged too, forming scouting parties to sift through the remains of nearby ruins.

Liz listens in wonder as Ruth describes all the scavenged mirrors they used to magnify light in the particular cavern where they could grow food. *That must have been quite a sight,* she thinks, *a stone room painted in mirrors and light.* Ruth lingers on this point, talking about how they would hang the mirrors, making frames for them when they could to keep them from breaking. She talks about the light reflecting between them, bouncing back and forth and back and forth, making the cave brighter with each pass. Liz listens, soaking it all in, allowing herself just a moment to dream that her mother could have found such a place, when she and Jackson were still little. Could they have lived in a stone room painted with mirrors? Could they have been a family? *Yes,* she thinks, but the word is a hollow bubble settling in her dream, creating an empty space where there should be joy. She blinks the thought away as Ruth continues, explaining how they hid the entrance to the cave, how they hid themselves.

It all seems plausible as Ruth explains it, but Liz doesn't fully understand. She won't ask the question but still wonders—how did a group of fifty-two people survive? Even in a cave, a large group would be hard to hide and even harder to sustain. Most survivors lived alone or in small family units, and for good reason. They needed to travel light and fast, without excessive burdens, so as to flee or search for food. Every hungry mouth was a competing demand, and only the closest of families endured the sacrifice and commitment required to keep someone else safe and fed. Outsiders were unpredictable—fickle and treacherous. Liz remembers her mom taking in a few, and it never ended well. The weak ones wilted into a burden, and the strong ones left with whatever they could steal.

"How long did you live in the cave?" Liz asks, trying to gain perspective.

Ruth's answer comes. "Nineteen years."

Nineteen years? Liz tries to keep her face slack, but she doesn't know if she's succeeding. Her mind is spinning. Nineteen years. She tries to imagine doing anything for nearly two decades, but the only thing she's done consistently for that long is breathe. She didn't even have a mother for nineteen years, or a brother. She tries to imagine living in the same place with the same people for that length of time, but she can't. Nothing in her life has been that consistent—not even Seth. Not yet, anyway.

Liz grasps for some clue, some explanation for how a group of over fifty people survived nearly twenty years without making a mistake, without getting caught by the New Generation. Mistakes are so easy to make, and people are so good at making them. Liz has seen it herself and heard countless more stories. People made targets of themselves by buying too many goods at the depot or bragging about things they found or had. Liz knows that some people would tip off the New Generation if they knew where survivors were hiding, in exchange for food or safety or whatever else they found of value. Even something as simple as making too much noise in a now-quiet world could tip off a raiding party. People make mistakes—it's just what they do. But this group survived for nineteen years without being discovered.

Liz's mind sifts through everything she's observed since she met these people, searching for some keystone or cipher that will make all of this make sense. Something about their situation seems off to her. Something isn't right, but she so desperately wants it to be. She saved these people—she needs it to be right.

She thinks about their first encounter at the depot, when Ruth asked her to help them. She remembers the children being shuffled to the front, closest to the fence.

Ruth asked her to take Zachary. Melissa and Will didn't object or complain. They didn't try to save themselves. No one did. She thinks about dinner last night, how no one touched their tray until everyone had one, even though they were starving. She thinks about story time, the laughter and memories.

Do they really love each other that selflessly? she wonders. It's the only explanation she can find, at least for now, and yet it's still nearly impossible for her to believe.

Does such a selfless love really even exist? Liz wonders, but she believes it does. She instantly thinks of her mother—her laugh, her smile, her starving face, her secret tears that Liz only heard when she was too hungry to sleep at night. Memories of her mother fly into her mind like arrows, memories of the sacrifices she made for Liz to survive, and she starts to feel sick.

Stop it, Liz commands her mind, *you still need information.* She swallows the bile rising in her throat, forcing it down with the grits she ate only an hour ago. She levels her gaze into Ruth's pine bark eyes, warm and alive, and forces herself to continue.

"Why were you at the depot that day? Did you know I was coming?"

"No." Ruth shakes her head. "We saw the shuttle land, but we were already on our way. We had to abandon the cave. The New Generation kept scouting closer and closer—I think they were onto us. It was just a matter of time. So, we took what we could and started walking to the depot. It took us two days, but we didn't know where else to go. I figured we had to try, for the children if nothing else. We couldn't just lie down and die. We almost didn't make it, but you know that part."

Liz nods dismissively. She doesn't want or need to rehash the events at the depot. She wants to end the conversation, to find a place to hide until she can wrangle her thoughts—or perhaps her memories—back into submission. She wants to think about what all of this means. She wants to decide if she believes it. But she doesn't have the luxury of time. Liz needs to learn everything she can before she meets with Seth. She'll need to tell him something he doesn't know so he will see that she still has value. So, Liz presses on, hoping Ruth can handle the part of the discussion that needs to come next.

"The number of children living in this group is … unusual. How did they survive?"

Ruth studies Liz's face before she answers. "We always put the children first. They receive the best and the most of whatever we have—food, medicine, anything." Her face turns bitter again, a look that could never suit her, as she concludes with, "The adults simply die off faster."

Liz knows she needs to press harder. "Will mentioned that some of these children might be … connected. To the New Generation. Does anyone in the group have New Generation ties?"

Suddenly, Ruth looks angry. "Connected? If you mean the product of rape and brutality, the answer is yes. Of course. But the children are innocent, regardless of how they come to be here."

"I'm sorry for asking," Liz says dispassionately, because she isn't really, she can't be. "But more questions like this will come. The New Generation terror isn't confined to the surface. We know they have infiltrated the space farms, so you can expect a lot of questions about any connections any of you may have to them."

Ruth nods in agreement, or perhaps acknowledgment, her composure wavering as she asks, "What's going to happen to us now?"

"I don't know," Liz admits. "I haven't been debriefed yet. But you are safe here, and if there's a way I can make this easier for everyone, I want to do it."

"Well, you got us this far," Ruth says with a tone of confidence Liz hopes is real. The old woman stands, straightening her shoulders as she beckons Liz to follow her. "Let's get you better acquainted."

The next few hours vanish in a whirlwind.

***

"I want to introduce you to our youngest member first," Ruth whispers, eyes settling on a young woman standing in the common room with a blanket wrapped around her. Liz recognizes her as the terrified young woman swaddled in a blanket the day before, the one Dr. Singh searched. "Gabriella," Ruth begins, "this is Liz, the woman from the depot." Gabriella looks scared, but if Ruth notices, she doesn't let on. "How is he this morning?"

Gabriella's deep eyes dart between Liz and Ruth. She smiles nervously. "He's good. He had a big breakfast, and he's sleeping." She removes part of the blanket draped over her shoulder to reveal a perfect little cherub face, much thinner than it should be, with dark hair and full lips. Liz gasps. She's never seen such a small baby. *Is this why Dr. Singh spared her being frisked by the security officers?*

"Liz," Ruth whispers, "this is Luke. He's ten months old." Liz's eyes fly to Gabriella's face, astonished. *How did either of them survive?*

"He's our miracle baby," Ruth continues, as if she can read Liz's mind. "We found Gabriella wandering alone, hungry and beaten. She was about seven months along." Ruth gently strokes the baby's face. His lips purse as he begins sucking his tongue.

"Gabriella," Ruth continues softly, "Liz is going to help us navigate all the questions we'll have to answer now that we're on the ship. She needs to know more about us. I know it's not easy, but can you tell her about your life before you joined our group?" The young woman bites her lip but nods slightly, clutching her sleeping baby closer.

Liz waits, but Gabriella is unable to speak.

"He has your face," Liz offers, hoping it will make her more comfortable. Of course, the tiny little human looks nothing like the woman, but Liz thinks it's the right thing to say.

"No," Gabriella replies, smiling wryly as she bundles the blanket back around her sleeping baby. "I'm sure he looks like his father. But, he's not his father. He's my angel, even though he looks like the devil."

"How old are you?" Liz asks softly, hoping to start somewhere that isn't too painful.

"Twenty-two," Gabriella replies, pausing for a moment as her brow furrows. "My father sold me to the New Generation when I was sixteen. He wanted to go south— past the flood basalt into Mexico. He said it made sense because his people originally came from Mexico. He said it was his right." She rocks back and forth from one foot to another, even though Liz is sure the baby is sound asleep. *Which one of them is the rocking meant to comfort?*

Liz knows Gabriella's father isn't unique—a lot of people talked about going south. There were rumors that it was still easy to grow food there, that it was still warm. Liz doesn't know the truth of it, but she's noticed tiny clusters of lights on the northern edge of South America when she watches the Earth from the window by the cafeteria. So, something must be going right down there. Liz waits for Gabriella to continue, but the young woman remains silent.

"What do you mean he *sold* you?" Liz prompts. Abduction was common, but she's never heard of anyone being sold.

"He traded me for a motorcycle," Gabriella replies, the emotion draining from her voice. "It was too far for him to walk to Mexico, so he traded me for a vehicle."

She continues mechanically, without further prompting.

"The man who bought me, Marco, he was a mechanic. He wasn't part of the raiding parties. He managed a New Generation fuel and repair station. It was mostly motorcycles, but sometimes there were trucks. He said he wanted a wife who was … clean. Not a woman who had been dragged off by a raiding party. So, he rebuilt an old motorcycle, filled it with New Generation fuel, and traded it for me."

Gabriella stares at Liz, deadpan, seeking some cue about what to say next. Liz considers the woman's dead eyes and slack face, debating what to say next. *She doesn't need pity right now,* Liz realizes, knowing that sometimes the only way to tell a story is to disconnect from all it makes you feel.

"What was it like to live with Marco? Was he good to you?" Liz asks.

"Sometimes," Gabriella responds flatly. "He protected me, and made sure I had food to eat. But he beat me sometimes, and he expected things—things I didn't want to do."

Liz sees something flicker in Gabriella's dark eyes as the young woman changes the subject. "Babies are prized in the New Generation—coveted. Someone in a raiding party noticed I was pregnant, and a group of men came a few days later in a van to take me away. I heard there was a place where the pregnant women go give birth. I heard once you go there, you don't come back. Marco didn't want me to go, so he fought them—said he'd defend me with his life. He killed two of the men, but there were too many of them.

"I was scared. I didn't want to go to the place where women have babies. But I didn't want to be beaten anymore either, or forced to do things I didn't like. So, I ran. I hid in the junkyard behind the house until the men gave up looking for me. Then I ran some more. I thought I would die, but I'd rather be dead than a slave that breeds more slaves.

"I don't remember much else before the cave. I remember a scouting party found me. I was scared, but the women told me I'd be free. Ruth took care of me—of both of us." Gabriella's eyes are blank again, exhausted.

"What else do you know about the New Generation?" Liz asks gently.

"Not much." Gabriella's brow furrows in thought. "The business is done by the men. Marco and I lived at the station, but I heard a lot of them live underground, in compounds they've built. I'd see the raiding parties when they stopped for fuel. Sometimes there were women—they could go if they kept the men entertained. But mostly I didn't talk to them. Marco didn't like me being around them."

Liz waits, but Gabriella says no more. She only rocks as she clutches her sleeping baby. Ruth approaches the young woman, murmuring promises of a book to read as she guides her back to a chair.

"Thank you, Gabriella," Liz says softly. "I'm glad you and Luke are here. You are both safe—and free." Liz nods to Ruth and turns away, surprised to hear Gabriella's voice echoing frantically behind her.

"I can work," she says quickly. "I'm a fast learner, and Luke won't be a problem. I'll get to keep him, won't I?"

Liz turns back and locks eyes with the skittish, distraught woman. "No one is going to take your baby," she says firmly. Gabriella nods, eyes darting around the room as if she needs more reassurance. Ruth smiles and steers Liz away.

"I hope you meant that," Ruth says quietly. "She won't let that baby out of her sight, not even for a few minutes."

Liz looks at her sidelong and repeats her vow. "No one will take her baby." They say no more about it.

***

"That man over there is Ruben." Ruth motions to a dark-haired man who looks a few years older than Seth. "He doesn't speak, but he understands everything you say to him. He can write notes, and he has a kind of sign language many of us understand. He's thirty-two now, and he's been with our group about five years.

"We know he was married. It seems his wife was abducted by a New Generation raiding party, and they left him for dead. He doesn't share much else, but you can try." Liz appraises him quickly as he approaches the group of children she saw earlier—Axle, Logan, and Sophia. He sits to play cards with them, flashing a toothy smile and motioning something with his hands that makes them laugh.

"Does he have children?" Liz asks.

"No, those aren't his children. Axle and Logan are orphans. I think that's why Ruben gets along with them so well. None of them have anybody."

Sophia is not an orphan. As it turns out, she is part of the largest intact family in the group. Liz meets Sophia's mother Olivia, Olivia's aunt Ava, Ava's husband Justin, and their two grown children Noah and Emily. They are all former Oxford residents.

Next, Ruth introduces her to Nora, who is Melissa's mom and Will's mother-in-law. She is also Steve's sister—the man with the electric car who lived next to Ruth. She is a quiet woman with empty eyes, in her fifties now. Ruth whispers to Liz as they leave Nora behind that she hasn't been the same since Steve died, since she saw him burning alive in his front yard, screaming and flailing to try to extinguish the flames. Then Liz meets Sarah, a widow in her sixties, and Colin, another former Green Grow employee who lost his job when the Denver depot closed. Colin is in his forties, and has a much younger brother, Ryan, just a couple years older than Liz.

There are so many new faces, so many new names, so many stories. Liz isn't sure if her head or her heart is in greater danger of exploding, but neither has space for another introduction, another face, or another story. She excuses herself from Ruth, who seems energized by all the activity.

Liz is determined to find a place in the crowded quarantine to be alone, even if it means locking herself in a toilet, but it doesn't come to that. Dr. Singh stops her in the hallway, wobbling along in her yellow biohazard suit, to remind Liz that she needs to complete a scan for anything contagious she might have picked up on the surface.

"How about now?" Liz asks, hoping that the rhythmic humming and pulsing of the scanner might drown out her thoughts. Even if it doesn't, at least she'll be alone. Moments later, she dons a thin medical gown and climbs into the scanner, praying that the lunch trays are delivered before she gets out.

CHAPTER 7

ZAG BRYANT

***

Liz crosses the threshold into Seth's office on Level 1 at precisely 1408. Her thoughts are spinning, trying to organize and assimilate everything she's learned about the survivors, adjudicating each piece of information for importance. Is any of it important? She doesn't know. She thinks about Will and Ruth and the faces of the children. She thinks about the stories she heard this morning. They are all compelling, but are they important? Are they enough to redeem her in the eyes of the Council? Will they undo whatever damage she's done to her relationship with Seth?

"Sit," he commands as he dismisses her escort. Liz studies his face, urgently seeking any signs of his mood as they sit in silence, waiting for the door to close. She registers his bloodshot eyes and tousled hair, how he sits behind his desk, cold and unmoving. *This is not going to be a good meeting,* she realizes as the ominous cloud surrounding him reaches out to envelope her in its dark, stifling embrace.

"Explain yourself," he barks, sitting tall in his chair as soon as they are alone.

Liz unlatches the bulky helmet and slides it off her head.

"I assume you're not really concerned about a contagion," she states coldly, meeting his hard gaze.

"Who are these people?" he demands.

"They are survivors—refugees. They came under attack by New Generation when I was at the depot, just outside the fence."

"So, you don't know any of them," he spits. Liz realizes this is an accusation, not a question, and the fear that has taken residence in her belly ignites into anger.

"Actually, it seems I do know one of them," she begins through gritted teeth. "Will Dabato and I worked together on a growing level several years ago, before he went to the surface and didn't return." Seth's callous eyes drill into her, but she meets his gaze coolly, unflinching.

"I'm not sure if that's better or worse," he growls, standing up quickly from his chair. Liz remains seated, oblivious to his towering hulk.

"What exactly is the problem, and why is everyone quarantined?" she demands, arching her neck to look at him.

"You go to the surface by yourself for supplies and bring back fifty-two unknown people from a depot surrounded by hostile forces. You alone decide to load them on the shuttle that the New Generation would stop at nothing to get. You jeopardize our entire operation, and you want to know what the problem is?"

"Why are we quarantined?" Liz keeps her voice even. "The medical scans are done. No one is dangerously sick. I'm not sick."

"Don't play dumb with me," he hisses through gritted teeth. "You know I had to tell the crew something while we attempt to check all of their backgrounds. Word has spread like wildfire. Everyone wants to know who's here and why."

"I heard," she replies casually. "Dr. Singh told me they're calling them 'Liz's fifty-two.' But you won't find anything useful. Most of them have been off the grid for years."

"You have no further explanation for your actions?" His face begins to flush.

"Seth," she asks softly, "why are you so angry?"

"Answer my questions or stop talking!" he roars, fists clenching and unclenching as he breathes sharply through his nose. Liz glares at him, measuring her words carefully as her patience began to crack.

"What's really the question here, Seth? I won't apologize for saving these people."

"Of course you won't," he cries, arms gesticulating violently in the air. He stabs a finger toward her in accusation. "You are too insolent to apologize for anything you do!"

Liz flies to standing from her chair, still lithe even in the bulky suit.

"Bushwa!" she screams, looking up to meet his fury. "Save your self-righteousness for someone who doesn't know you as well as I do. This is about your mother, isn't it?" A darkness flickers in his eyes as he turns away, raking his fingers through his hair. He doesn't respond.

Everything Liz wanted to say at the Council meeting suddenly begins to gush out of her mouth. "I know just how dangerous the New Generation is—I've lived it for far longer than anyone on the Council! But it's not right to blame me for that danger, it's just easy! It's easy for your mom to blame me because I do the dirty work! I do the things that have to be done while she sits safe and comfortable on the Council, trying to clutch you in her lap!" She stares defiantly at Seth's back, knowing that she could say more, but it wouldn't serve any purpose other than hurting him.

"How do you know we can trust these people?" he asks, voice low and deadly.

"I don't," Liz replies sharply. "Seth, we know the New Generation has spies on this ship. We can't trust anyone. But you searched the survivors for contraband and communication devices and found nothing. They aren't any less trustworthy than anyone else here." He remains distant, his face a mystery as he stands unmoving with his back to her. "You weren't there, Seth! I made a decision in the field. Circumstances happen. Decisions have to be made. I didn't know they would be there, but they were. I made a decision!"

"Circumstances? Decisions? What about the circumstances you created?" Seth's voice cracks. "What about the decision I had to make, Liz? I thought I might have to blow you to stardust!"

"Seth, there were innocent people involved—children. What would you have done? Watch the New Generation slaughter them?" Liz spreads her hands in front of her, pleading with him as he stands with his back turned.

Finally, he speaks, his voice even and low. "My mother isn't the only one on the Council upset about these refugees. Four days ago, Jarrod intercepted new messages to the New Generation. We couldn't pinpoint where they originated on the ship or who sent them. Best we can tell, whatever device transmitted them was destroyed immediately after the communications were sent."

"Four days ago?" Liz is incredulous. Why is she hearing about this only now?

"They know we have the antimatter drive, and they know we'll be leaving as soon as its installed."

"You didn't find this relevant for me to know before I went to the surface?" Liz demands, feeling sick as the realization settles on her that the New Generation would be even more desperate now to find a way onboard. If she had known, she might have … *What?* she asks herself. *Left the survivors to die?*

"I'm not sure it's relevant for you to know now, given what you've done!" he shoots back, finally turning to face her. "You know we've been infiltrated. You know how careful we need to be."

"Careful?" she demands. "At whose expense? Over fifty survivors? Seth, this makes no sense. Nothing about our present situation is *careful.* What we *need* to do is get our asses out of here, and I fail to see how saving these people has any bearing on that!"

"Oh Liz." Seth's voice is caustic. "You fail to see so many things. I'm trying to save the lives of everyone on this ship. Who exactly are you saving?"

Liz reels, speechless. She doesn't know which hurts worse—his words or his tone. But maybe he's right. *I'm certainly not saving my mother,* she thinks. *And I can't even find my brother, much less save him. This would be so much simpler if Ellen had killed me in Minneapolis.* But Liz knows things will never be that simple; her heart has already died a thousand times over, but the rest of her body can't even manage it once. Her lungs begin to burn, swimming in the tears she knows she can't hold back much longer.

"At this point," she replies through gritted teeth, "it seems I'm saving strangers. Am I dismissed yet, *Captain?*"

"No, you are not," he replies, his voice as cold as his eyes. "You and I both know you didn't turn in all your weapons. Turn it over to me now." Liz freezes. Her knife. He wants her knife. No one touches her knife. She starts to speak but has no words, just the emptiness of all those who have abandoned her.

"Z," Seth says softly, "I'll give it back to you as soon as you're out. This shitshow is only going to get worse if one of these refugees steals it and hurts someone."

Liz's eyes narrow. *He's only taking it because he can.* Ripping open the fastenings of her biohazard suit, she reaches under her tunic, where the large survival knife is strapped to her bare skin.

"Save your lies for the crew!" she hisses as she launches the blade end over end, stabbing into the plush carpet less than an inch from his right boot. "Don't forget, Seth. None of us got here alone." Her voice has a ragged edge, and he isn't sure if she is threatening him or reassuring him.

She unbuckles the thin leather sheath and tosses it unceremoniously at his feet, biting her lip as if considering whether to say more. She doesn't. Instead, she turns her back, attaches the bulky helmet to her suit, and waits for her escort to take her back to quarantine.

"You forced my hand, Z." His voice is soft. "Do you have any idea how precarious all of this is? Really, do you have any clue?"

"I'm well aware," she replies nasally through the mask, "of the lies you've told this crew and everything that involves. I've helped you tell every single one."

"Well then," he starts sarcastically, "I'm glad you realize we're both neck-deep in this fresh hell. Get some rest. We have a Council meeting and an all-hands meeting tomorrow. I want you to be the one to explain the refugees to the crew—you'll know best what to say to them."

She hears his words but doesn't respond.

***

Liz sheds the biohazard suit in the decontamination chamber, feeling naked without the leather sheath pressed against her belly. She fixes her eyes to the ground as the door opens into the quarantine, heading straight for her cot. She curls into a ball, pulls the blanket over her head, and buries her face in the pillow, sobbing the burning tears that refuse to be denied.

Does he really not understand why I did what I did? she wonders, as the pain of his harsh words transforms to fear. She can't lose Seth—he's the only one who matters to her now. How will she go on if he turns his back on her? *Would I even want to?* She squeezes her eyes shut tightly, sucking in air between sobs as her broken, empty heart whispers words of comfort. *He didn't mean it. You misunderstood. Everything is okay. You'll see.*

Her tears fade to a trickle, leaving Liz weak and tired, withered and deflated. She flips her pillow over, finding a dry spot to clutch under her chin as she closes her eyes and searches for happier thoughts. She can see Seth's shiny dark hair, his vibrant eyes—sometimes lightning, sometimes steel. *He needs time to understand,* she tells herself. *He hasn't even been to the surface since ...* The realization pierces her fragile heart. Liz knows exactly when Seth last went to the surface. She took him, seven years ago.

The day Liz smuggled Seth onto one of her routine surface runs was a turning point in their relationship. Of course, she'd liked him since she first came to the Green Grow 3. She was only twelve then, although she told everyone she was sixteen. But she was old enough to feel her heart flutter when her eyes met his, her curiosity about him even more powerful than the fear she felt trying to lie her way into a job on the station.

But who wouldn't like Seth? He was handsome and smart, and she quickly learned he had connections – lots of connections. She wasn't the least bit surprised to see how all of the other girls on the ship looked at him, how they pursued him—sometimes with reckless abandon. Indeed, Liz liked him a lot, even from that very first moment, but she couldn't imagine asking anything more of him than he gave her in those first few minutes. Seth smuggled her onto the ship and into a job, and that favor was big enough to last a lifetime. If she could be his friend, it would be enough.

Besides, they were so different. He was important, and she was nobody. So, she left him in peace, although it was always a pleasant surprise when he sought her out, to share a meal or watch a film. He was the first to congratulate her when she worked through a series of promotions to become a shuttle pilot, and she had only completed three surface runs when he whisked her away to a corner of an orchard and asked if she could smuggle him aboard one of the flights.

She stared at him, mouth agape, struck by the realization that maybe it wasn't all fun and games to be cloistered away in comfort and privilege. Maybe he was lonely, or bored.

"Of course I'll help you," she said, "but why? You know I fly cargo shuttles, right? I'm sure your parents could get you onto a passenger shuttle." As he sighed deeply and slumped against a tree, she was struck by another realization. *He doesn't want his parents to know. He wants to go unseen and unknown—like me.*

That was all she needed. She didn't judge or question him; she simply helped him make it happen. He showed up at the dock when she told him, and she hid him in the cargo bay while the rest of the crew was distracted. When they landed at the Denver depot, she helped him blend into the warehouse as the cargo was unloaded.

As a pilot, Liz had a four-hour break while the shuttle was unloaded and then loaded again with supplies to go back to the ship. Usually she spent those four hours napping, eating, or checking for news of her brother, but that day she spent the time seeing the depot through Seth's fresh eyes. She showed him the storefront and the warehouse. She took him up to the fence where he could see the people coming from all around looking for food, medicine, and news.

The experience seemed to overwhelm him, and Liz's first thought was that he was a little soft—perhaps a bit weak. But as he began to ask her questions, and as his excitement grew to incomprehensible levels, Liz realized he wasn't weak at all, just inexperienced in a world that she knew intimately. In fact, she realized he was far braver than she could have imagined. Who else would have pushed the bounds of his world like this? Who else would trust himself to her for the day, functionally blind and deaf in a world he had no clue how to navigate, just to find out what it was like? Only Seth.

It took her longer to understand why he found the adventure so enthralling. What was exciting? Everyone looked so downtrodden on the surface—everyone *was* downtrodden. But she eventually realized that he wasn't excited about *what* he saw; he was simply excited that he managed to see it. Seth wasn't satisfied with the small world his parents had created for him. He wanted to know more, to experience more, and that day he did.

When they docked on the Green Grow 3, he casually strolled off, carrying a notepad she'd given him, just like they'd planned. No one noticed or cared. No one would have imagined someone like Seth Harris would so desperately want to see the surface that he'd stow away like a rat. But they didn't know him like she did, not after that.

She met up with him later in the orchard, and he was still exuberant from the day. That was when Liz realized that he wasn't just handsome—he was beautiful. He grabbed her by the waist, laughing as he spun her around. Then his face grew serious as he set her gently down, pulling her close to him. She thought he might kiss her. She hoped he would. But as he leaned in, a curious look spread across his face.

"What in the world?" He tugged on the front of her tunic, just enough to see it. "Holy bearcats, what the hell is that?"

"My knife?" she asked, disoriented and wanting to hold on to the moment. "I ... I always wear it. Please don't report me. My mom gave it to me." Weapons weren't allowed on the Green Grow 3 unless the company issued you one.

"Report you?" he laughed. "We're so far past that. Anyway, I'd be afraid to report you. You scare me, girl." He didn't kiss her, and it was probably for the best.

That's what Liz tells herself, anyway. Whatever romance they might have had was quashed, but their friendship deepened to a whole new level. Now, back in the present, her knife is gone, and Seth is furious with her. But somehow it seems a little better than before as she closes her eyes and dozes.

***

When she wakes, Liz's face is sticky with tears, eyes still swollen. She checks her tablet, finding a note from Seth.

I'M SORRY. DINNER AT 1700? I'LL COME GET YOU.

She checks the time. It's almost 1600. Rising from her cot, she sees the old woman on the other side of the room, intently studying another Green Grow orientation video. *She made it to the part about the space farms,* Liz notes, deciphering the murmur of the narrator running through the growing level statistics. "… Over fifteen hundred acres of arable land, which can feed thousands of people when cultivated properly. Each ship is outfitted with a complete bioengineering lab to manage livestock such as pigs, goats, and cows …" Liz quietly pads out on bare feet to wash her face and collect herself in the bathroom.

When she returns, Ruth pauses the video, smiling kindly at her.

"Are you okay, dear?" she asks. "You seemed a little unsettled earlier."

Liz is startled by the question. *Dear? Mom used to talk that way sometimes.*

"I'm okay," Liz replies. "There was a lot to discuss with the captain. We're reconvening in an hour. I'm sorry to say that I don't have much to report yet."

"Oh, we're fine," Ruth assures her. "You're the one I was worried about."

Liz doesn't know what to say, so she changes the subject. "I see you made it to the videos about the space farms."

Ruth glances back at the monitor, her expression changing to mild disgust. "Yes," she says curtly. "I'd love to know why the depots are closed and empty, given three space farms with almost five thousand acres of growing land."

"It's a good question," Liz replies, meeting her gaze squarely, "although actually now there are only two space farms. The New Generation hijacked one of them and blew the entire ship."

Ruth's eyes widen as Liz continues.

"Plus, there were all the surface attacks on the depots. Their raiding parties would overrun the security systems, kill the Green Grow employees, and take whatever food and equipment they could carry. The Green Grow Executive Board has been in peace talks with them for over two years now, but progress has been slow. The New Generation obliterated everyone who attended the first peace summit—including our former captain. Until a treaty can be reached, we've been told the routine surface runs are simply too dangerous for everyone—even survivors trying to make their way to the depots."

Liz doesn't mind telling the lie about ongoing peace talks. She is certain that whatever remains of the Executive Board is still trying to negotiate a peace with the New Generation, even if they aren't returning any of the communications Seth sends them. And if the board has been obliterated, which she knows is a real possibility, Seth will figure out how to negotiate peace once they are safely out of orbit.

"Is that why you hate them so much?" Ruth asks, eyes still wide. "The New Generation, I mean."

"Doesn't everyone hate them?" Liz asks.

"I certainly have no love lost for them," Ruth replies bitterly, "although their numbers seem to be growing."

"The New Generation took everything from me," Liz replies, a fresh wave of grief washing over her heart. *How does it still hurt so much?* she wonders. "Hopefully a peace will be reached soon. We all want to get back to the business of bringing food to people on the surface."

"It seems to be an impressive operation," Ruth concludes. "I can't wait to see it in person." She turns back to the video as Liz speaks again.

"Captain Harris is coming to collect me in an hour, to continue our debriefing. Would you like to meet him?"

***

Liz is waiting in the improvised common room when Seth strides into the medical unit to collect her for dinner. She stands to greet him. Everyone else in the room freezes, all attention focused on him.

"No biohazard suit?" she asks.

"Everyone's tests came back clear," Seth replies as he approaches her.

"I see you combed your hair," Liz notes softly, giving him a critical stare. He still looks tired, but otherwise seems composed.

"And I see you washed your face," he replies, eyebrow cocked.

A corner of Liz's mouth turns up as she looks for Ruth, who is sitting at a table with Melissa, Will, and Zachary. "There's someone I'd like you to meet," she says, motioning Seth to follow her. Everyone at the table stands as Liz approaches for introductions.

"Captain Harris," Liz begins, "I'd like to introduce you to Ruth—she's the leader of The Fifty-Two." Ruth's eyes scan him, almost too quickly to notice. She smiles warmly and extends her hand.

"Captain Harris," Ruth begins, as Seth delicately shakes her hand, "I'm so pleased to meet you. Thank you so very much for all of your help and hospitality."

Seth smiles broadly. It's the smile Liz loves best when it is directed to her, although seeing it in any form always makes her feel lighter. She knows he doesn't mean it. She knows he's only being polite. She knows he will never reveal to Ruth his fury at her appearance here. She knows all this, but she likes his smile anyway. Liz admires his ability to hold his true feelings so close, even if it is a bit deceptive.

"Ruth," he says warmly, "welcome aboard. I'm so glad you are here. You can imagine I was a bit surprised when Liz told me she found survivors at the depot, but I'm so glad you found each other. I'm sorry for all of this." He waves his hands in a flourish. "It's all just precautionary."

"Of course, of course," Ruth replies, although her expression seems guarded.

"And this," Liz interjects, "is Will Dabato, his wife Melissa, and their son Zachary. Will and I worked together years ago in the orchard." She motions to the couple, who stand clutching a studious Zachary in their arms.

Will extends his free hand. "Hello, sir, I don't think we've met before."

"I don't think we have," Seth agrees as he shakes his hand heartily. "I'm sure Captain MacAbee was in charge when you were here last."

"Yes," Will agrees with a tentative smile. "Liz told me he met an unfortunate end at a peace summit with the New Generation."

"Indeed," Seth agrees, eyes going dark. "Peace talks continue, but it's not clear that the New Generation wants peace."

"Oh?" Ruth replies, startling Liz. "What do they want then?"

Seth studies her, eyes still dark. "I wish I knew."

Ruth nods, returning Seth's intense gaze. "Well, they certainly seemed intent on exterminating all of us at the depot. The horrors and suffering they've caused us are staggering, although I'm sure you've heard many such stories."

"Yes, but you're safe now." Seth's face lightens, filling once more with a smile. "I look forward to speaking with you further. I hear everyone is making good progress completing the Green Grow employee orientation, and the medical scans are complete. Hopefully we can get everyone assigned to jobs and quarters soon. Is there anything you need in the meantime?"

Liz detects a hint of a flush creeping across Ruth's weathered face. "We're fine, thank you again. Is it possible for our quarters to be near each other? We've been together for so long, it would be a comfort to still be close to one another."

"Of course," Seth replies, smile widening as he continues. "Liz, why don't you work with Harry on the arrangements? Ruth, Will, it was a pleasure to meet you. Liz, shall we go for debriefing?"

They turn toward the exit, but Liz suddenly stops, looking back to find Ruth's eyes.

"Ruth? Is there story time tonight?"

"Yes, dear. We do it every night after dinner."

"I might not be back in time," Liz says quickly. "Will there be another one tomorrow?"

"Of course. You're welcome anytime."

Liz nods and turns back to Seth, breathing in deeply to fortify herself for whatever is to come.

***

Most people eat in the cafeteria, and Seth often does as well. But he also has a dining area in his quarters where he can entertain or take meals. So, Liz follows him silently, unsure where they are going or what to expect.

She is accustomed to walking silently with him in the corridors. It's a comfortable silence, one that protects them from the scrutiny of the crew. When he presses the button for Level 1 in the lift, she knows they will be eating in his quarters. This seems like a good sign.

Liz knows that two places will be set at the rich, mahogany table. And indeed, he has set it precisely, with large covered bowls of food nestled between the two gleaming, empty plates, adorned with shiny cutlery and crowned with sparkling glasses of water. She smells marinara and knows instantly that the bowls hold cheese ravioli and salad—Seth's favorite meal. Her stomach growls. The meals in quarantine have been increasingly substantial, but they are less than her body craves.

She knows which seat is hers as soon as she sees the table. Her knife lies neatly wrapped in its sheath to the left of the salad fork, its muted black blade peeking ominously out of the leather.

"I told you I'd give it back as soon as you got out," Seth says gruffly, as she gently runs her finger over the rubberized handle.

Liz doesn't want to mince words or beat around the bush with him.

"I'm sorry," she says, eyes locking with his. "I mean, I'm not sorry for helping those people. But I'm sorry for the position it put you in. And I'm sorry for the things I said to you in your office."

"I'm sorry, too," he says softly, stormy eyes searching hers for an answer to an unknown question. "I'm sorry for putting you in quarantine, and for the things I said. I'm sorry I took your knife. I know how much it means to you, even if it is a bit weird."

Liz laughs at his honesty.

"This looks great," she says, eyeing the covered bowls and plate of bread.

"I wasn't sure what you'd want, so I figured I might as well get something I like. That way at least one of us will be happy." He smiles playfully.

"I fully intend to eat my share, so don't be too pleased with yourself." She winks at him as she takes her seat, serving herself and diving into the plate.

"We have a lot to discuss," Seth begins as he takes his own seat and prepares his own plate. "We have the all-hands meeting tomorrow, followed by the Council. You know the department heads are going to have all sorts of questions for you."

"And your mom? Where does she stand in all this?"

Seth sighs heavily.

"She's completely beside herself, and you know what that means. She's livid." He stabs at his salad with his fork. Liz exhales, feeling the weariness and dread pool in her chest.

"All I can do is tell the truth," she says quietly. "I knew the Council would have concerns about The Fifty-Two, but I couldn't let them die for the sake of the Council being less angry at me." She looks at him, pleading.

"I believe you, Z, and I'm behind you. Completely." Seth rests his fork on the table, focusing on Liz. "But, about telling the truth … There are some things we need to get straight before tomorrow."

Liz eats slowly as Seth tells her everything that transpired when she was flying back from the surface, starting with the private channel he used to communicate with her on the shuttle.

"I had no idea what had happened or what you needed to say, so I thought it best I talk to you alone," he explains.

Which of us doesn't he trust? she wonders. *Jarrod, Mathilda, or me?* He goes on to tell her about the emergency Council meeting he convened, leaning in to make sure he has her full attention.

"The Council believes that you were still sitting on the runway when I spoke to you on the radio. They believe our conversation happened before you loaded The Fifty-Two onto the shuttle. I told them I directed you to bring them back here."

Fresh hell, I can't imagine how that went over with Claire. Why did he feel the need to protect me? He seems to know what she's thinking.

"Yes, I lied. How do you think they would have taken the truth, especially after the meeting we had right before you left? Mom would go off the rails. She already wonders whether you're unhinged. I know that she shouldn't blame you for this mess, but for some reason she does."

"Is she the one who insisted I be quarantined?"

"Yes, she brought it up, and it seemed like a good compromise," he says gruffly, avoiding her eyes.

"I'm sure it was," she says, her voice soft, "and it gave me a chance to learn more about these people. I'll tell you everything I know."

Seth continues, "Mathilda has been investigating everyone's backgrounds, but you were right. Other than the two former employees, we couldn't find much. Most of them have birth records, and we found a few old government records—marriage certificates and tax records. Some of them have medical records from the Green Grow clinic at the Denver depot, but it's spotty at best."

"Their statements will be compelling," Liz adds quickly.

Seth exhales deeply, raking his fingers through his hair. "I'm not sure we should even get into that. I told the Council we are integrating those who can be employed, and relaxing the policy on crew family members for everyone involved. Hopefully it won't piss off the rest of the crew. I know they had to make their own hard choices between this ship and the surface."

He takes her hands in his, eyes burning holes into her. "Tomorrow at the all-hands meeting, I need you to explain to everyone who The Fifty-Two are and why they are here. I need you to make them understand." Liz nods.

"You also need to know," he continues, leaning back in his chair and pushing his plate away, "that tomorrow may be your last Council meeting. Mom is convinced you are a liability, and I think she's persuaded Jarrod and Mathilda."

"Jarrod and Mathilda think I'm a liability?" Liz sets her fork abruptly on the table.

"Well, they didn't use that word, exactly. It's more that they think you're … *unnecessary.* To the business of the Council."

Liz is speechless, but not surprised given her discussion with Harry the day before. Seth waits a moment to let her respond, but she remains silent. After a moment, he continues.

"There's something else, Z. Jarrod found a spy. We think it's the person who leaked the status of the antimatter drive to the New Generation."

"What? Who?" Liz's back is rigid, as she perches on the edge of her chair. Why didn't he tell her this first?

"One of the engineers," he says. "Zag Bryant."

Liz doesn't know him, but it makes sense. Jarrod's senior engineers can't build the antimatter drive without the specs. Any of them could have leaked it.

"Where is he now?" she asks. "Is he talking?"

"He's in the brig. Jarrod was questioning him but getting nowhere. Mom has him … medicated. I think she overdid it. He's talking now, but a lot of it sounds like gibberish. I don't know if it's useful."

Medicated? Shitbiscuits, he's lucky he's not a frog!

"What if I talk to him?" Liz offers.

"Do you know him?" Seth asks, surprised.

"No, but if his gibberish is about the surface, maybe I can help."

Seth considers this, then nods. "I don't see how it could hurt. I'll take you tomorrow, after the Council meeting. Maybe he'll be lucid by then."

"Anything else going on?" she asks, wondering just how deep this rabbit hole goes.

"Not really," he says dismissively. "I'm glad you're out. I've missed you."

This sounds promising, but she desperately squeezes his hand anyway, needing to know that they're okay.

"Seth, are we jake?"

"Right as rain, Z." He looks tired and emotional. Can she believe him? She doesn't know.

"Okay," she says, standing to secure her knife around her waist. "I'll go so you can get some rest."

Seth nods, acknowledging the end to their evening.

"You're released from the quarantine," he says, rising from his own chair. "I'll deal with the rest of the group tomorrow." He sees her to the door and closes it behind her without ceremony.

***

Liz takes the stairs to Level 2 and sits in silence in her quarters. She stares at a blank wall as thoughts tumble through her mind. What will she do if she's dismissed from the Council?

It feels like the Council has been her life forever, although it's only been a couple of years. Seth approached her about joining the same day Jarrod convened all the shuttle pilots to tell them the department was being disbanded until further notice. He indicated they would each receive new assignments, and Liz assumed she'd probably get assigned to the orchard again when Seth pulled her aside and told her he still needed her to fly.

"Aren't the shuttles grounded now?" she asked, confused. "Does Jarrod know?"

"We don't need a team of pilots," Seth told her, "but I still need one—one I can trust." He explained that she would join the Council and report directly to him.

It was surreal at first, sitting in the same room as the department heads every morning. Liz didn't think of them as peers—she had worked under both Harry and Jarrod, and she found Claire extremely intimidating. She appreciated the warm, reassuring glances Mathilda frequently cast her way, but she didn't know Mathilda well enough to feel reassured. Over time, she better settled into the role.

Seth moved her quarters to Level 2, with the department heads, and she left the crew and her old life behind her. She started spending her days planning and training for surface missions, choosing crew members to assist, requisitioning the necessary equipment, and then executing the missions. She made sure the shuttles were maintained and ready to go, starting her practice of daily inspections on the dock with Charlie. She carefully managed the information any assisting crew members received, and she provided updates and briefings to the Council.

Most importantly, she organized surface intelligence. In the beginning, this was the part she was most excited about. This was the part of her new role that fanned her dying flame of hope that she might still find Jackson.

Of course, by that time it had been thirteen years since she'd seen him, thirteen long years since he'd walked away from their small farmhouse without looking back. That was a very long time to be missing, a very long time to look for someone who couldn't or wouldn't be found. Liz knew death was the only plausible ending to his story, but she couldn't stop trying to find out what had happened to him. A part of her, albeit an increasingly small part, still hoped she might find him alive. It was definitely against the odds, but wouldn't she feel it if he were dead? Wouldn't she know for sure in her heart?

So, she scoured camera feeds from Green Grow surveillance systems, as well as satellite images Mathilda shared—not just to plan her missions, but to find Jackson. She dug in with fervor, but her enthusiasm quickly dwindled as she began to realize how sparse the information was.

She didn't doubt that the Green Grow Corporation had gathered extensive intelligence on the New Generation, but none of it was available to her. Headquarters' systems were offline or locked down. Record centers were destroyed. More and more surveillance cameras began to fail.

Now, two years later, it's nearly impossible to get any useful data. The Green Grow 3 is cut off and flying blind, unaware of what transpires on the planet below. This is why they need to leave, at least until they can establish contact with someone and ensure their own safety. And this is why, with her last mission complete to the Denver depot, she has to give up on finding her brother.

Maybe Claire is right, she ponders. *Maybe I am unnecessary now.* Liz remembers how meticulously she planned her first mission, how thrilling and fearful the whole experience was. She went to Philadelphia, to retrieve an offline server Seth thought might help them find the Executive Board. Part of her hoped she'd actually find the Executive Board, holed up in the secure bunker and desperately working to reestablish communication with the Green Grow 3. She remembers how carefully she briefed the Council every single morning until mission day arrived, how she broadcast a live video feed from her helmet to the bridge while the Council watched. She remembers the empty bunker, the brief wave of disappointment quickly overtaken by satisfaction as she retrieved the server. She remembers the fearful thrill when her radio scanner detected a strange signal, and she intercepted a message from a New Generation scout that a Green Grow shuttle had been spotted landing. She and her team bolted back to the shuttle, server in hand, and took off just as the enemy came into sight.

The Council was there to greet her team on the dock. Later, after everyone was debriefed, Claire complimented her bravery, how cool she'd remained under pressure. Harry congratulated her on a smooth and effective operation, boasting that there couldn't have been a better person for the job than Liz. She was a hero then, lavished with praise that pushed her to embarrassment. Now she's a wild card. Not a team player. A loose cannon. Now, she's *unnecessary.*

Nothing lasts forever, she tells herself. *Every beginning has an end.* Now she is at the end of this, and she has no idea what will come next. Perhaps she'll go back to work in the orchard for Harry. But can she go back? Can anyone ever go back? She loves the trees and the fields, but she knows it can't be the same as before—not after everything she's seen and done on the Council. Perhaps she'll learn a new skill—something mechanical. Maybe she can find a place for herself on the dock. Maybe Jarrod will take her back.

What else will change? Will Seth move her back to crew quarters on Level 3? Will he still be her friend, or will he disappear, too, when she's no longer allowed to hear what he can tell her? Exactly how many endings will all of this involve?

Fresh hell, all I can do is wait and see what happens, she thinks, frustrated that she's never been able to cultivate patience. She doesn't like to wait. She likes to do. She needs to do something now, to move her body before she goes completely insane. And so, she rises from her couch. She exits her private Level 2 quarters, telling herself that the space never meant anything to her, anyway.

***

Liz walks down the corridor, one foot in front of the other, even as she still decides where she is going. Level 7, maybe? To the trees? No, the trees keep their own counsel, and she already feels alone. She considers the goats on Level 16; they're fun. *Except when they try to eat my clothes,* Liz thinks wryly, remembering the first time she felt that telltale tug on the bottom of her tunic. She had no experience with goats then, and had no idea that such small adorable creatures would truly eat anything. The ragged edge of her frayed tunic taught her otherwise.

Story time. The words pop into her mind so unexpectedly, they startle her. She stops in the empty corridor to consider this further. Maybe she can catch the end of the session. Or, even if it's over, maybe some of the group will linger. She quickly walks toward the lift and approaches the quarantined medical unit moments later. The man posted outside the door seems surprised to see her.

"Back so soon?" he asks, his eyes shifting briefly before he manages a smile. Liz doesn't recognize him, but that isn't unusual. There are plenty of people on the ship she doesn't know. He seems to know who she is, but that isn't unusual either, especially these days.

"The captain released me from quarantine," Liz says, "but I wanted to pick up a few things." She studies him. Does he seem nervous? He shifts his weight from foot to foot, and she senses a damp glow of sweat on his forehead. Yes, he seems nervous.

"Do you think the captain will release the rest of the group soon, too?" he asks.

"I'm sure he will," she says, deciding that he probably doesn't want to get assigned to guard duty again. "I hear the tests are all done, but they still need quarters assigned. I'm sure we'll know more tomorrow." This seems to allay his curiosity, and perhaps even his nervousness. His hand twitches violently a final time as she moves past him into the decontamination chamber, but she chooses to ignore it.

Liz enters the common room and is surprised to see Ruth sitting alone at an empty table, close to the door. Ruth looks equally surprised to see her, but the expression vanishes in an instant and is replaced by a warm smile.

"Back so soon, dear?" she asks, rising from her chair to approach Liz.

How long did everyone think I'd be gone? Liz wonders, as she replies, "The captain released me from quarantine, but I left my tablet here." Was it a mistake to come? Why is everyone so surprised to see her?

"Of course," Ruth replies, taking Liz's arm and walking with her down the hallway. "Hopefully we'll be out of here soon, too. Is there any news?"

"I'll talk to Harry about the room assignments tomorrow," Liz assures her as they enter the shared sleeping space. Her tablet lies exactly where she left it, and the room is bustling with movement, chatter, and laughter as several others get ready for bed. This seems normal, so Liz relaxes as she gathers the tablet and yesterday's clothes, sitting for a moment on the cot she doesn't need anymore. She can't help but feel a twinge of sorrow that she's leaving this community for her own solitary space.

"I'm sorry I missed story time," Liz adds. "I was looking forward to it."

Ruth pats her arm and sits next to her. "Don't worry, there will be plenty more," she replies warmly. This makes Liz feel better. She takes a last appraising look around the room, knowing she has no reason to stay here any longer. Ruth walks with her back to the common room.

"I'll check in on you tomorrow," Liz says, "after I talk to Harry about the room assignments. I'm sure he'll stop by as well." She turns to go, but Ruth catches her arm.

"Liz," Ruth says, her brown eyes intensely misty, "I will never be able to thank you enough for bringing us here. I'm so glad we had a chance to get to know each other, if only for a couple days."

"Don't worry," Liz says, a corner of her mouth turning up. "There will be plenty more."

Ruth smiles and nods as Liz turns to go. The doors hiss closed behind her, and the outer doors open again. The man standing guard is still there, looking nervous. Liz studies him for a moment before she bids him goodnight and begins to walk down the corridor toward the lift.

Strange man, she thinks, as a flash of movement catches her eye ahead. *Was that someone peeking around the corner?* She quickens her pace, making her way quickly to the intersecting hall and looking both ways. Seeing no one, she turns toward the stairwell, walking quietly and hugging the wall until she reaches the doorway. She shoves the door open, hearing a solid thwack and a groan as the door smashes into a person. Liz runs into the stairwell, hand reaching for her knife, to see who awaits.

"Will?" Liz is stunned. "Will Dabato? What the fresh hell are you doing here?"

Her old friend, who is supposed to be quarantined, meets her eyes as a small trickle of blood drips from the hand he's raised to cover his nose.

"Evidently, I'm running into doors!" he replies, letting out another groan.

"You're supposed to be quarantined! Why are you out here sneaking around?"

"I know, Liz, I know," he says, giving her an evaluating glance. "I heard Captain Harris say the tests came back clean. I thought that meant the quarantine was over." He takes his hand away from his face, inspecting the drops of blood now smeared on his hand as he waits for Liz to respond.

"Bushwa!" she growls. "There's still a security officer posted at the door. How did you get past him?"

Will sighs deeply, focusing his full attention on Liz.

"That guy?" he asks casually. "I just asked him to help me out. He remembers me from when I was here before."

"Help you with what, exactly?" Liz demands, eyes narrowed. Will gives her another look that infuriates her. She doesn't wait for him to respond. "Do you have any idea what a shitstorm I caused by bringing all of you back here? I'm probably going to lose my job over it! And what else do you think is going to happen to me if you get caught wandering around when you haven't been cleared to leave quarantine?"

Will's eyes soften.

"I'm sorry, Liz," he says quietly. "I didn't know." She glares at him, arms crossed and foot tapping.

"Look," he continues, "I asked the guard to help me out. I know him from when I was here before. I got into an argument with Melissa, and she's mad at me. I wanted to pick some flowers for her. It's been so long since she's had anything nice like that, I figured she wouldn't stay mad at me for long. So, I asked the guard to let me out for a little while, but I guess I don't remember the ship as well as I thought I did. I got lost, and it took me forever to even find my way back here."

Liz's eyes narrow again as she considers him, arms still crossed and foot still tapping.

"I know I shouldn't have left, but I didn't think it would be that big of a deal," he says, delicately touching his nose with his fingers as he waits for Liz to respond. She waits for him to say something more, but it seems he's done explaining.

"I don't see any flowers," Liz says, uncrossing her arms.

"I told you, I got lost. I remembered flowers by the bee hives in the Level 7 orchard, but I forgot how big the level is. I never even found the bees, and honestly, it's creepy there in the dark. Besides, I'm sure Melissa will be plenty satisfied when she sees my face. I'll tell her where to send her thanks."

Liz stares at him, exasperated. Part of her wants to laugh like she would have done years ago. Another part of her wants to punch him. She considers what to do, knowing that if she reports this to the Council, her current situation, which is already precarious, will probably just get worse. No, she really doesn't need any more chastising. Besides, why report it? The quarantine was a ruse. She doesn't need this trouble.

"You're going back to the medical unit," she says through gritted teeth, motioning Will out of the stairwell. They walk in silence. Liz fixes a glare on the security guard, who starts shifting from foot to foot. She refuses to look away, her fiery gaze drilling a hole in him until she's inches from his balmy face.

"I'm sorry, Greg," Will says ruefully as he turns toward the decontamination chamber. "I told her it was all my fault. You know, flowers for the wife and all. It was stupid."

"Greg?" Liz cries incredulous. "The same Greg who was assigned to guard me on the dock?" He wilts as she turns her heated gaze to him once more. He doesn't need to answer. She remembers now—he shifted from foot to foot in his biohazard suit, too.

"I'm staying in my lane!" he yelps, raising his hands as if she might pummel him. Will stops, looking confused by this, as Liz suppresses a smirk. *Stay in your lane,* she told Greg on the dock. *If you step into mine, we're going to collide.* She must have made an impression on him.

She says nothing as she motions Will toward the decontamination chamber. He hesitates on the threshold, lightly rubbing his swollen, bloody nose as his eyes shift between Greg and Liz. He remains silent, however, and turns to enter the quarantine, shoulders slumped in tired defeat.

Liz watches the door close behind Will before she turns again to Greg. He looks as if he might melt into a puddle on the floor.

"I suspect you have enough challenges as it is," she hisses inches from his face, "so I am not reporting you. But, do not let anyone else out of this quarantine until you are expressly told to do so by Captain Harris or a department head."

Liz doesn't give him a chance to respond, but she can see his head working a stiff nod as she turns on her heel and stalks away. She goes back to her Level 2 quarters, where she will spend the night in a lonely comfort she would gladly trade for a cot in the quarantine, back with the people she risked so much to save.

CHAPTER 8

THE MOUSE

***

The scientist locks himself in his makeshift lab, determined to work undisturbed even if only for a few hours. It is a secret lab, of course, but it's the purpose of the space that's secret, not the location. In fact, it's an abandoned room next door to his quarters. His colleagues know he uses it, although they think it's a library. They all know how much he loves paper books, so it makes sense he would want a space for his collection. He's not impossible to find here, so he locks the door for his peace of mind.

The rest of his day is done, and no one should be looking for him. They *shouldn't* be looking for him, but he simply cannot abide the possibility of interruption—not tonight. He's on the verge of frustration but determined not to succumb. He is the conqueror, not the conquered. He refuses to be defeated, especially by that pathetic waste of space who hides behind his mother's skirt—Seth Harris. He takes a moment to center himself, to start again from the beginning, if only for a moment. He calls up the image of the woman and the baby, thinking about her smiling face until his thoughts settle. Then he brushes it out of his mind.

Time. Space. Matter. They are the building blocks, intertwined in complex ways to create everything from his beating heart to the supervolcano eruption that transformed his world. He has come so far in understanding how they work together—far enough to build the machine. He calls it the transporter, although he could legitimately call it many other things: a portal, a time machine, a creator of wormholes. He knows he should feel accomplished, but for this scientist, it's a tease, just enough success to make him hunger for more. The real success will come in getting it to work properly.

It works, of course. He wouldn't credit himself with building it if it didn't work. But it needs fine-tuning. Truthfully, the machine itself needs nothing. It's his understanding of how to use it that is lacking. He has so much to learn, and time is essential.

Technically, he's not bound by any deadline, but there are practical matters that concern him. He knows the Green Grow 3 will be leaving Earth's orbit soon after the propulsion drive is complete. He doesn't know exactly when they will go. No one but the Seth Harris does, and despite his woeful inadequacies as a captain and human being, he's done a good job of keeping this information secret. It annoys the scientist, because he'd like to complete his mission while they are still in orbit.

As long as the ship orbits the earth, its speed and movement remain highly predictable, especially over short timeframes and distances. When the ship leaves orbit, it will undoubtedly be traveling faster, and its movement will be harder to predict. His calculations will have to be much more precise; his margin for error will shrink to nothing. If he's off by even a fraction of a fraction, he'll wind up freezing in the cold depths of space, instead of safe on the Green Grow 3. It would be like diving off a cliff only to have the ocean beneath you suddenly recede seconds before you smash into the sea bed. And that would be a shame—a terrible shame.

He cannot imagine such an anticlimactic end to his story. Not him. For he is no mere mortal, or he won't be for long, anyway. He will be a god when he can bend the time-space continuum to his will. His machine will fold the space-time continuum and connect the points that he designates with a wormhole, a wormhole he can step through just like a doorway.

The hard part is calculating his destination accurately, because everything is always in motion. Take the Green Grow 3, for instance. At this exact moment, it occupies a precise location. He could transport a mouse from his lab to the Captain's quarters. But if he transports a mouse to that location a minute later, where will it arrive? The captain's quarters have moved. Will it arrive in the cafeteria, or on a growing level? Will it arrive in the emptiness of space, where the Green Grow 3 used to be, as it suffocates in the wake of the ship that has already moved on?

Time is even trickier. Do you go forward? Back? And in which reality? The scientist knows the possibilities are endless, and the circuitous questions and implications of what he is doing threaten to overwhelm him. He takes a deep breath and tries again to empty his mind as he surveys a clear fiberglass box, looking for the scurrying bits of life hiding between the wood chips and the water bowls.

"Which one of you is ready for an adventure?" he murmurs, as he reaches into the mouse house to extract tonight's test subject. He knows it would have been wiser, or at least kinder, to start the experiments with inanimate matter—a rock or paperclip, perhaps. No doubt, in his real lab, his colleagues would have pressured him to follow more conventional protocols. But this is his secret lab; he can do whatever he wants, which will be even more important when he's ready to test his machine on a human. He hasn't worked out all the details yet, but he certainly intends to test it on someone besides himself. Someone less valuable. It's a shame he can't test it on Seth Harris.

He tries to let go of this negative judgment, silently reciting his mantra that all lives have value, even if that value isn't obvious to him.

"And yet," he whispers to his tiny, beady-eyed companion, "sacrifices must be made."

His experiment design is simple: bend the space-time continuum enough to transport a mouse through the wormhole from one side of his secret lab to the other. But even over such a short time and distance, he knows that he's tinkering with the magic of the universe every time he experiments. And until he works out the kinks in his calculations, he can't be entirely sure what is happening to his test subjects.

This is a problem, and the results of prior experiments weigh on his mind. Some of the mice just disappear. He doesn't know to when or where. Some of them arrive in ways that are odd—crushed, singed, or substantially older or younger than when they started. These things shouldn't happen. Something must be occurring in the wormhole, but he doesn't know what.

Answers are elusive, and the universe is reluctant to yield its secrets to him. He's made several attempts to fit the test mice with sensors, devices intended to record sight, sound, and biometric readings. They all come back fried. Why does the biological matter fare better than the inanimate sensors? It's a worrisome problem, because the body is an electronic device in many ways—the nerves, the heart, the brain. They all require electrical impulses. Perhaps the mice are damaged, and he just hasn't detected how yet. He could explore the possibilities for a lifetime, but he doesn't have that much time. He needs a protective barrier, and he's testing his first theory tonight.

He fits the furry test subject with a series of sensors and recording devices. Half of them are wrapped in protective mesh, and half are not. The wormhole may be generating electromagnetic pulses, which could explain why the electronics fry but the mice live. Mice are mostly water, which is more resistant to electromagnetic energy. If the mesh protects the sensors, there's a good chance he's dealing with electromagnetic pulses. If the mesh doesn't help, he'll have to consider other options.

He activates the machine, which generates a pulse of light. Then the mouse is gone. He starts his timer and stares at the test pad across the room, waiting for the creature to appear again. He sees nothing. Where is the mouse? Dead in a wormhole, ripped apart into atoms and subatoms? Arriving in the future? Arriving in the past? He curses aloud. He didn't think about the past. He should be continuously recording video—in case the mouse shows up early. But he hasn't recorded anything.

He's tired and frustrated, and this oversight pushes him over the edge. In a rage he kicks the least valuable piece of equipment in the lab: his trash can. Papers and small bits of refuse fly. He sighs, chiding himself for behaving like a child as he dutifully begins to collect the bits of garbage.

That's when he sees it, in the corner. It's the mouse. Rather, it was the mouse. Now, it is a carcass—an emaciated one. He carefully scoops it up into a glass dish, realizing upon further inspection that the mouse isn't simply emaciated, it's mummified. Completely dehydrated. And all of the sensors are melted, even the ones covered in mesh.

"What happened to you, my dear?" he asks the withered remains of the body. "And when did you get back?" He goes to his desk and types a few notes. The mouse completed the journey, but arrived too soon, and in the wrong location. Plus, there's the issue of it being dead.

What does the scientist know that he didn't know before? All he really knows is that the mesh failed to protect the sensors, but he supposes that's something. He has to keep going. It's too late to turn back now; he's closer to the end than he is to the beginning. After shutting down his computer, he carefully takes the remains of the mouse with him and leaves the lab. He will try again tomorrow.

CHAPTER 9

MESSAGE BOARDS

****

"Thank you, everyone, for coming," Seth booms, quieting the crew who occupy the large meeting space on Level 1. He makes a few other opening statements but quickly turns it over to Liz to talk about the Denver operation and The Fifty-Two. It's a nice reprieve to let someone else bear the scrutiny of everyone's gaze for a while.

Seth is in a room full of people, but it's funny how that only makes him feel more alone. He imagined he would be relieved to tell the crew they are leaving Earth's orbit, and yet, his heart feels no lighter. He has no idea how they will react to the news. He's not sure they will see the merit in the plan if they know it's his, which is why he continues to let them believe he's getting orders from the Executive Board. They haven't questioned him so far, but he knows the winds of fate are fickle and could turn at any point.

For all he knows, they may have turned already. He sees everything beginning to slip away, right before his eyes. The Council is at odds, the ship is infiltrated with spies, and the crew doubts him—he knows they must. Leaving orbit won't solve those problems.

He wonders if leaving orbit will actually solve any of his problems, and the thought settles in his brain like a sledgehammer. It doesn't matter. There's no going back now. They have to leave, especially since the New Generation knows about the antimatter drive. But, even when they go, he can see that the Council will still fight, the crew will still doubt him, and the New Generation will still be a threat. He adds another mistake in judgment to his mental tally.

He closes his eyes, only for a moment, as yet another heavy realization settles on him. He is at a crossroad, and it's time to choose a direction. Either he can take charge of this crew and command this ship, or he can continue to let the Council distract him as he watches everything fall apart. He can't do both, not anymore.

Making the choice is easy. Seth knows he's done himself no favors by allowing the Council to steer him. He will rise to his position and take command of this ship. But how? He has no idea, not even a clue. The pieces of the puzzle need to come together, but instead, everything is flying apart at the seams. All he can see now are his mistakes, again and again.

He berates himself once more for trying to appease the Council. He should have spent his time earning the crew's confidence instead. He should have been gathering intelligence on the New Generation, grooming his own spies who could tell him everything he needs to know. He should know his enemy and how to come to terms with them, but he doesn't. The New Generation is completely hidden from him, behind an impenetrable and invisible wall, and it's no one's fault but his.

And Zag Bryant? He's the most infuriating piece of the puzzle. Everything Seth needs to know about communicating with the New Generation is probably in Zag's head, but Zag can't tell him, even if he wants to. The man is completely incoherent—barely alive, in fact. Who knows what Zag might have been willing to divulge if his mother hadn't completely scrambled his brain with her truth serum? Seth will likely never know. It's just another example of his world flying apart at the seams.

A pillar of fury starts to rise in Seth's chest when he thinks about how little respect his mother has for his authority. He takes a deep breath and turns his attention to Liz, who is talking about The Fifty-Two.

"I expect you have two pressing questions," she says, speaking clearly into the microphone as she addresses the crew. "Who are they, and why are they here? First and foremost, they are people—human beings just like us, except their path in life left them hungry and vulnerable instead of safe and fed. They are the same people we served at the depots before the New Generation attacks forced us to close."

Seth likes Liz's way of getting right to the point, her way of skipping past all the niceties and saying what needs to be said.

"We've all been forced to make choices," she continues. "Choices about where to go, what to do. Choices between families and jobs, between safety and home. We've made hard choices, and many of you—as well as me—have lost those who matter most dearly. When I became aware of these survivors, I had to make a hard choice: take a risk and help these people, or watch them die. I can't help the past. I can't help the people you've lost, nor the people I have. But I could help these people, and I've seen enough survivors die."

Seth scans the faces in the crowd. He studies the unwavering eyes of a man in the first row completely immersed in what Liz is saying. He sees an enraptured young woman two rows back who is perched on the edge of her seat, wringing her hands in her lap. A shade of jealousy darkens the shadows of his awareness. Why can't he command the crew's attention this way?

Of course, he knows why—the crew can't relate to him like they can to Liz. Most of them lived and suffered on the Earth, and they know he didn't. They think he's sheltered, a pampered idealist who never had to work for his success because his parents were connected. Seth knows no one would say such things out loud, not now and not to his face, anyway. But he heard it plenty growing up, and he's sure nothing has changed. Well, he's changed. He's worked so very hard to be more than the boy his parents raised. But how can he get the crew to see this?

An idea hits him. Maybe they don't need to see it. Maybe he needs to think about this differently. He turns his attention back to Liz, although the hum of her voice cannot compete with his own thoughts. His mom wants her off the Council, and the other members don't disagree. He hoped to persuade the Council to let Liz stay, to convince them of her merit. But he's changed his mind about that. It's his Council. He's not going to bother with their approval. He knows now that he needs Liz even more than he imagined. She is his ambassador to the crew, his ticket to gaining their confidence.

And yet, even in the light of this epiphany, he can't deny why he really wants her on the Council. It's the same reason he's wanted her there since the beginning. She does something no one else has ever done—she *sees* him. Liz doesn't get lost in the haze of who he *could* be or who he *should* be. She sees who he *is*, and he's come to realize he desperately needs to be truly seen by someone. It's why he needs Liz more than the air he breathes, and part of him wants even more.

Could they be more? Could he envelop her in his arms and claim her lips in a passionate kiss? Could he nuzzle her neck and run his fingers through her soft blonde hair? Would her skin be warm on his if he unveiled her body, one piece of clothing at a time? The idea intrigues him, and he thinks it intrigues her too, because they have both pressed the boundary of their friendship.

But boundaries aren't the only thing that might be broken, and he knows there are far more important questions. Would he be everything she expects, everything she needs? Would she meet his expectations? And most importantly, would they still be friends? At the end of it all, that is the only question that matters, because Seth knows the truth. Liz is the only person who sees him clearly, and he needs to be seen even more than he needs to be loved. He can't lose her friendship, even if it means foregoing her love.

Quieting his thoughts, Seth tunes in to her words again. She's telling the crew how proud and inspired she is to report to a captain who so dearly holds the ideals of Green Grow—to ease people's suffering and nurture humanity. Nice, although he wishes she would have said something besides *ideals*; the crew already thinks he lives in a dream.

He chides himself for being petty and steels his face with a broad smile. He knows his reprieve is almost up, and it's time for him to step into the spotlight of the crew's scrutiny once more. Now he has to tell them they are leaving orbit.

***

As Seth rises, Liz takes her seat, exhaling deeply and trying not to slump. She had never addressed the entire crew before, and it was unsettling. The sea of faces looked at her with familiarity, although she knew far fewer of them than seemed to know her.

There has never been a time when she's known everyone on the ship, but there was a time when she knew more of the people who filled her world—back when her world was smaller, neatly bound by the edges of the growing levels. Now her world may once again shrink, if she's removed from the Council, but not without consequence. Everyone will still look at her, imagining far-fetched reasons why she was dismissed, scrutinizing and judging her behind her back. She shouldn't care what anyone thinks of her, but she doesn't want to be constantly guarding what she says and what she does like some kind of spectacle who will be rated for entertainment value at the end of the show.

She monitored the sea of faces as she spoke, watching their expressions and reactions to measure her own words. She thought that seeking a familiar face might bring her comfort, and instantly one appeared—Albert Wyndham. His face was too familiar though, not only in its own right but because he looked so much like Sam.

Every time she tried to look away, her eyes managed to find their way back to him. She saw tears form in his eyes, which he quickly wiped away before they could spill over his cheeks. She watched his face become drawn, and she did not know what it meant. Was he sad? Angry? She witnessed a full array of stoic, heated, and sometimes unreadable expressions spill over his face, but they revealed so little about his thoughts.

How long will he blame me? She knows she has no right to wonder. All he's been told is that Sam died in a training accident, and Liz has done nothing to help him learn the truth. *Shitbiscuits, it shouldn't be this hard. All I need is a simple 'yes' from Seth.* Except, of course, she knows it's not entirely that simple. Once she gets Seth permission, she will have to talk to Albert, and that's when the hard part will begin.

You're a hypocrite, Liz. You've spent years trying to find out what happened to your own brother, and you won't even do the work to have a ten-minute conversation with Albert about what happened to Sam.

Liz feels her insides start to churn. She sits up straight in her chair and pushes her focus outward, to the people around her. She hears murmuring and senses people shuffling in their chairs. Seth is still standing tall and proud as he speaks. She likes how he maintains that confident posture, even when the people around him get unsettled.

"… and we now think the New Generation may have used similar weapons against the Green Grow 1," his voice echoes. "To assure our safety against any such missile or laser weapons, we must put distance between ourselves and the New Generation while peace negotiations continue. The new propulsion system is almost ready, and we'll be leaving orbit in a matter of days."

Liz can sense the waves of shock and fear growing in the crowd around her, making her arms and the back of her neck tingle. *How fearful would they be if they knew the truth?* she wonders, knowing this is why Seth lies to them. The ship might unravel into chaos if the crew knew that headquarters had gone dark, the Green Grow 2 had disappeared, and New Generations spies had infiltrated their own ship.

Murmurs and whispers grow into a clamor, as voices cry out from behind Liz as Seth opens for questions.

"Why?"

"Where?"

"For how long?"

Seth raises his hands to quiet the group. "We'll travel to Mars, slingshot around the planet, and return to Earth's orbit—six months there, and six months back. Hopefully by then, a peace can be reached, and we will be in constant communication with the Executive Board. What other questions do you have?"

"Does this mean the peace talks are failing with the New Generation?"

Liz notices Seth's expression falter for half a blink, smile frozen on his face. In a flash, his steely eyes reanimate, and he responds, voice once more booming.

"I'm not privy to the details, but there is still hope. We have to trust the Executive Board and do what they tell us. I know each of you will do your part.

"This is no small request," Seth continues, before anyone else can ask a question. "The Executive Board is asking for our trust, cooperation, and obedience. I've assured them there is no better crew for the mission than this one. If you have any questions, please reach out to your department head. They are important members of my advisory Council, along with Liz Goeff, and you can be sure that all of your questions and concerns will receive due consideration.

"Thank you for your attention," he concludes. "Let's get this done."

Seth casts an intense gaze across the crowd, then turns promptly toward a side door that leads to the captain's conference room. He strides long and powerful steps, quickly catching up to his mother, who is seated much closer to the door as the crew begins to flow toward the elevators.

Liz hops up from her seat and walks quickly toward Seth, hoping to talk to him before the Council meeting. As she reaches out to touch his shoulder, he leans forward, close to his mother's ear, and growls, loud enough for her to hear, "Do not test me at the Council meeting. We can talk about Liz later."

Liz pulls her hand back, a ball of ice suddenly settling in her stomach. She doesn't want to be part of this discussion. Instinctively, she turns away, staring first at the ground and then directing her gaze up, across the backs of the crew still exiting the level. One man still faces her, eyes burning and mouth pursed into a thin line. Albert Wyndham. Their eyes meet for only a moment before Liz looks away. His tear-stained face is filled with raw hatred.

***

A half hour later, Liz sits motionless in a chair in the captain's conference room, eyes flickering between Jarrod and Claire as they argue. She's dreaded this meeting all morning, wondering if it will be her last, but she's surprised to gather that the question of her Council membership has been resolved. She will remain on the Council. Nonetheless, remnants of her earlier dread still linger inside her chest, refusing to be dismissed, making her feel weak and pathetic. She keeps her face impassive, taking in the scene as her heart flutters in her chest.

"The man is barely coherent," Jarrod hisses. "Whatever you dosed him with has accomplished nothing except wasting time."

"I told you the serum might need to be adjusted," Claire retorts, face flushed and dark. "At least I've made progress, which is far more than we can say about any of your interrogation methods."

"He's a human being, Claire, not a lab rat." Jarrod's face looks like it might pop. Liz has never seen him angry. She finds herself surprised that he is capable of so much feeling, and yet there it is, written in red and purple all over his face.

"He's a spy!" Claire reminds him, clapping her hands on the table like an ominous thundercloud. "I've adjusted the serum, and I'm ready to try it again."

"Enough!" Seth bellows, glaring at his mother. "You know he is in no state to receive another dose. We'll continue with the questioning, and I'll make a decision about the serum when he's lucid. We're moving on." Claire sighs heavily, slumping back into her chair. *Did she really just roll her eyes?*

The room is so thick with tension that Liz can barely breathe, and she's glad to have no role in the discussion. In fact, she hasn't said anything since she sat down. When Seth asked her to provide an update on The Fifty-Two, Claire interrupted before Liz could even open her mouth to speak.

"The captain reminded all of us yesterday that this is not a democracy," she said, "so there's no point talking about these people. We have more pressing business." Claire's tone could have melted the outer hull, a pointed reminder that Liz did not want to be on the wrong end of the woman's wrath yet again. She was glad to be overlooked, but the ease with which Claire dismissed her offered another troubling reminder—Liz couldn't be further out of her element on this Council.

Why does Seth want me here? she wonders again, glad that she will continue on the Council but unsure what her role will be. She studies the bulging veins on Jarrod's crimson neck, feeling impotent and on the edge of lunacy in this sea of politics and personalities she can't understand or influence.

Seth asks Jarrod for a status update on the propulsion drive. Liz watches the engineer attempt to calm himself, but it only takes a moment for him to lose the battle and launch into another tirade about Zag Bryant, the New Generation spy currently in the brig.

Liz has already gathered that when Jarrod's questioning didn't yield immediate results, Claire took matters into her own hands and injected Zag with a truth serum she whipped up in her lab. Jarrod's fury is beyond measure, and his tirade provokes Claire into a new round of the same argument.

This really is a shitstorm, Liz muses, as Seth demands they stop the fresh volleys of insults and accusations. Jarrod's face is purple again, and Claire looks at her son as if he is a pesky toddler. Silence descends, but only for a moment before Jarrod erupts with renewed fury. *Precarious—that's the word Seth used,* Liz remembers, thinking back to hiss cutting remark that she didn't realize how finely he had to balance order on the ship. Liz now realizes that his description was too kind. She watches, knowing she is powerless to help as she waits for the room to implode. Seth observes as well as the two department heads continue to rage at each other, oblivious to the rest of the Council.

When Seth reaches his limit moments later, he slams both hands flat on the table, palms making a sharp crack as bone meets with wood. It's enough to get everyone's attention, at least for a moment. It's long enough for Seth, who appears tired and perhaps even resigned, to abruptly close the meeting, casting a menacing glance as he commands everyone to be prepared with status updates next time.

Jarrod and Claire begrudgingly stop exchanging insults as a frazzled Mathilda and troubled Harry leave the room. Claire exits haughtily and Jarrod stiffly, leaving Liz alone with Seth. She sits silently in her chair as he slumps back and closes his eyes. She waits for him to look at her before casting him a questioning glance, mouth half-pursed and eyebrows raised, that asks, *Are you jake?* He inhales deeply and replies, in a casual voice, "Let's go see if Zag is awake."

***

Liz is surprised to learn that the brig is on Level 5, adjacent to the dock. Objectively speaking, it's as good a location as any, especially if the idea is to transport troublemakers to Earth. The location is fine; it's her lack of knowledge she finds unsettling. She's spent countless hours on the dock, and she thought she knew this level inside and out. But she did not know the brig was here. *Foul mother of hell, how many times have I walked by this place?* Liz instinctively sucks in her belly as they approach the entrance, lightly brushing the ever-present knife under her tunic—the one she's not allowed to have.

Seth swipes a key card, and a metal door hisses open. Liz follows him past an office area and then to a second door, which also hisses open after he lays his palm on a scanner. She crosses the threshold to find a long row of cells along one wall and a single familiar face.

"Charlie?" She recognizes the head mechanic.

"Hi Liz." He flashes her a familiar smile, but it clashes with his black tactical uniform. Liz eyes the taser and pepper spray prominent on his belt. *At least it's not a shotgun,* she thinks as images of Greg fill her mind. *What a hapless fool.* She wills him to be anywhere other than the brig today.

"Is he in the interrogation room?" Seth asks brusquely, motioning for Liz to follow him.

Charlie's smile freezes. "Yes, Captain, but he looks a little poorly. I'd recommend medical attention."

"Thank you," Seth replies evenly. "Please call Dr. Singh." The man nods, then turns to go.

"Does he have any security training?" Liz whispers harshly, her mind still trying to absorb the sight of Charlie with a taser.

"I'm working on it, Z," Seth replies in a hushed voice.

Liz surveys the empty cells as they walk past. They look like the loneliest, least private place a person could be. Each is sealed with a clear pane that spans the entire width of the cell. The remaining three walls are solid and appear to be made of concrete, along with everything else. Other than a thin mattress on top of a concrete slab, the only other fixtures are a concrete sink and toilet.

Seth pulls open a heavy door at the end of the hallway, revealing a stark room with a metal table and chairs. The figure of a man lies slumped in a chair, head resting between his arms. He wears handcuffs, which are chained to a large metal loop on top of the table.

"Zag?" Liz can't tell if Seth is greeting the prisoner or trying to validate that he is conscious. *Is that blood dripping out of his ear?*

"Captain Harris," he slurs, raising his head from the table to look at them. Liz is horrified to see that one pupil is substantially larger than the other.

"Zag, this is Liz Goeff. I thought you might want to talk to her."

"Elizabeth?" he demands. "Elizabeth who?"

"No," Liz replies loudly. "Liz Goeff. Two words. G-O-E-F-F."

Zag's mouth falls open. *Is that drool?*

"Lizzie," he whispers as he scrutinizes her with pupils that seem to shrink and grow independently of each other. Liz refuses to look away, although his freakish stare makes her feel dirty.

"Zag, why did you help the New Generation?" she asks, taking a seat across from him. Seth continues to stand.

Zag looks at her quizzically. "Pinkerblew?" he asks, then repeats the word like a mantra. "Pinkerblew. Pinkerblew."

Sweet shit sauce, Claire totally fried his brain. She decides to take a different approach.

"Zag, tell me about your family. Are your parents still alive?" He stops chanting, brow furrowing as he shakes his head from side to side.

"Nooooooooo." The part of his brain that should tell his lips to close seems to glitch. He finally runs out of breath and coughs.

"Brothers? Sisters?" Liz continues.

"Like you?" he asks, his eyebrows jumping up in an exaggerated swagger.

"You have a sister like me?" she asks. *Maybe we're getting somewhere.*

"Nooooooooo," he drones, going on until he runs out of breath.

"Do you have a wife or a girlfriend?" she continues, determined to maintain eye contact as she struggles to decide which eye to look at.

His mouth falls open. "Pinkerblew. Pinkerblew. Pinkerblew."

This must mean something, she thinks, trying to siphon through all of her memories of the New Generation. She breathes in sharply.

"You do, don't you?" Liz leans in closer, determined to transcend her revulsion. "She's at the place women go to have babies, isn't she?" *Pink or blue.* Zag's muddled face goes slack, eyes large and suddenly leaking tears. *Gotcha.*

Then his face contorts. He screams, enraged, "What do you care? Your bread is buttered on both sides!" He tries to jump up from the table only to be yanked down by the restraints. His body falls into a heap on the floor, catching the edge of his chair on the way down. The seat crashes into the wall behind him as his hands continue to twitch, straining against the handcuffs supporting his body weight.

He begins to wail, words slurred and barely intelligible. But Liz knows exactly what he's saying. "I want to go home." Dr. Singh enters and rushes to the heap of person on the floor as Seth leads Liz into an adjacent observation room, looking at her quizzically.

"One of The Fifty-Two escaped from the New Generation when she was pregnant," she explains. "She told me there's a place where women go to have babies. Zag's wife must be there."

"But he's been on this ship for two years!" Seth exclaims, bewildered. "If his wife is having a baby now, it can't be his."

"I don't know," Liz replies, deep in thought as her mind generates possibilities. "Maybe she's not pregnant now. Maybe she was pregnant then. Maybe the New Generation took her. Or maybe …"

Liz suddenly feels the urge to vomit.

"What?" Seth demands. "Maybe what?"

"Maybe he agreed to spy for the New Generation so they would take care of her. He wouldn't have had very many options, Seth." Liz's voice trails off.

"If she wasn't a Green Grow employee, he had no way to bring her to the ship," Seth concludes softly, choking out the words as if someone punched him in the gut.

"The New Generation must have a way of recruiting people like Zag, people who still have ties to the surface." Liz can only think of one place the New Generation could have accessed Green Grow employees—the depots. They must have used the depots, at least when they were still open.

"Seth, I have an idea, but I need to talk to The Fifty-Two," she says urgently, following him out of the brig.

"Let me know what you find," he says as she steps onto the lift, clearly knowing that she intends to meet with them alone.

***

Liz doesn't realize how anxious she is until Ruth's warm brown eyes wash over her, soothing her with instant comfort. *She's warm, like the sun,* Liz thinks, *and I'm falling into her orbit.* She knows she shouldn't feel so comfortable around someone she's only known a short time. She knows she shouldn't trust Ruth, or any of them, really. She knows that things are often not what they seem, not even things that seem obvious. But it feels so good to be around these people who accept her without reservation, who welcome her as if she belongs—as if she's always belonged. She knows she shouldn't succumb to the ease, but she thinks she will; it's only a matter of time.

Liz is surprised to see Harry Goodworth sitting across from Ruth at a table in the common area of the quarantine, engrossed in his tablet. She intended to talk to him this morning, but hasn't done it yet. She makes her way over to the table.

"Since everyone's medical scans came back clear, the quarantine has been lifted," Harry says, still engrossed in his tablet and not yet aware of Liz's presence. "Everyone can stay here another day or two, but we need to get the medical unit back to normal operations soon."

Liz catches Harry's glance as he leans closer to Ruth to show her his tablet. He smiles at her warmly then turns his tablet so both women can see the schematics he's pulled up. It's Level 3, where the crew bunks.

"There's plenty of open space, so here's what I propose," he begins, highlighting a series of connected hallways that encircle a large block of empty rooms. "If you agree that this space works for the group, you can decide amongst yourselves who bunks in what room and provide the directory back to me for entry into the ship's records."

Ruth looks surprised and confused. "Why are all these rooms empty?"

"Our crew is only at 30 percent capacity," Harry explains casually, as if he receives this question a lot.

"Is that why there's no food on the surface?" Ruth asks, face growing tight. Harry studies her before answering.

"Here's the bottom line," he says firmly. "Until a peace is reached with the New Generation, none of this works like it should. The ship, the land, the people, and the depots are all connected. We've been under constant threat of extermination for over two years now, and everything has ground to a halt."

Ruth's eyes narrow, her lips pursing. "Look at these children, Mr. Goodworth. Look at these people." She motions around her. "Don't you think they deserve something better than that?"

Liz is puzzled. She knows Ruth is grateful to be safe on the ship, and yet she seems angry. *Maybe she's not angry,* Liz rationalizes. *She's only asking questions. A person doesn't have to be angry to question things, right?* But why isn't it enough to be here? What more does Ruth want? What more is even possible? Liz doesn't know, and she can't afford to think about it now.

Before Harry can respond, she excuses herself to find Will. She finds him on his cot.

***

"I don't understand what you're asking." Will looks confused and slightly distracted as his gaze darts between Liz and his boisterous son, who's playing nearby. His nose is still swollen, and he instinctively rubs it gently when he sees her. "You saw the message boards at the depot just like I did. You were looking for your brother, right?"

"I must have missed something," she says bluntly. "Is that where the they posted it? On the message boards?"

"Yes, they posted fliers—a lot of them, urging everyone to join the New Generation."

"How would a person join, if they wanted to?" Liz asks, thinking back to her conversation with Zag.

"I don't know, Liz. I wasn't interested in joining," he says, rubbing his still-swollen nose and casting a nervous glance toward Zachary, who has disappeared under a cot.

"Think, Will! It's important!" she demands, drawing his attention back to her.

"The fliers advertised monthly meetings. They said you could show up to a meeting and talk to New Generation leaders, join up without having to interact with any of the raiding parties. I guess once you joined, you got some kind of credential that would keep you safe."

"Seriously?" Liz is incredulous. "The New Generation walked right onto the depot and put up fliers recruiting members? Where were the meetings?"

"The fliers I saw mentioned different locations—often old schools or abandoned buildings. They usually listed an address and provided some directions. I'm sure once you got there, it wasn't too hard to spot."

Right under our noses. Liz is disgusted, but also afraid. Anyone who rotated to the surface could have seen the posters and joined at any time. And everyone rotated to the surface—for meetings, assignments, or surface leave—until Captain MacAbee suspended the routine surface runs two years ago. For all she knows, the entire crew could be spying for the New Generation. It isn't likely, but it's not impossible.

"Look," Will says as he reaches under the cot to fish out his squirming son, "after I found my mom, I stopped checking the message boards. I don't know anything else."

Liz can see that Will is ready for this conversation to end. There's so much more she wants to know, but she doesn't press him.

She walks purposefully out of the medical unit, noticing that Ruth and Harry are gone, probably on Level 3 by now, looking at the new living space. Liz wonders if Ruth is still plying Harry with questions, and what she thinks of the barren, utilitarian accommodations. No doubt, it's better than a cave, or at least Liz hopes it is.

Either way, Harry will have to handle it. Liz needs to find Seth, and she needs to find him now. She doesn't waste time waiting for the lift. She bounds up the stairs two at a time to Level 1, offering only a cursory knock on his office door before she enters and finds him squinting at his monitor.

"Seth," she says, out of breath. "I think I know how the New Generation was recruiting spies. You're not going to like it. And someone needs to examine Zag's body, closely. For scars or tattoos or anything that might resemble a permanent credential. Shitbiscuits, why couldn't I manage to bring back Ellen's body? We could have compared any markings."

Seth looks up with bloodshot eyes, bewildered, as Liz sits down and begins to explain.

***

Seth terminates the call to his bewildered mother, who is on her way now to the brig to scan Zag Bryant for any scars, tattoos, implants, or other markings that might serve as a New Generation credential. He made her agree repeatedly that she would not inject him with anything, and as far as Liz can tell, she thinks Claire means to keep her word.

"There's no point sitting here, Seth," she says patiently as his eyes dart between his email and his phone every few seconds.

"But what if she finds something?" he asks, his eyes pleading for knowledge she doesn't have to give him. "Besides, what else do we have to do?"

Seth probably thinks this is a rhetorical question, but Liz considers the options. For her, anything would be better than sitting here in his office waiting for a call or email that may not come tonight. She stands quickly, his bloodshot eyes twitching as she reaches for his hands, determined to pull him out of the chair if need be.

"We'll get dinner," she says with resolve.

"I'm not hungry." He takes the hand she's offered but makes no move to get up.

"I don't care. We're going." She pulls on him, leaning back with all her weight. He relents begrudgingly and stands, tucking his tablet into his waistband. "Besides," she continues, "there's something I want to share with you."

"Z," Seth says with a tired voice, "I'm not sure I can take any more revelations tonight."

"You'll like this," she assures him, hoping she's right. She's going to introduce him to story time, and she hopes it's a hit.

***

Seth and Liz stand on the edge of the circle as Ruth announces that it will be the group's last night in quarantine. Liz basks in the woman's glow, glad to be back among these people even though she was here just hours before. She's glad Seth is with her too, and except for a few quizzical looks when they arrived, no one seems to be paying him any attention. In this fleeting moment, Liz lacks nothing. She is safe within his protective aura, among people who accept her.

Tonight's theme is music, and Ruth shares memories of her favorite songs and concerts. "Etta James, and B.B. King," she says, working through a list of artists Liz doesn't know.

"ZZ Top!" someone else cries out.

"The Rolling Stones!" another voice challenges.

Seth probably knows these bands, Liz muses, considering the vast collection of music he curated as part of the ship's virtual library. She studies his rugged face, watching it transform from disinterested to enraptured as the banter escalates among the group. The debate progresses to laughter, and Seth gasps audibly as Ellis, an older member of the group who seems especially close to Ruth, pulls out a guitar and begins to play.

"Z," he hisses, eyes still glued to the battered duo of man and music, "that's a guitar."

Even I know what a guitar is, she thinks as she laughs, but Seth is too engrossed to notice. A lively melody fills the air as Ellis strums the strings, and The Fifty-Two begins to split off into pairs and small groups, stepping in time to the music.

"Do you know how to dance?" Liz asks as she watches Will and Melissa twirl and glide. Seth casts her a skeptical sidelong glance.

"No," he says. "Do you?"

"Nope." Her foot taps to the beat as she studies the bodies moving before them.

"It looks easy enough," he says. "We could try." Seth offers his hand, pulling her close to him when she takes it. She laughs as he almost steps on her toes, hopping quickly to the side before his feet land on hers. Soon they find an easy rhythm to their steps.

Liz is sure they lack grace, but no one seems to be watching—except Ruth. Glancing over, Liz sees her warm brown eyes studying them intently, mouth set in a line of concentration. Liz meets her gaze, and Ruth smiles, quickly turning her attention elsewhere. The music carries them all away. Elsewhere.

Liz can't remember the last time she had this much fun. Nor can she remember ever feeling so carefree. Even Seth seems without worry, smiling and laughing as they dance until the music fades. Ruth closes out the evening much too soon, and all the tired, happy souls depart for bed.

Liz isn't ready for it to end, and she gets the feeling Seth doesn't want it to end either. He follows her off the lift on Level 2 to walk her to her quarters.

"I hope you don't mind," Liz begins as they amble alone in the corridor. "I asked Harry to help me find a special place to keep having story time, maybe a garden on one of the unused levels."

"I don't mind," Seth replies. "People have used story-telling for thousands of years, and I see why you enjoy it. Thank you for inviting me."

"You mean for dragging you out of your office?"

"That too," he says, one corner of his mouth tipping up into a smile. "You seem especially fond of Ruth. I don't think I've ever seen you take to someone so fast—except me, of course." He flashes her the broadest, most charming smile Liz could hope to see.

"I suppose," she concedes. "I know it's only been a few days, but she reminds me of someone."

"Anyone I should know about?"

Liz laughs. "My mother. She reminds me of my mother."

Seth stops to face Liz squarely, playfulness giving way to a probing stare. "You don't talk about her much."

"True." Liz takes his arm as she starts walking again. "I find it's best to leave the past in the past."

"Do you miss her?"

Every day, she thinks as she responds, "Sometimes."

"Tell me something I don't know about her," he challenges.

She killed herself, Liz thinks as the familiar guilt and sadness fill her. Instead, she says, "She loved roses. There was one particular bush she especially loved, just outside our living room window. The flowers were incredibly fragrant, with pink and yellow petals. Somehow, she kept it alive for years."

They arrive at Liz's door, but Seth catches her arm as she turns to open it.

"Liz," he says, looking at her with lightning intensity, "I'm going to do things differently. I'm going to lead this ship and keep us safe, with or without the Council." She regards him curiously but says nothing.

"I need your help," he continues. "Will you help me? Are you with me?"

Liz isn't entirely sure what he's asking, but the way he's looking at her makes her belly flutter.

"Of course, Seth," she replies breathlessly. "I'll do anything to help you. Always."

"I need you to help me win the confidence of the crew. I know they doubt me." Seth's brow furrows, his eyes burning. "I can lead this ship, Z. I know I didn't grow up on the surface like everyone else, but ... we're not on the surface anymore."

"The crew?" Liz is confused, distracted by the strange feelings that continue to well inside her. "Seth, I haven't been part of the crew since I joined the Council." He waits as she thinks, her mind racing as she flails for something meaningful to say. "Of course I'll help you, Seth. Let me get my bearings with them again. I'll talk to Harry about working some shifts in the orchard."

"Sure," he says, still looking at her strangely, "if you think that's the best way."

Is he biting his lip? she wonders. Seth doesn't bite his lip—at least, Liz has never seen it before. *Why is he looking at me this way?* The fluttering in her belly grows. She tries to quash the feeling, telling herself it's the leftover thrill of dancing.

"I don't know," Liz replies, "but it will give us a place to start."

Seth's gaze wanders away, and he absently reaches for her hand, stroking her index finger softly with his thumb. The sensation sets her fluttering belly aflame. *Sweet shit sauce, I'm melting,* she thinks as she stays a wave of panic. She feels her eyes grow big, glad that Seth isn't watching.

"We could use a place to start," he says softly, still looking away. Liz waits for him to continue, trying to compose herself and unsure where this conversation is going.

"I'll always protect you, Z," he finally says as he looks back at her again, "if you let me."

Liz doesn't know what she expected him to say, but this isn't it. Her mouth falls open, but no words come out.

Seth looks away quickly, straightening himself and releasing her hand, which falls limply by her side. He tells her to get some rest and turns to go before she can reply, but that's okay with her. She opens the door to her quarters and steps inside quickly, not waiting to see if he looks back.

If I let him? she wonders, feeling weak in the knees and sitting down hard on her sofa. She thinks she knows what he's getting it, but Seth is knocking on a door she's not sure either of them should open.

Can I let him? She tries to imagine what it would be like to surrender completely to Seth—body, mind, and heart. The fluttering returns to her belly, making it dance with anticipation and perhaps a bit of fear. She makes her way to her bed and sits on the edge, staring into space, as she tries to decide if she likes the way this makes her feel and wonders what the future will hold.

CHAPTER 10

DR. HARRIS

***

Seth looks at the stairwell door wistfully, knowing he can't yet go back to his own quarters. No, this has to be done, and he might as well do it now. Procrastinating will only make it worse, and besides, he's feeling strong now. Purposeful.

He continues down the Level 2 hallway, down past Harry and Mathilda, beyond Jarrod's quarters where his parents reside. He knocks softly on the door, and his father answers, a look of concern flashing briefly across his face until Seth smiles, sending the signal that everything is okay.

"I know it's late, Dad, but I need to talk to Mom. Is she here?"

Seth appraises his father, a tall and angular yet unassuming man. He has a quiet, gentle nature, and Seth thinks this makes his parents a good match. His fiery, domineering mother seems to be much calmer when his dad is around, anyway. But what can a child truly know about his parents' relationship? Seth finds himself wondering whether his father's quiet gentleness is really just resignation.

"She's just gone to bed. Can it wait?"

"Who is it?" Seth hears his mom's voice from the bedroom.

"It's Seth, dear. Perhaps you can catch up with him tomorrow. You've had a long day."

"Don't be ridiculous," she says, not unkindly. "I'll be right out."

His father acquiesces, as he always does, and ushers Seth toward a couch in the small living area. Seth sits, noticing a well-used book of poetry on the table beside his father's chair. He smiles, remembering how his father reads the same poems over and over again, relishing them anew each time.

His mom, the formidable Dr. Claire Harris, comes out of the bedroom, wrapped in a bathrobe over her pajamas. The emotional distance Seth has worked so hard to build instantly crumbles, and the strength he felt holding Liz's hand in front of her door abandons him. He tries to see the woman before him as an impertinent department head, an unruly colleague. But here in this moment, she is neither of those things—she is his mother, and he is her child.

And yet, that's exactly why he's here. He's not a child anymore. Seth knows his mom hasn't accepted this, but she has to. She has to see him more clearly, although even as he prepares to speak, he knows that she's not the only one who needs to change. They both need to open their eyes and see each other clearly, but will either of them like what they see? Seth feels a pang of sorrow as he looks at the woman who gave him life. He knows this conversation won't go well.

"What is it, dear?" she asks, accustomed to familiar affection when they are in private. He stands to embrace her as she stretches her arms out for a hug.

"I want to talk about the Council," Seth begins. "And Zag Bryant."

"I haven't found anything definitive on Zag yet," she says hurriedly, "but I'll pick it up in the morning before the Council meeting. I need fresh eyes."

"That's not why I'm here." Seth's face is serious.

"Oh?"

"Mom," he starts cautiously, knowing he cannot unsay what comes next, "you went too far, with the truth serum. Your behavior has been increasingly erratic, and you are undermining my authority on the Council."

Claire's mouth falls open, eyes growing. Seth knows he's hurt her, and his confidence erodes even further. Was it a mistake coming here? Maybe he should have tried another approach. Maybe he should have waited.

"What are you talking about?" she demands, face flushing. "I've done nothing but help you!"

"Help me?" Seth momentarily forgets his lack of confidence as anger sparks at her indignation. "Zag Bryant is completely useless now. And you spend your time in the Council meetings talking over me and arguing with everyone about Liz!"

Claire's eyes narrow.

"She is a liability," she mutters, hands clenching into fists.

Seth meets her fierce gaze. "You know that if Captain MacAbee were still here, you'd be disciplined for drugging Zag without permission."

"Well, Captain MacAbee isn't here!" she yells. "If he were here—why do you think I'm trying so hard to help you?"

Seth crosses his arms, her words sinking in. Claire's face goes soft.

"Seth, I don't mean you're incapable," she says quietly, although Seth knows that's exactly what she means. "You're my child. I'll always do everything I can to protect you."

"Protect me from what, Mom?" Seth demands. "Independence? Success? Myself?"

Claire's mouth falls open, but Seth goes on before she can reply. "Yes, you always try to shelter me—to the point of embarrassment! But I'm not a child anymore. I need you to understand that."

"Seth …" his father begins, rising from his chair. Claire shoots him a fierce glance, and he sighs, shaking his head in resignation. "I'm going for a walk," he mumbles, laying his book carefully on the table before exiting the quarters. Claire turns back to her son.

"Embarrassment?" she huffs. "How dare you? What should we have done, Seth? Push you out in the cold to suffer and hope you lived? Why? For the principle of it? So other people would find you credible? I'm sorry if other parents had so little to offer their children. Your father and I did everything we could to keep you safe."

Seth feels the wash of shame he's been expecting. Even before coming here, he knew he would feel ashamed at some point, because his mom is right. Any decent parent would have jumped at the opportunity to move into an underground Green Grow bunker after the extinction event. Any decent parent would have wanted their child safe underground, inside walls of concrete and layers of security, while people on the surface reeled in tragedy and drowned in ash.

It's the same reason they moved again, just as Seth turned eleven, to the Survival Saucer, taking up residence with other scientists while the growing levels of the Green Grow 3 were still being built. Most parents didn't have options like this—it just so happened that Seth's parents were prized Green Grow scientists, the lynchpin of the space farms and the cornerstone of the future. And it just so happens that his mother brings this up anytime he criticizes her behavior.

This is why Seth avoids these conversations. He ends up feeling ashamed and confused, like the little boy his mother seems to think he is. But this conversation is different—it has to be. He can't keep sitting by idly, like the obedient child she wants him to be, while she undermines his authority. He's worked too hard for this. There's too much at stake.

He reminds himself that this isn't about decisions she made when he was a child, it's about decisions she's making now. He's thirty years old, and he is the captain of this ship. If she doesn't respect him now, she never will.

"I appreciate everything you've done," he says in a low voice, "but I don't need you to keep me safe anymore. Things need to change now, Mom. If you can't trust my judgment or don't think I'm capable, perhaps you and I shouldn't work together anymore."

"What are you talking about?" Claire snaps, locking eyes with Seth. He refuses to look away.

"Seth," she continues softly, unclenching her fists, "I know things are hard right now. But it won't be this way forever. When we can communicate with the Executive Board—"

"Mom, it's been two years!" He feels his anger rising, in concert with his voice. "They're gone. By force or choice, we'll never know. We can't keep waiting for them to magically appear and solve our problems. If we are to have peace with the New Generation, we need to make it ourselves."

Claire laughs, a full-bodied sound that tips her head back.

"And how exactly are we going to do that, Seth?"

"I don't know yet," he says, disregarding her obvious sarcasm, "but Zag Bryant might be able to give me insight if he was even remotely coherent."

He sees a flush rise on his mother's face.

"Yes, I was wrong, and I'm sorry," she says gruffly. Seth knows this apology will have to be enough. He knows that pressing her would be a mistake, and he thinks he's made his point.

"I know this isn't easy," he says, reaching out to take his mother's hands, "but our very lives are at stake here, Mom. You must know that. We can't waste any more time arguing."

Her chocolate eyes fill with tears as her brow creases and her lips purse. Seth can't tell what she's thinking, and it's probably better that way.

"Okay," she says, nodding her head in agreement. "I'll tone it down. I don't want you to push me away. I know you're capable but you can't do this alone."

"I know, Mom." Seth reaches to embrace her again. "And I love you."

One of her eyebrows cocks. *Really?* it asks, even though Claire doesn't vocalize the question. Seth can still see the hurt in her eyes, and he knows she'll have to work through it on her own. He feels her trembling, undoubtedly with pent-up emotions she doesn't want him to see.

"I hope Dad didn't go far," Seth says, trying to bridge the silence as she pulls away.

"Oh, I'm sure he's right outside the door," Claire says casually, composing herself. She wipes her eyes and regards her son, suddenly reaching out to squeeze him tightly. She seems so slight, perhaps even fragile, and so he gives to her pressure and hugs her again, until she is ready to let go.

"I love you more than you know, Seth," she says, voice thick with emotion as he opens the door. He sees his father pacing the hallway. Seth smiles—he really does love his parents very deeply—as he bids them both goodnight and leaves them to the privacy of whatever conversation they will have about his visit.

He walks slowly down the corridor, feeling lighter and heavier at the same time. He pauses in front of Liz's door and briefly considers knocking, but what would he say? Seth shakes his head and walks away, knowing it's better to go back to his own quarters and plan tomorrow in solitude.

CHAPTER 11

MOTHER

***

Liz lies in bed, eyes wide open. She doesn't know which is more troublesome, her strange conversation with Seth or the memories of her mother's roses. *She killed herself,* she thinks again, knowing that it's her mother keeping her awake. She sighs deeply, sitting up and swinging her feet to the floor. Her hand instinctively finds her knife, sheathed and resting on the table beside the bed. She pulls the blade out slowly, carefully returning it to the table.

She pads into the bathroom, squinting as she activates the light. As her eyes adjust to the brightness, she leans over the sink, splashing a trickle of water on her face before she straightens, steeling herself to look in the mirror. Tonight, she won't look away.

Her hair is tousled from tossing and turning, tangled on one side in a frizzy mess. But it's her face that jars her—the strong cheekbones beneath her blue eyes, the square jaw framing her face, the straight, narrow bridge of her nose. It is her mother's face.

She doesn't have any pictures of her mother, only the image she holds in her mind. But all she has to do to call it up is look in a mirror. Normally she turns away, avoiding the memory, but tonight she continues to look, stepping precariously onto the precipice of a grief that threatens to consume her.

She studies her eyes as her fingers comb through the tangles of her hair, pulling it away from her face like her mom used to do. They share upturned, almond-shaped eyes, part human and part feline. Liz's bright blue irises are flecked with silver; her mother's were flecked with jade.

She studies her pink lips, neither full nor thin. Her mom's were dry, and they cracked a lot. But they always promised a radiant smile. She hums a few notes of a tune she barely remembers until her heart begs for mercy, aching with misery as tears spill down her face. It must be a lullaby—she remembers her mom humming it anytime Liz needed comfort.

Would she still be here if I had been stronger? Liz wonders, going back to that familiar place her mind often visits, that never-ending path of doubt and criticism that calculates every scenario that might have led to a different outcome. *I was plenty old enough to do something more.*

Liz was twelve when it happened—not an adult, but so much more than a child. Jackson had been gone four years by then. Somehow they'd managed, but their luck was running out. Liz was thin and hungry all the time, and her mother was worse off, weak and listless from starvation. They were out of food and hope, and they were out of options.

The day her life changed forever started off like any other. It was cool and a little breezy, a harbinger of the cold, ashy, hungry winter that was coming. She kept her eye on the road, hoping it would be the day Jackson came home. He had to sense how much they needed him; he had to know it was time to come home.

Liz watched her mother from a corner of the living room as she began to stow a collection of items in a backpack. There were some leather scraps, a piece of rope, a small blanket, and a piece of plastic tarp, along with an extra shirt, a pair of heavy socks that had been mended several times, and a wool hat and scarf. Beside them lay a bag of dried apples and some nuts, the remainder of the food they had to share between them, and a plastic container full of water.

Liz remained silent as her mother worked quietly, wondering but afraid to ask what was happening. Her mother wasn't strong enough to travel anywhere, and where would they go anyway? Green Grow offered her a job as a produce picker, but it required her to rotate to the space farm for weeks at a time. She wasn't allowed to take Liz with her, and she had refused to leave her alone on the surface. Instead, they'd gone home to ration their supplies and hope for better times, a waiting game Liz knew they were losing.

Finally the bag was packed, and Liz's mother closed it, leaving only a large knife resting on her lap—not a kitchen knife, but a survival knife with a muted black tactical blade that peeked out of a thin leather sheath. Liz watched her mom unsheathe it, turning it over in her hands as she ran her still-nimble fingers up and down the length of the sinister blade.

"Are we going somewhere?" Liz finally asked, no longer able to bear the knot in her stomach. She knew by then how to tune out hunger, but she didn't seem to have any control over this growing, nauseating knot.

"Yes," her mother answered quietly, eyes downcast and vacant.

"When will we go?" Liz asked, trying to stifle a growing panic.

"Today," her mother responded, pausing to study her face. "But we're not going to the same place." Liz thought she was suffocating, even as her breathing quickened. Her mother continued, "Sweetheart, you're going to have to walk to the Green Grow station by yourself this time. Get a job and don't ever come back. I won't be here, and there's nothing for you here."

"What do you mean, Mom?" Liz remembers the hot tears that ran down her face, the snot she wiped from her face with her sleeve. She remembers the silence, as she waited for a response that never came. She remembers the panic that overtook her, sobbing and clutching her mother's frail body.

"No!" she cried. "Let's go together! I can carry you, or pull you in the cart. Then we'll come back. We have to wait for Jackson."

Her mom smoothed her hair and kissed her head, murmuring under her breath something sweet and faint. "No, sweet girl," she whispered in her ear, "it's your time now. My time is over, and your brother isn't coming back." She wiped Liz's tearstained cheeks, lifting her face to meet her gaze. "Stay hidden. Trust no one. When you get there, to Green Grow, don't take no for an answer. Remember, you have to tell them you're sixteen. You have to find a way to carry on. You'll be fine. You're stronger than you know."

"Let's both go, Mom. We can make it!"

"I can't make it any further," she replied simply. "I love you more than you can imagine. And I'm sorry. But you have to know there's nothing left here for you. You have to be certain. I'm so sorry."

Liz remembers screaming as her mother ran the knife deeply across one wrist, steeled with determination as she then cut the other. It didn't take long at all, even though Liz's world was standing still. While the blood spilled out of the woman's body, she wiped the blade of the knife quickly on her skirt and carefully slid it back into its sheath, tossing it next to the backpack. Her mom's determined face became weary and then peaceful. The last words she whispered were, "Now you have to go."

Liz sat there for a while, crying next to her mother's lifeless body slumped in her chair, pools of blood at her feet. She thought she would stay there crying forever. But eventually she ran out of tears, and a feeling welled up from deep inside her, a feeling that she had to leave.

Liz strapped the knife to her torso, drops of her mother's blood staining her skin. She donned her only coat and threw the bag over one shoulder, closing the door as she walked out of the house. She put one foot in front of the other, refusing to look back, too sad and afraid to be angry at her mother for taking away all her other choices. But her mom was right about one thing. She couldn't wait for Jackson to come home any longer. She'd have to go find him.

She walked that first day until well after dark, when she was too afraid to walk any farther. She could see nothing and hear everything, and it was terrifying. A snap here, a rustle there. Was it the wind, or the New Generation? She crept toward a stand of dead pine trees, burying herself in the thick bed of pine needles where she tried—and failed—to sleep until morning.

Why didn't I grab the knife? she wonders. *I could have carried her to the depot. Why was I too weak to protect the only person left who loved me?*

Liz tries to stop the sea of questions flooding her mind. She knows the past is gone. Not even saving fifty-two people can change what happened to her mom. Shutting off the bathroom light, Liz returns to bed, fearful of what awaits her when she begins to dream.

CHAPTER 12

THE CREDENTIAL

****

AUGUST 18, 2059 – MONDAY

For the first time, Liz feels like she's right where she belongs as she sits in the Council meeting. It's a strange and unexpected feeling, different than the sense of belonging she's found with The Fifty-Two. She concludes that it's not so much a feeling of belonging as it is acceptance, but it's still a welcome surprise. Although she knew her discovery about the New Generation was important, she hadn't expected it to unlock the path to the Council's good graces. And yet, even Claire seems welcoming, listening attentively when Liz speaks and replying with thoughtful questions and comments.

However, Liz realizes that the lack of criticism may have nothing to do with her. Whatever concerns the Council may harbor about her are undoubtedly eclipsed by the shock of what Claire found when she closely examined Zag. Even Liz becomes aware that everything she thought she knew about the New Generation now means nothing as she studies the strange credential Claire found. There is obviously much more to the New Generation than any of them suspected.

The symbol itself is foreign to Liz—an inverted triangle, bisected about a third of the way from the bottom with a horizontal line. *Are those letters above the line?* Liz wonders. *A "v" and a "y" maybe?*

"It's a rune," Mathilda states abruptly. "The inverted triangle with the line is an old runic symbol for the earth."

"And the letters are Greek," Claire continues. "Lower case nu and gamma—or NG. New Generation." Liz isn't surprised they have a secret symbol to identify each other, although the symbol itself is unusual and strange. It's how Claire discovered the symbol that has everyone flummoxed.

"So, it was behind his ear?" Seth asks again, only slightly less dumbfounded than the last time he asked.

"Yes, under the skin on the upper edge of the mastoid process," Claire repeats. "I missed it in the cursory scan because it was so close to his ear canal. It wasn't until I palpated the area that I activated the credential."

"So you pressed on the tiny chip behind his ear, and this symbol began to glow on the palm of his hand?" Harry asks.

"Yes, the chip must be depressed for at least three seconds, and then the symbol on the palm glows."

"But there are no chips in his hand?" Seth asks again, no less confused or astounded than anyone else in the room.

"I couldn't detect the source of the hologram, but it was quite large—more than two inches across. It appears to be a light, not a dye. A dye might be easier to explain, but a light ... I wouldn't know where to begin."

"I couldn't find any explanation either," Jarrod adds, looking just as unsettled as everyone else in the room. "I can't detect any kind of signal or radiation activating the chip. I have no idea what kind of technology this is."

So much for the New Generation being nothing more than roving bands of psychotic idiots, Liz thinks as she ponders aloud, "If they have better technology than we do, why do they need to steal a shuttle to take control of the ship?"

"Maybe they have technology but lack materials or manpower," Mathilda offers.

"Jarrod, do you think they stole these microchips from Green Grow?" Seth asks.

"I don't think so. All of Green Grow's technology development projects are accessible from the corporate research files—the ones I hacked to get the specs for the propulsion drive and the location of the antimatter. I looked through the files again this morning and couldn't find anything resembling these microchips. However they got them, it wasn't from us."

Seth breathes in deeply, lips pursed together. "This leaves us with a lot more questions than answers about the New Generation, but perhaps we now have a way to rout any remaining spies. Can we systematically detect these chips?"

"I don't know," Claire says pensively. "We could inspect everyone's ears, or require body scans …"

"But that might tip our hand," Harry concludes.

"What are we doing about security in the meantime?" Mathilda asks. "Is the antimatter drive safe?"

Jarrod replies, "I'm overlaying the controls with a new security system. Captain, you'll need to input your biometric information."

"What kind of a system?" Mathilda asks. "Clearly, we underestimated the New Generation. Do we need to re-evaluate what we're doing?"

"The new system will ensure that the drive can only be activated from the bridge. The captain will have to biometrically confirm his identity, as well as a second person designated by him."

"Who is the second person?" Mathilda presses.

"Mathilda," Jarrod says abruptly, "I think the less we know the better. The captain can designate the second person after I set him up in the system."

"Of course," she concedes, "but what about the physical security? Is the drive safe in the tube?"

"I've reprogrammed the access doors to require the captain's key card," Jarrod responds. "It's not foolproof, but it will have to suffice for now."

"And what about our security?" she presses, looking squarely at Seth.

"I'm assigning all of you Level 1 quarters," Seth begins as he projects a list of room assignments onto the monitor. "The rooms are fully furnished, and I expect you'll move any personal effects today. Starting today, the lifts and stairwells will also require fingerprint and keycard validation to enter Level 1."

Liz tunes out the discussion about the room assignments. Her mind is still stuck on the radiant blue credential, wondering exactly how deeply she has underestimated her enemy. She leaves the meeting quickly, as soon as Seth adjourns the group, needing to distance herself from the chatter, to process what she's seen and heard.

***

Liz sits in silence in her new Level 1 quarters, achieving no profound insights but grateful that the noise is subsiding in her head. Her tablet buzzes—a message from Seth.

NO EMERGENCY, BUT COME TO THE BRIDGE WHEN YOU CAN.

It only takes a minute to get there. She remembers Jarrod mentioning final tests on the propulsion drive at the Council meeting, but Liz can't imagine what that has to do with her. The doors hiss open, and she hears Jarrod's voice, hitching as she crosses the threshold and then fading out altogether.

"So, voice recognition and a retinal scan?" Seth asks, pulling the man's attention back to him.

"Yes," Jarrod confirms, quickly pressing a sequence of buttons on his tablet and motioning Seth to sit in the captain's chair. "Okay, you can confirm now."

Seth speaks clearly, "This is Captain Seth Harris activating the propulsion drive. Tango. Delta. One. Charlie." Liz watches a red beam of light as it scans his eye, and she waits. Nothing happens.

"Is that it?" Seth asks. Jarrod nods.

"Once the security program reboots, we'll be good to go," Jarrod says as Liz moves to stand in front of the large, panoramic window that spans the bridge. To the right looms the dark side of the Earth. It's nighttime in Asia, and Liz wonders if the people who remain below are sleeping. Or are they looking at the countless stars she can see off to the left? Are the stars even visible tonight on the surface?

"Can we see it?" she hears Seth ask.

"Sure," Jarrod replies, tapping a sequence of commands on his tablet as the large window darkens. A live camera feed fills the space, from a drone that is zooming along the outer surface of the Green Grow 3 just on the other side of the hull. Jarrod navigates the drone past the bridge to the top of Level 1, into the round opening of the tubular channel that runs through the core of the ship.

The tube protects the thrusters, and now the propulsion drive, from space debris, but it isn't sealed on the ends. It flows directly into space on both sides and doesn't have gravity or air. Liz knows that years before she came to the ship, people worked in the tube wearing clunky space suits. Even now, fully functioning airlocks remain on Levels 1, 6, 7, and 37, still equipped with the bulky and presumably functional suits. But these days, have drones to work in the tube.

The drones are stored and maintained on the dock, adjacent to the shuttle parking, so Liz has seen them up close numerous times. They are nearly twice her size, and she finds them ominous—faceless, wingless beetles with an unnatural number of thin metal legs. The large machines are just as versatile as they are frightening, capable of flying, welding, cutting, riveting, hammering, and collecting samples. But they are complex to operate, and only a handful of people on Jarrod's team possess the skill and precision required to control them.

Liz realizes she is holding her breath as Jarrod navigates the drone past the thrusters, revealing the new propulsion drive. The drive itself looks unremarkable, a sleek compilation of thick casings and metal rings, but somewhere underneath the polished exterior is the antimatter that people died to retrieve. This is what makes her heart flutter, her mind filled with a memory of Sam's lopsided smile and Ellen's betrayal. She hopes this propulsion drive is worth the cost, except she knows it never can be. All she can really hope is that it works the way they need it to.

"Do you want to practice it now?" Jarrod asks, gaze darting nervously between Seth and Liz. Seth nods, tapping buttons on his console and repeating the security sequence. Liz can't help but gasp as a blue light begins to emanate from the cold metal. It's beautiful—breathtakingly beautiful, in a cold and lifeless sort of way.

"Now you can control it from the console," Jarrod explains, apparently unmoved by the enormity of what they are seeing. "You'll see a message to approve all of the specifications input by myself or Mathilda. After you approve the specifications, you'll have to approve again to engage the drive."

"And I can designate a different approval code for each action?" Seth asks, engrossed in the screen.

"Yes," Jarrod says, turning back to his own tablet as the drone begins to change position. "Are you ready to shut it down?" Seth studies the console and taps a button that makes the blue light dim and then disappear completely. The picture lurches as the drone zooms off, flying past the drive and the thrusters. Jarrod cuts the camera feed, and the large window becomes clear again, the dark side of the world once more floating before them.

"Do you think we'll leave soon?" Jarrod asks, smiling nervously.

"Mathilda wanted to recheck the calculations, so I told her she could have the day. Any concerns?"

"No, we're ready. It just feels strange—I'm not sure whether to feel like a pioneer or a refugee."

Seth nods thoughtfully. "I can understand that."

"I'll be glad to get this behind us," Jarrod concludes, tucking his tablet under his arm, "literally and figuratively." The bridge doors hiss open and then closed again, leaving Liz and Seth alone. He motions her over to the captain's chair.

"Will you be my second?" he asks. She looks at him, perplexed, and he motions to the console.

"Your second to activate the drive? Is that why you asked me here? Seth, this isn't the same as flying a shuttle—"

"It's not about flying the ship," he interrupts. "It's about the security of the propulsion drive. If you won't do it, I'll ask my mother."

"I'll do it!" she says quickly, mostly out of reflex. *Sweet shit sauce, his top two choices are me and his mother?* Liz is glad that Claire is the second of the two.

"Good." Seth looks pleased as he starts tapping buttons on the console to add her to the system. "I'm going to make an announcement to the crew after dinner tonight. Tomorrow morning we will leave orbit, and tomorrow night, I'll hold an open hearing for Zag." He looks at her sidelong, trying to gauge her reaction to what he just said.

"You're going to try him in front of the crew?" Liz is surprised by both his timing and his method. The Green Grow Code of Conduct outlines some judicial proceedings, but ultimately the captain is responsible for sentencing any crimes. It hasn't come up before because there is very little crime on the ship. A safe and secure position on the Green Grow 3 is a prized commodity, not something a crew member would jeopardize lightly. Liz remembers hearing about a few issues when she worked in the orchard, but they were minor things that supervisors chose to overlook— scuffles between crew members, contraband, or petty theft.

She hasn't forgotten that Seth told her he was going to do things differently, but she didn't imagine this. She thought Seth would adjudicate Zag's case privately with the Council, and Mathilda must have assumed that as well, since she asked about the hearing at the morning's Council meeting. Seth brushed her off, saying he didn't yet know how he wanted to proceed. *Seems like he figured it out pretty quickly.* Liz looks at him expectantly.

"What are the charges?" she asks, oblivious that he hasn't yet answered her first question. Neither question articulates what she really wants to know, but she doesn't know how to ask him how far he intends to take this.

"Mutiny," he says gravely, eyes fixed on hers.

"Are you prepared to execute him?" Liz asks, suddenly feeling like she is in a dream. This is the question that matters, but does she really want to know the answer? Is Seth willing to address the gravity of Zag's crime? Charges of mutiny will force him to deal with the possibility of ending Zag's life, something she assumes he wants avoid. Is Seth prepared to make a hard choice, to render a judgment that could cost a person his life? Liz can't imagine choosing to end someone's life if other choices are available. She has killed plenty of times, but it never seemed like a choice in the heat of the moment.

Seth's face clouds, his voice dark. "I have to keep order, Z. Zag well understood the severity of what he was doing."

"You'll make an example of him," she whispers, as a heavy realization settles on her. *It's a show of strength.* She has no words. Her world spins around her, shifting and changing even as it spins. She's dreaded this moment. But now it is upon them, and she can do nothing but watch it unfold.

Liz knows that she is adept at the art of surviving—a ferocious fighter and a master of tactical strategy. She is intimately familiar with the leading edge of violence, and shows of strength come as easily to her as the air she breathes. In her world, weakness is deadly. And now, her world has become Seth's. It's time for him to prove himself, or rather to reveal himself.

He will either show that he is strong enough to do what needs to be done, or he will cower. She will know what kind of man he is, and once she knows, she cannot unknow. He will either be the man she believes him to be, or he will be someone else. If he's someone else, she has no future with him. But even if he's the man she believes him to be, will he still need her in his life once he knows he can stand on his own? If not her strength, what does she have to offer him?

"I have something for you," Seth says, pulling her attention back. Liz studies the rubberized wrist band he offers her. It looks like a watch.

"Jewelry? Why Seth, you shouldn't have." She flutters her eyelashes. "Although if you did, I'd much prefer something shiny."

"Oh, I doubt that," he murmurs, narrowing his eyes at her. "You are all tactical, girl. But to answer your question, no. It's not jewelry. It's a wristband communicator. I have one too." He holds up his hand, showing her the matching device he's already secured to his arm. She extends her arm as he attaches it.

Studying her, he continues, "This is a direct line to me. If you need me for any reason, just press the button here, and I will answer."

"Does everyone get one of these?" she asks, not sure whether she should feel privileged or distrusted.

"Nope," he says as he finishes securing the communicator, flipping her palm up to gently trace a line with his finger that makes her feel like she's melting again. "Just you. I want you to have direct access to me, always."

Liz commands her thoughts to come together.

"I'm on my way to Level 7," she says. "A few of The Fifty-Two were assigned to work there, and I want to pop in on the last half of their orientation. I'll buzz you when I get there—to test our communicators."

"Good," he responds softly as she turns to go. "I'll be in my office."

Liz fondles the flexible band that presses against the flesh of her wrist as she waits for the lift, deep in thought. Everything seems to be coming together and falling apart all at the same time. She thinks she should feel good about leaving orbit tomorrow, and also about routing out a spy, but nothing feels good about knowing Seth will have to judge a man and decide whether he lives or dies. Nor does it feel good to know that yet another crew member betrayed them. She tries to dismiss the thoughts from her mind as she steps onto the lift, knowing that there is no easy answer to this situation.

The lift stops on Level 3. Her heart lurches as she sees Albert Wyndham's face, the rest of his body obscured by two other crew who stand in front of him. She tries to keep her own face impassive as he makes his way to stand right next to her, arm brushing her shoulder even though there is plenty of room on the lift to allow space between their bodies. *Is he trying to intimidate me?* she wonders, concerned more about his strange behavior than his physical size or strength.

"Albert," she greets him evenly.

"Liz," he replies. His voice is calm, but his roiling eyes give him away. "I want to know what the Council is doing to investigate my brother's death."

"I'll talk to the captain," Liz replies. "You deserve to know what's happening."

"I know he didn't die in a bushwa training accident," he mutters.

"I need the captain's permission to give you any details," Liz says cautiously.

"I deserve to know how my brother died," Albert growls through gritted teeth, "and Sam deserves justice."

Liz briskly steps off the lift when the doors open onto Level 7. She gives Albert a final glance, but he refuses to look at her, standing rigid with his eyes fixed straight ahead of him as the doors close again.

***

Liz breathes in deeply, reveling in the smell of damp soil and everything green, determined to leave her troubles behind her. She hasn't worked on Level 7 in years, but she still likes to come here, to walk among the trees on the soft green grass planted between the rows. She fondly remembers pruning branches and thinning apples, but there is more to Level 7 than apple trees. There are cherries and peaches, plums and apricots, and a vineyard. Liz also worked in the tropical orchard on Level 8 where they grow citrus, coffee, avocados, mangos, cacao, and bananas. It was there that she came to love the smell of oranges and lemons as they were harvested in the thick, humid air, but Level 7 is the one that feels like home.

She sets off with purpose, following the most logical path for an orientation tour. She passes a team of people picking cherries, working with ladders in pairs. Their quiet murmurs and buzzing conversation make it seem like the trees are whispering secrets to each other—or maybe to her. Liz passes a woman who is reaching up to take a full basket from someone standing on a ladder, handing up an empty one in return. Liz remembers the work being tedious but peaceful, the cherries delicate. As she reaches the end of the row, she hears a telltale sign of The Fifty-Two—Zachary's little voice.

"Where are the mirrors, Mama?" His question pierces the drone of adult conversation.

"I don't think they have mirrors," Melissa replies, as Liz finds the row where the group is currently standing, surrounded by peach trees.

"But then how do they get the light, Mama?" Zachary asks.

"I don't know," Melissa replies, "but Mama needs to listen to what the man is saying right now."

Liz smiles as she approaches, bending over slightly to say in a loud whisper, "Your dad used to work here, Zachary. I bet he can tell you all about the lights later." Zachary starts, taking a step closer to his mother.

"I'm sorry, it's all a bit overwhelming," Melissa whispers. "Harry said it would be okay for the children to come." Liz smiles and nods, looking for other familiar faces in the group—one in particular. She finds the warm brown eyes and makes her way toward Ruth, who is standing next to the tour guide, a young, clean-cut man Liz doesn't recognize even though he acknowledges her with familiarity.

"Now here we have a veteran," he proclaims, speaking to the group. "Liz Goeff! Have you been assigned to work here as well?" He winks at her dramatically.

"I could do far worse," she responds jovially, "but today I'm only tagging along."

"Very well," he says. "Let's move on to the vineyard. We'll pay a careful visit to the bees, and then we'll wrap up with the compost pile and the tool barn."

"Bees?" Ruth whispers loudly.

"They pollinate the trees," Liz explains softly, soaking up the life around her. "Many of the levels have hives, but you'll also see hummingbirds and some butterflies."

Ellis moves up to Ruth's side, and Liz falls a step behind, breathing in the warm air. She follows quietly, listening to the young man guide them through the rest of the level. Liz is impressed by his deep well of knowledge, and it reminds her how much work the orchard requires. Planting the trees and harvesting the fruit is only a small portion of what they do. They also prune branches, maintain the drip irrigation system, thin the fruit as it matures, shred compost, maintain the grass that grows between the rows, and maintain the equipment necessary for all of it. The cycle never ends, but rather flows in a satisfying current that Liz finds appealing.

The young man is explaining the climate control system and wintering protocol when Liz hears a distinct series of tones—the ship's broadcast system. *I thought Seth said he wasn't making his announcement until tonight,* she thinks as she turns toward the tool barn, eyes trained on a large monitor.

A face fills the screen, a man that Liz feels like she should know but doesn't. His eyes are stony, not the eyes of anyone she know, and framed by a ragged scar that starts above his left eyebrow, runs down his cheekbone, then slithers back toward his ear. His mouth looks familiar—the top lip thin and the bottom lip full, set on an angular jaw right above a dimpled chin.

As the man's voice begins to fill the air, Liz's knees buckle. She falls to the ground, needing every bit of life energy it can offer her. *This can't be real.*

"To the crew of the Green Grow 3," he starts, his voice cutting and severe, "this is Jackson Goeff. I am a captain in the New Generation, and I am bringing you a message of truth." Liz's mind flashes back to the brother she loved, his boyish smile and soft waves of dark blonde hair. This can't be him. This man looks callous and cruel, hair cropped close to his bony head. *He can't be alive,* she thinks, remembering all the days she watched for her brother outside her mother's window. *He wouldn't have abandoned us if he was still alive.*

"Your captain—Seth Harris—and your Council have been lying to you. Accept the truth, my friends, and rise up! For time is short. If you do nothing, your captain will lead you out of Earth's orbit tomorrow—away from the planet that is your home. Rise up and join me to prevent this. The New Generation is not the enemy. How can we be your enemy? We have been taking care of your friends and family on the surface, the ones the Green Grow Corporation forced you to leave behind as they cut off our food supply and starve us into submission."

Tears sting Liz's face. *This can't be real.* But despite the severe tone, she knows it is his voice, the same voice that bade her farewell at the end of the driveway, cheeks flushed and eyes full of hope as he left to find a better life. *He promised to come back. He promised to find somewhere safe for us.*

"Come to your senses," he continues, "just like your colleagues who have already seen the truth and are working to disable the deep space propulsion drive as I speak. Help them! Rise up! The Council doesn't control the ship—you do! Seth Harris doesn't control the ship—you do. Choose to stay here. Choose to save the people of Earth. You will be rewarded."

Liz's chest tightens. *He had to know how much mom and I needed him. Didn't he know?*

"And to my sweet sister Lizzie … What a beautiful woman you have become. Come home to me, Lizzie. I've made a place for you here. Blood is thicker than water. Don't abandon me now. Rise up!"

Jackson's face disappears from the screen, and a symbol remains—the New Generation credential.

Don't abandon me.

Liz looks wildly around her, taking in the shock on everyone's faces as she feels her wrist vibrate madly. *Seth.* She presses the button on the device and begins to speak.

"Seth! What the hell is going on?" she demands, releasing the button so he can reply.

"We've been hacked. Someone has taken control of the drones, and they're trying to disable the propulsion drive in the tube. They're trying to hack the bridge controls as well. Jarrod isolated the signal to Level 5, but I don't know where. I need to quash this. Where are you?"

Liz reaches for the button to respond, but another voice cuts through the air. It's the young man who led the orientation. He raises his right hand high above his head, left hand flying behind his ear as he shouts, "Rise up! Liz, will you do what's right? Will you lead us?" The blue light that radiates from his palm stuns everyone, except Liz.

"Bushwa!" Liz hisses, knowing that even such an impressive credential doesn't change the truth. She leaps up from the ground, propelled by a rage that is ready to feast on something more than her sanity, running full speed toward the man as she pulls her knife from its sheath.

"The New Generation lies!" Liz screams, as the young man drops his palm and reaches behind his back, producing a pistol he isn't allowed to have. She is on him before he can level it, launching herself through the air and landing a brutal kick that sends him sprawling, gun flying into the grass. She rolls on top of him, using the weight of her body to force her knife through the soft hollow at the bottom of his throat. She rips out the blade, blood flowing onto the grass as she presses the button on her communicator again.

"I'm on Level 7. Are you on the bridge?"

"No," Seth responds. "I was in the cafeteria when the broadcast started. I made it down to Level 5. I'm here with Charlie."

Liz smashes a bloody finger against the communicator.

"I'm coming, Seth. The spies are using their credentials. They're trying to rally the crew to mutiny, and they have weapons."

"Liz, stay where you are. I don't understand what I just saw, but if that really is your brother, no one will know whose side you're on."

"My brother is dead," she hisses, drawing the communicator close to her mouth, "and no one will wonder whose side I'm on."

"Liz!" Ruth howls, pleading for Liz's attention. "What's happening?"

"It's mutiny! You have to hide! I'll come back when it's safe!"

"Where? Where do we hide?"

"Take everyone to the trees!" Liz shouts. "Any traitors looking for weapons will descend on this tool barn." She can see the leaves of the vineyard start to rustle. People are coming. She wonders how many as she picks up the pistol.

"Ruth," Ellis commands, "keep the children safe. Gabriella, go with her. The rest of you come with me." Liz looks at him quizzically as Ruth and Gabriella begin to swiftly herd Zachary and two other children toward the trees.

"If you don't hide, we don't hide," he snarls, grabbing an axe from the tool barn before motioning the others to follow. Liz can hear the pounding of footsteps in the vineyard getting closer.

"I don't know whose side they're on!" she screams to Ellis. "We need to get to Level 5."

Ellis turns to the small group of men and women holding shovels, axes, and saws. "Secure the stairwell before they flank us," he commands. "Noah and Ruben, you're on point. Melissa, take up the rear with me and Liz. Patrick, Eli, and Ava, keep it tight!"

The seven individuals instantly transform into a unit, moving with speed and precision toward the stairwell. As Ellis beckons Liz to follow him, a group emerges from a tangle of grape leaves. Liz turns to face them squarely.

"Rise up!" a woman cries to the people behind her.

Liz doesn't see a credential on her palm, but it doesn't matter. She's chosen her side and her fate. Liz levels the pistol and shoots her twice in the chest.

"The New Generation lies!" Liz bellows as the woman falls to the ground. The rest of the group stops, apparently unsure what to do. Liz trains her pistol on a stocky man who stands frozen a few feet away from the woman's limp form.

"Who do you serve?" she demands, as the man raises his hands in the air. He looks around quickly, as if he isn't sure who she is addressing.

"Captain Harris!" he squeaks. "I serve Green Grow. The New Generation killed my family!"

Liz lowers the pistol. "If you don't want to end up like the people on the Green Grow 1, I suggest you arm yourselves and follow us to Level 5 to subdue this shitshow!"

She runs to the stairs where the others are waiting for her, pushing her way to the front of the group. "I still have fifteen bullets in this clip," she says when Ellis starts to object. "You have axes and shovels." She opens the door to the stairwell and hears the wailing echoes of hell somewhere above her.

"We have to contain them," Liz barks, bounding up the stairs with the pistol in her left hand, knife in her right. They've just passed the door to Level 6 when a screaming mass of rabid bodies tries to crush them.

Liz doesn't look closely enough to recognize any of the faces before her. In this moment, she's not capable of seeing the people she's worked with and lived with for years. They all have the same face—the face of her enemy. They aren't human to her now. Her first bullet sails through a glowing blue palm, shredding the Greek letters before it devours the man's eye then settles in his brain. She gets off two more shots before the group starts to flow around her, swinging wildly with dowels and lengths of pipe as she slashes their legs and torsos with deadly cuts.

A hulk of a man launches himself at her from two steps up. She sidesteps his lunge, sinking her knife into the small of his back just as Melissa lands a crushing blow to his head with the blade of a shovel. Blood flows down the stairs like a sacrifice on the altar of ancient gods.

Moments later, Liz crashes onto Level 5, adrenaline-fueled fury ready to conquer whatever awaits. But the level is quiet, the floor littered with bodies attesting to earlier violence. Her breath hitches as she takes in the scene. There must be at least fifty bodies here, probably more. Some of them are still, while others groan and shift. Liz doesn't know who is friend or foe, so she picks her way carefully through them, crouching behind the landing gear of the farthest shuttle as she reaches toward her wrist.

"Seth," she hisses into the wristband communicator. "We're on Level 5. Where are you?" The channel goes silent for a few seconds. Just as she reaches for the talk button again, Seth's voice comes across.

"I'm in the server room. One of them ran in here—"

Liz hears a splash of static and replies, "I'm coming," as she takes off at a run, toward the maze of mechanical rooms on the far side of Level 5. She rounds the edge of the dock, hurtling down the corridor that houses the server room. Then she slams into the ground, a crushing weight on top of her as she begins to lose consciousness.

Liz's ears ring as her eyes flutter open. She tries to push herself up, to sit, but her body is leaden. *What fell on me?* she wonders as she tries again to rise, taking in the barren hallway that looms before her. A drip tickles across her face, warm and thick as it slides down her jaw. She touches her ear, and her fingers come away bloody. Her head begins to pound, thumping in rhythm to her heart beat as the ringing gets louder. The world starts to go dark again as she fights to stay conscious and loses.

She wakes again to Dr. Singh's face hovering over her. The world is still spinning precariously, and she can't hear anything as she feels herself lifted onto a medical transport.

CHAPTER 13

THE SUBJECT

***

The scientist stands in front of his transporter, but this time he's not alone in his secret lab. He has a human subject—one that exceeds his wildest expectations. He hoped to find someone who wouldn't be missed if the experiment went awry, and that was a tall order. Even the most seemingly insignificant people seem to know someone who will eventually start asking questions about why they aren't around.

The scientist could, of course, craft some story or explanation, but he doesn't want to spend his energy that way. He has enough distractions as it is. So, he needs someone who won't be missed. But to find someone who is also willing to help him, someone who comes of his own volition—now that is a dream come true.

The scientist knows that testing on humans isn't something to be taken lightly, and so he worked with mice as long as he could. The mouse trials allowed him to work out the kinks in his calculations and coordinates, to consistently transport the mice when and where he intended. Plus, the trials allowed him to perfect the biofilm capsule technology, which effectively shields living creatures as well as electronic sensors from the perils of the wormhole. Of course, this means that he now gets no useful readings from the sensors about the nature of the wormhole, but at least he knows the environment inside the biofilm capsule remains stable as it passes through. He knows he should feel good about this and relegate the nature of the wormhole to future learning. Setting priorities is necessary, after all.

He turns his attention back to his test subject. The subject looks scared, and so the scientist offers him a slight smile. *My sweet pet,* he thinks, reminding himself that the man's name is Alex. Does his name matter? Perhaps, but the scientist believes that most people are inconsequential. What have they done with their lives, after all? What have they done that matters? But Alex matters. Alex will help him conquer the mysteries of the universe.

Suddenly, the scientist feels a seed of fondness begin to blossom for the man, the trust he's given so freely, the fear he tries to stifle—not for the sake of science or knowledge, no, Alex offers himself for nothing more than the sake of pleasing the scientist.

He doesn't know if Alex will survive these trials, and it's probably easiest if he doesn't. The scientist must protect the secrecy of his work at all costs, and he can't afford even someone as simple and well-meaning as Alex slipping up and saying something he shouldn't. He can't risk exposing his work. He may have to kill Alex, if it comes to that, and it may come to that indeed.

So far, Alex has survived every trial, although the process seems to be taking a toll on him. The first time, he came back a bit singed—evidently because of a leak in the biocapsule the scientist had overlooked. The second time he came back rather dehydrated and looking noticeably older, sporting a full inch of new facial hair that was already going gray. The scientist thinks he's solved those problems, and tonight he will know for sure. And if Alex survives the remaining trials, he will have exhausted his usefulness, and the scientist will most likely have to kill him.

Unless …

Something occurs to the scientist, and he feels his seed of caring blossom into a wave of emotion as he looks deep into Alex's fearful and vulnerable eyes. It's an impulse that flies in the face of all logic, but the scientist knows, he simply knows with all his being, that he wants Alex to survive. In fact, he will do everything he can to make sure Alex survives. He can always use a loyal follower—a devoted assistant. Of course, it will be challenging to make this work out the way he needs it to, but the scientist loves a good challenge.

His smile broadens, and it's as genuine a smile as he's ever given. Alex seems to relax, at least for a moment, as the scientist secures the last of the sensors to his body. His fear returns, however, as he steps into the biofilm capsule.

"I'll see you on the other side," the scientist reassures him as he fits the top of the biofilm capsule in place. He can't see Alex anymore, but he can feel the slight trembling of the capsule as he begins to seal the edges with a liquid bio-glue. And so, he begins to hum, to soothe his frightened pet, alone inside the dark capsule with nothing but a few sensors to keep him company. He doesn't know if the humming helps, but he continues anyway as he calibrates his machine and checks the coordinates one more time.

He's still humming when the transporter flashes briefly. In an instant, the capsule is gone. He has one hour before it returns. If Alex comes back alive and undamaged, he might be ready to transport himself. Well, maybe after one more trial. He can't afford to be reckless, even though he is running out of time. Nor can he afford to let his vision be clouded by his insatiable desire to kill Seth Harris.

The scientist makes a note of the time then turns to his computer. He sees a message from Mathilda. What can she possibly need from him at this hour? All of his joy evaporates as he reads her message. He reads her words again and again, angry and confounded. She needs his help, but he doesn't know how to help her. Not yet.

He stands and begins to pace, pulling at his hair. Time was short, he knew this, but now he realizes it's gone. He's out of time, and the transporter isn't ready. What is he going to do now? A whirlwind of thoughts consumes him—he needs to clear his mind.

He knows he can solve this problem. He can solve any problem, and he is unwilling to forfeit the game to a pathetic excuse of a man like Seth Harris. There is opportunity here; he only needs to see it. Where is the opportunity? He holds his breath until it comes: an idea. In a flash, his anger is gone. The scientist has no energy for anger. He only has energy for the idea. Returning to his computer, he begins to sift through his old records. After jotting a few notes, he returns to his search. His focus is singular. He knows how to help Mathilda, what she needs to do now. He sits, immovable, hashing out the details, until Alex returns from his journey through time and space, exactly when and where he is supposed to.

CHAPTER 14

WILLOW BROWN

****

AUGUST 20, 2059 – WEDNESDAY

Liz becomes aware of a steady beep and the soft hum of equipment around her. *I can hear again,* she realizes as she opens her eyes slowly, afraid that the world might still be whirling around her. But the spinning has stopped, so she opens them wide, taking in the dimly lit room filled with medical equipment and three other beds. She's starting to push herself up when a set of warm familiar eyes comes into view. Ruth's hand rests gently on Liz's shoulder, a wordless suggestion that she not get up.

"Welcome back," she says, smiling. "I'll get Dr. Harris."

"Wait!" Liz's voice is raspy. "The children! Is everyone okay?"

"Everyone is fine. There's nothing for you to do now but rest." Ruth shushes Liz as she tries to protest, stepping out of the room and into a light that sears Liz's eyes. The door closes, and Liz tries to blink away the spots in her vision as her eyes begin to readjust to the low light. She squints toward the other beds, trying to see who's in them. They appear empty.

The much-too-bright light reappears as Claire enters, pointing a scanner at Liz's head while she scrutinizes the readout on a tablet in her other hand.

"What do you remember?" Claire asks, setting her tablet on the bed as she hands Liz a glass of water. Liz sips it slowly, rewinding her memory to the Level 7 orchard and everything that followed.

"I was running," Liz recounts, "trying to get to Seth in the server room on Level 5. Then something fell on me. I remember being dizzy. I remember my ears ringing. Then I woke up here."

Claire smiles. "Good. No memory loss."

"What happened?" Liz struggles to sit up, splashing water on her thin medical gown. "What fell on me?"

"Nine G's of acceleration," Claire replies evenly, as she presses a button to raise the head of the bed. "It hit all of us. You suffered two ruptured ear drums and another concussion."

"Is there still fighting?" Liz asks, prepared to launch herself out of bed.

"No," Claire replies in the same even tone. "You've been unconscious for thirty-six hours."

"What?" Liz gasps. "Why?"

"I was worried about your head. You suffered a severe concussion. You were combative when my staff brought you in, and I knew you wouldn't comply with my order to rest. So I put you in a medically induced coma until I could be sure your brain wasn't swelling dangerously."

Liz considers a response but sees no point in complaining. Claire's presumptuousness is annoying, but not surprising. *At least she didn't inject me with truth serum,* Liz rationalizes, thinking back to Zag's lolling head.

"I would have left you under another twelve hours," Claire continues, "but Seth insisted I wake you. He wants you present at the hearing tonight, so I'm releasing you with orders to rest. I realize you may not follow these orders, so you should know that if you traumatize your brain again before it can heal, I will put you right back into a coma."

The hearing—Seth was going to announce it before Jackson hijacked our broadcast system. Jackson. Even the idea of his name makes her head hurt. She can't think about her brother right now. In fact, she never wants to think about him again.

Liz swings her legs over the side of the bed as Claire turns to go, feeling vulnerable as a rush of air caresses her bare skin through the opening in the back of her gown. She manages to stand up just as Ruth reappears, clean clothes in one hand and Liz's boots in the other. The rubberized handle of her knife peeks over the top of one boot.

"I thought you might want these," Ruth says, setting the clothes next to Liz on the bed. "That's quite a knife you have there."

The old woman's gentle tone washes Liz with shame; she knows the knife is a fearful weapon, one that transforms her into a fearful beast. She knows it's taken many lives. Well, technically not *it.* She knows *she* has taken many lives. But she meets Ruth's warm brown eyes and answers simply, "My mom gave it to me before she died."

"That's quite a gift." Ruth blinks in surprise. "She must have been a formidable woman,"

Not nearly as formidable as she needed to be, Liz thinks ruefully as she examines the pile of clothing.

"The children—" Liz starts, turning her back to the woman as she sheds the gown and begins to dress. "You said they were okay. Did they ... see anything?"

"We sheltered them as best we could," Ruth says, her vague answer telling Liz everything she needs to know. "But children are resilient. They are safe now, and loved and fed. The rest will heal with time." Liz exhales deeply, hoping Ruth speaks the truth.

"Speaking of healing," Ruth continues, voice brighter, "I must say, the medical care on this ship is extremely impressive." Liz turns to see the old woman studying her own forearm. "I tried to brace myself when I fell and broke my arm. But look, it's all better now."

Liz smiles. "You got the machine, didn't you?" She knows it well—the bone mender.

"Indeed," Ruth replies. "I thought I'd be in a cast. But I got a shot of painkiller, or something, and then the next thing I know, these little red lights are pulsing over it. It didn't hurt at all. Not only is my arm better, but my arthritis is gone in that hand." Ruth flutters her fingers nimbly.

"I've been in it a few times myself." Liz chuckles as she secures her knife around her waist.

"Why didn't they use it for your injury?" Ruth asks curiously, motioning to Liz's head.

"It doesn't work on soft tissue—only bone."

"Fascinating," Ruth says, giving Liz a thoughtful look. "I'm sure you have plenty to do, but I'm a good listener if you ever need to talk. You seemed ... unaware. About your brother."

An even hotter flush of shame washes over Liz's face. She nods briskly, wanting to forget what Jackson has become. As Ruth turns to go, Liz clicks the button on her wristband communicator, waiting for Seth to answer.

"You jake for a briefing?" Seth asks, dispensing with formalities.

"Affirmative," she replies, walking out of the dimly lit recovery room. She wonders exactly how much she's missed in the last thirty-six hours.

***

Seth rushes toward the door of his office, wrapping Liz tightly in his arms the moment the door closes behind her.

"Holy bearcats," he breathes in her hair, "am I glad to see you. How do you feel?" He ushers her to a comfortable chair.

"Like I don't know what's going on," Liz replies with an edge. "Why did your mother tell me I got hit with nine G's of acceleration?"

"We all did," he says absently, pulling another chair close to hers and perching himself on the edge.

Liz sighs deeply, knowing that she needs answers before she runs out of patience.

"You were in the cafeteria when the broadcast started," she prompts. "And you went down to Level 5. Can you start there?"

"Right," he says. "My first thought was to go to the bridge, but then I remembered most of the weapons were stored in the security office on Level 5. The broadcast ended just as I got to the dock. A woman activated her credential, raising her palm up over her head and telling everyone to rise up."

Seth looks at Liz with wide eyes. "Z, it's a good thing we discovered Zag's credential before the broadcast. Everyone on the dock was stunned by the light radiating from her hand. I would have been too if I hadn't seen it before. I would have lost valuable time. I'd probably be dead now.

"As soon as the woman recognized me, she pulled a pistol. If I'd hesitated, I'm sure she would have shot me. I was close enough to wrestle it away from her. I tried to restrain her, but by then some of the crew had started to turn. Charlie came out of the security office to help me, but I had to shoot two of the crew members—and then the woman …"

Seth goes on to explain that when he called Liz on her wristband communicator, he was in the security office with Charlie, scanning camera feeds across the ship and deploying security teams. The broadcast hit at the beginning of the lunch rush, so most of the crew were on Levels 3 or 4, on break in their quarters or the cafeteria. Charlie rallied the security officers, quickly assembling ten five-man teams that were deployed on Levels 3-6—fifty security officers to bring order to a crew of over six hundred. Seth stayed on Level 5, putting himself in charge of the team that defended the security office and stairwell.

"We managed to get the crew quarters on Level 3 under control," he continues, "but the insurgents overtook the security teams on Level 4. At least a hundred people came down the stairwell. It was hard to tell who was fighting whom. Complete chaos. The bulk of them broke off on Level 5, and you met the remainder, who were apparently on their way to Level 6 to disable the mechanical systems.

"I really don't know where the guy came from that I chased into the server room. He wasn't part of the mob that came down the stairwell. I think he might have been hiding on the dock, waiting for the right moment to breach the servers. When I saw him break for the mechanical rooms, I left Charlie in charge and took off after him.

"I found him typing frantically on a tablet he'd plugged into one of the servers. I probably shouldn't have barreled into him like I did," Seth says thoughtfully, brow furrowed. "The tablet shattered on the floor, and the cable he'd connected to the server started to spark. That might be why the propulsion drive malfunctioned."

"What do you mean it malfunctioned?" Liz asks as Seth's attention seems to drift away.

"It engaged—much too fast and much too soon. We catapulted out of orbit. It's a miracle we survived the acceleration. As the gravity stabilized, Jarrod managed to get the drive under control and shut it down, but it was too late."

"Too late for what?" Liz asks.

"Jarrod stopped our acceleration," Seth says, "but that doesn't diminish our speed."

"So where are we now?" Liz asks, astonished.

Seth checks the time, squinting one eye as he calculates.

"About halfway through the asteroid belt, I think?" he offers tentatively.

Liz's mouth falls open.

"The asteroid belt? But that's farther than Mars!"

"Yes," he affirms. "We've gone further in thirty-six hours than we planned to go in six months, although not in the same direction. We're technically still in our solar system, but we aren't on a trajectory to intersect with any of the planets—not even close. We're headed for deep space, and we're going so fast, all Mathilda can do is try to keep us from crashing into any major asteroids. She has no idea where we're going, but wherever it is, we're getting there fast."

"I guess at least we're safe from the New Generation," Liz murmurs.

"Perhaps," Seth replies darkly, "but we can't be certain. When the spies realized they were on the losing end, they started killing themselves and each other. We're holding one in the brig, but she's not talking. I ordered all the remaining crew to be scanned for New Generation credentials, but we didn't find any. I'd like to believe that means we're safe, but I'm not confident. How can we know where anyone's loyalties lie?"

Seth puts his hands on Liz's shoulders, seeking her eyes. "Z, we're more vulnerable now than ever. Eighty-two people are dead. Twelve of them had the New Generation credential, and thirty-two were from the security force. At least fifteen people died during the acceleration. The ship wasn't designed to accelerate that fast or that long, and we're repairing damage on several levels—damage to the land as well as mechanical systems and electronics. We're lucky the whole thing didn't shred, and we certainly never intended to leave our solar system. We need to turn around and get back to our solar system."

"So basically," Liz says evenly, "the ship is damaged, the crew is diminished, we don't know where we're going, and we have traitors in the brig who aren't talking."

"It's not all bad news," Seth says, closing the shade on the round window. "It seems that some of your survivors are actually very well trained. It turns out that Ellis was an army medic, and he fought with the infantry in Iraq. I've put him in charge of training, and Charlie is leaning on him heavily to manage security operations." Liz remembers how quickly Ellis mobilized The Fifty-Two in the orchard. *I wouldn't have made it to Level 5 without them.*

"Oh, and there's this." Seth strides to his desk, reaching into a drawer and handing her a black woven tactical belt with a holster similar to his own. She pulls the dull black pistol out of the holster, feeling the familiar weight in her hands. It's the same type of pistol she used on her surface missions. "I've issued them to everyone on the Council," Seth explains, "although I'm requiring everyone else to train with Ellis before they get theirs."

Liz looks at him skeptically as she checks the safety and holsters the pistol.

"Don't worry," he grumbles quickly. "He already spent an hour with me, and I've been instructed before. Look, yours has a place on the left where you can clip your knife, too."

Before she can comment, Seth changes the subject again.

"How are you doing?" he asks softly. "I mean, seeing your brother and all …"

Liz considers his question, then shakes her head in disbelief. "I really can't think about it right now. He seems to know a lot about us—about the ship. How did he know when you were planning to activate the drive? Zag didn't have that information."

"It's troubling," Seth agrees. "Only the Council knew about the schedule. We might have a leak, but who would it be? We've worked so closely together, and everyone has played a critical part in getting us where we are. If any of the Council members turned, we'd be finished. So, I don't know what to make of it."

"Maybe we're bugged?" Liz offers.

"Jarrod scanned Level 1. He didn't find anything, but maybe they have technology we can't detect. Or maybe they knew some other way. We'll have to be vigilant, even with the Council, but for now the crew needs to see a united front."

Liz nods. "That's why you wanted Claire to wake me for the hearings, isn't it?"

A corner of Seth's mouth pulls up in a wry smile. "If anyone had any doubts about whose side you're on, I'm pretty sure you crushed them on Level 7. But still, I don't want anyone to wonder where you are—especially since you know the New Generation spy we captured. You used to room with her."

"What? Who?" Liz's eyebrows shoot up as Seth scans his tablet, looking for her name.

"Willow Brown."

"Willow? Oh no!" Liz feels sadness well in her belly, remembering the dark-skinned, somber girl only a few years older than her. They shared a room on Level 3 with two other women when Liz worked in the orchard. "How could she have turned against us?"

"You could ask her," Seth replies. "Ellis and I have both questioned her, but she hasn't given us anything useful. At this point, given our current situation, I don't think she could give us anything useful even if she wanted to. I think the best use for her now is to serve as an example. So, if you want to talk to her, you should do it now. I can't promise she'll be alive when the night is over."

***

Once more, Liz sits in the brig's stark interrogation room. She is alone with the prisoner. This time, instead of a drooling, incoherent man, she sits across from a stunning woman with full lips. Willow Brown is one of the most beautiful people Liz has ever met, with rich bronze skin that glows caramel and cinnamon. Even now, her regal composure suggests that she owns the room, although the chain that binds her hands to the metal table tells a different story. Willow's sleek black hair is tied in a knot, her dark eyes relentless, pelting Liz with stony glances.

Liz returns the gaze, struggling to make sense of everything she feels. She doesn't pretend to know Willow well, nor does she imagine they were ever friends. But Liz still feels a connection, a sense of intimacy and familiar affection that grows from sharing a space with someone. She knows things about Willow other people don't know. She knows Willow sleeps on her stomach every night with one foot and one arm draped off the bed. She knows that the woman stashes snacks in her bedside table, mostly oranges and muffins, because she gets hungry during the night. Willow is brilliant, and sensitive, and evidently a traitor.

"I don't understand," Liz pleads softly. "After all the raids on the depots—after everything they did, how could you turn to them?"

Willow's eyes cast icy daggers, but she says nothing.

"I don't understand," Liz repeats. "You, of all people. How did they manipulate you?"

"I don't expect you to understand, Liz!" Willow's words crack like a whip in the air. "You haven't understood anything since your *boyfriend* swooped in and plucked you up the moment he became captain."

"I'm not trying to criticize you," Liz replies flatly. "I'm trying to understand."

"Well maybe you can't understand! As much as you complain about having lost everyone, you are surrounded by people everywhere you go. You were always one of Harry's favorites, and Seth has been smitten with you since the day you showed up. Even on the surface, your brother is in the top echelon of the New Generation. Everywhere you turn, you have someone!"

Liz leans forward, instantly furious. "I thought my brother was dead!" she hisses. "And as far as I'm concerned, he's better off dead than where he is now. Willow—the raiding parties! The brutality! What could they offer that makes that okay?"

"Did you really not know he was alive?" Willow's eyes widen just enough to betray her curiosity. "I assumed you knew. I assumed you were …"

"Working with him?" Liz adds, articulating Willow's question. "No, I am not working with him, and I did not know he was alive. Willow, he abandoned his family. He left our mother to starve and me to fend for myself. I assumed he was dead because no other explanation made sense. How else could he leave us like that?"

"Liz," she replies evenly, "you need to open your eyes. Things have never been as simple as you make them."

"Simple?" Liz replies, incredulous. "Have you ever seen a New Generation raiding party, Willow? Have you seen what they do? There's nothing complicated about it!"

"Yes, I've seen them," she rebuts, defensiveness growing in her narrowed eyes. "And they didn't give me any problems. I'm aware of what's in the past—it's full of things we can *all* regret, Liz. You need to start looking to the future."

"There is no future with the New Generation," Liz retorts. "They aren't yesterday's problem and tomorrow's solution! They're terrorists, and they'd rather destroy us than build peace!"

"You want to know the difference between Green Grow and the New Generation?" Willow counters. "Green Grow *tolerated* me. The New Generation *welcomed* me, from the very first day. I was on surface leave, and I saw a flier at the depot for a meeting. I had nowhere to go and nothing to do, so I hooked up with some other pickers and went to the meeting. I even met your brother. He reminds me a lot of you." Her voice drifts off for a moment.

"What did they offer you?" Liz asks, not sure that she can bear to talk anymore about her brother.

"They offered the credential, Liz—to me and everyone else there. I didn't have to commit to anything. They simply told us they appreciated us coming with open minds and wanted us to be safe. And they gave us a way to report information to them, if we thought it would help make a better future. Unlike Green Grow, and unlike Captain MacAbee, they gave me a choice, not an ultimatum."

"They manipulated you," Liz hisses.

"They *welcomed* me," Willow corrects. "And what did Green Grow do? Besides cut us off from the people on the surface who need our help? You want to know why I didn't have problems with raiding parties? All I had to do was show them the credential, and I was safe."

"And what about the people without credentials?" Liz demands. "A New Generation raiding party almost killed the fifty-two people I rescued from Denver!"

"What does Green Grow do for people without credentials, Liz? Are they any better?" Willow sighs deeply. "Look, you need to understand. The New Generation has technology, stuff that we don't have. Look at this credential—isn't it amazing?" She presses behind her ear, staring in wonder at the blue light that emanates from her palm. "They bring boxes of these to the meetings, and they just … give them away. They have other technology, too. Communications and computer stuff. But they need the ships. Don't you see? We each have a piece of the puzzle."

"I assume you have no intention of telling me about this technology," Liz says coldly.

"No, I don't." Willow's voice is flat. "But all you would have to do is ask your brother. I'm sure he would tell you. Besides, I only know what I've seen; I'm not exactly in the inner circle."

"How do you communicate with them?"

"I'm not telling you that either, but I will tell you this. They monitor radio frequencies. Send your brother a message, and I have no doubt you'll hear from him. Liz, he only had a few precious minutes of airtime on the broadcasting system, and he used some of them to talk to you—just to you! You tell me he abandoned you, but it's Green Grow that abandoned all of us!"

Liz looks quizzically at Willow, who chokes out a bitter laugh before she continues, "Didn't your *boyfriend* tell you? This business about the Council getting orders from the Green Grow Executive Board is all lies. The headquarters are empty. They have been since Captain MacAbee flew to Detroit with a shuttle full of cargo that, best we can tell, he and the rest of the Board used to buy their way into India."

"Buy their way into India?" Liz is flabbergasted.

"Oh yes, using the food and the shuttle as collateral. That's why they didn't show up to the peace talks."

"No, the New Generation sabotaged the peace talks. No doubt, Captain MacAbee had to blow the shuttle to keep it out of their hands. He piloted it himself. He would have had the ability—and the obligation—to blow it."

"You're right," Willow says, voice turning smug, "he did pilot it himself. You don't find that odd? Think about it, Liz. No security team? No flight crew? The New Generation never stopped reaching out to Green Grow for peace talks. They still monitor Detroit for activity, in case the Board surfaces again. Green Grow abandoned us, and so did Captain MacAbee. Can't you see? They saved themselves and left us for dead. The New Generation is all we have left."

Liz doesn't know what to say. Willow's accusations sound like New Generation propaganda, but the story isn't impossible. The only impossibility now is knowing for certain what happened at the peace summit or to Captain MacAbee.

"Lives are at stake here," Liz says plainly. "Your life may be at stake. What else can you tell me about the New Generation?"

"My life?" Willow rolls her eyes, shaking her head in exasperation. "You and I both know the dice are already cast. No doubt, your boyfriend won't be inclined to redeem me. But what does it matter now? I'll make you a deal. I'll tell you what I know, and you tell me what you know."

"What do you think I know?" Liz asks suspiciously.

"What's going to happen to me now?" Willow asks, her eyes and voice softening.

"Seth will hear your case tonight, along with Zag Bryant's," Liz replies, knowing she can't speak to the captain's intentions even if she wants to. "Your turn," she continues. "What do you know?" Willow gives her a long glance.

"Jackson told us that he had a way to get to the ship, but he couldn't get here in time to prevent us leaving. He asked us to overtake the Council, until he could join us and assume command. I don't know the details, or how or when he would have come. But I think we'd all be better off if he had."

Liz absorbs the words, then nods as she rises and silently exits the room. The heavy door clicks closed behind her, severing any lingering connection she might have with Willow Brown. Liz looks down the long hallway, but instead of going back the way she came, she knocks softly on a solid metal door a few feet away. It clicks open, and she enters to see Ellis, studying the woman on the other side of the one-way mirror. Her hands are still chained to the metal loop in the middle of the table, and she slumps in her chair, undoubtedly thinking she is alone.

"Did you get all that?" Liz asks.

"Audio and video," he replies. "She had a lot more to say to you than anyone else."

"What do you make of her story?"

"I don't know," Ellis says, deep in thought. "It's a lot to take in. All I know for sure is the New Generation was hellbent on killing us on the surface, and they were willing to take the ship at any cost. None of that sounds *welcoming* to me."

"Not at all," Liz agrees, checking the time. She needs to get back to her quarters, to prepare for the hearings.

***

Seth insisted the Council arrive early for the hearings so that he could lock down the rest of Level 1. Liz wasn't sure what he meant by "lockdown," so she arrives a half hour early, quietly pacing as the remains of a sandwich churns in her belly.

Her heart flutters watching Seth tonight. He usually dresses in the same tunic and pants as everyone else, but tonight he wears his captain's dress uniform. He isn't just handsome—he is majestic. The charcoal gray coat falls below his hips, adorned with a single row of elaborate silver closures that runs from his neck to the thick black belt at his waist. He wears trim dark pants that flow across his legs like a second skin, retreating into gleaming, knee-high leather boots. Liz notices the pistol holstered on his right side, surprised at how natural it looks on him.

The rest of the Council trickles in, also dressed in uniforms they rarely wear. Theirs are a lighter shade of gray—waist-length jackets with a single row of silver buttons, above trim pants and ankle boots. Liz is the only one without a dress uniform, although her gray tunic and black leggings are clean and her well-worn boots polished. Formal attire isn't issued to the crew, and despite her position on the Council, she isn't interested in pretending to be something she's not.

Besides, as far as Liz is concerned, her clothing is the most normal thing in this room. They all just gathered here four days ago, but now everything is different. The meeting four days ago was intended to bring people together, to build them up. Today, they are here to condemn. Four days ago, Seth wanted the crew to believe in him, but tonight, he seems ready to command them, indifferent to how they feel.

She studies him as he stands nearby, immersed in the codes he's typing into his tablet. After several fingerprint scans, retinal scans, and voice confirmations, Liz hears the whirring of thick metal plates descending from the ceiling, sealing off every corridor and doorway. Other than the lifts, the only visible opening is the door to the captain's conference room, where the prisoners will await their hearings.

Liz climbs the few stairs to the top of the dais that was assembled at the head of the room just hours before. A heavy wooden desk sits in the middle, bare except for a gleaming palm gavel and wooden sound block. Behind the desk is an imposing leather chair from which Seth will pass judgment. On the far side stands a metal pole, topped with a metal loop and bolted to the dais. On the near side sits a cluster of five seats for the Council—formal chairs with high backs that demand propriety. Liz moves to the seat on the end and perches on the edge, sitting tall with her knees together, feet crossed at the ankles.

Ellis stands at the bottom of the dais, along with three other security officers wearing black tactical uniforms. They handle shotguns with ease, attentive to everything going on around them. Seth and Ellis exchange a few quiet words and then pause to watch as a five-man team, also armed with shotguns, escorts the two prisoners off the lift and into the conference room.

The crew will be coming soon. Seth stands on the dais, waiting and watching as they begin to flow off the lifts and into the 550 seats that have been arranged. He stands tall and rigid, his broad chest and muscular body imposing— perhaps even menacing, although Liz is unafraid. *He will prove himself tonight,* she realizes, feeling her heart flutter again. *This is the man who would protect me—if I let him.* But will she let him? She still doesn't know.

The murmur of the crowd hums as Seth takes his seat of judgment and raps the hand gavel. His voice rings out, cutting through the silence he just commanded. "The prisoners will be heard in the order in which they were arrested."

Zag is dirty and disheveled, but he looks far more coherent than when Liz saw him last. Ellis escorts the man up the dais, locking the chain between his handcuffs to the loop on top of the metal pole. Zag looks awkwardly out across the crew before straightening himself to face his captain.

"Zag Bryant," Seth bellows, voice echoing through the room. "You are charged with mutiny. You have been identified as a member of the New Generation by the electronic credential you bear. You were caught in the act of transmitting to the New Generation confidential specifications related to the antimatter propulsion drive. How do you respond to this charge of mutiny?"

"I can't deny it," he says, voice faltering.

"Do you plead guilty or not guilty?" Seth demands.

"Guilty," he says softly, the chamber so silent that even his whisper echoes.

"Zag Bryant, your acts constitute the highest form of treachery. Given your guilty plea and the evidence against you, I sentence you to death."

Seth rises from his chair, strides to the prisoner, draws his pistol, and shoots him between the eyes. Liz's ears register cries and gasps as her own eyes widen, struggling to process what she just saw. The captain stands squarely, unflinching as he holsters his pistol. Then he wordlessly returns to his seat behind the desk as Ellis removes Zag's lifeless body and retrieves the second prisoner.

Moment later, Willow tromps haughtily onto the dais. As Ellis secures her chains to the pole, the woman's eyes rest on Liz, who quickly looks away. She cannot bear the plea for mercy she sees in those dark pools of mystery. Instead, she fixes her gaze on Seth. His expression is unmoved, although Liz detects the hint of a twitch in his right eye and a single bead of sweat trickling toward his ear. When he speaks, his voice is steely.

"Willow Brown, you are charged with mutiny. You have been identified as a member of the New Generation by the electronic credential you bear. You were caught in the act of inciting rebellion, and you are complicit in the deaths that occurred during the hijacking of the antimatter propulsion drive. How do you respond to this charge of mutiny?"

"This is outrageous!" Willow cries, turning away from Seth and addressing the crew. "Do you not see how wrong this is?"

The crowd begins to murmur.

"Willow Brown," Seth commands, "what is your plea? Guilty or not guilty?"

"Listen to me," she pleads with the crew. "If you would just listen, you would understand. The New Generation is not your enemy! This man is your enemy—Seth Harris!"

An angry voice rises above the murmuring, "Guilty! She's guilty!"

Seth pounds the gavel, commanding silence.

"Willow Brown, your actions directly contributed to the death of eighty-two people. Do not try to appeal to those who remain. You have already shown how little regard you have for their lives, and they have no authority to decide your fate. I find you guilty of mutiny, and I sentence you to death."

Willow screams as Seth rises from his chair and purposefully spans the distance between them. She tries to shield her face with her hands, but it doesn't change what happens next. In the blink of an eye, her life is gone, terminated by the sentence that Seth issued and carried out. Her body lies on the floor as he holsters his pistol and addresses the crowd that has once more fallen into stunned silence.

"The last two days have been nothing short of tragic," he begins. "Eighty-two people lost their lives during the insurrection and unrestrained acceleration that followed—eighty-two friends and coworkers. Justice required that two more die here tonight, but the necessity of it doesn't make it any less heart-rending. We need to put this travesty behind us.

"Our mission is unchanged. We will find a way to get home. We will continue to work toward peace with the New Generation—not domination, but peace. I will do whatever is necessary to maintain order and keep all of you safe while we complete this mission. We can succeed together, but divided we will fail. Insubordination will not be tolerated. We don't have time for it, nor can we afford to lose any more precious lives. Any additional infractions will be dealt with as they occur. These hearings are concluded, and everyone is dismissed."

Seth stands at silent attention, straight and tall as the crew exits the room. The Council remains seated, soberly absorbed in private thought. Liz notices Seth's hand begin to tremble at his side, but he clenches his fist and the shaking is gone. No one speaks until Ellis breaks the silence, confirming that the last of the crew has left Level 1 to return to their respective parts of the ship.

"Everyone is out," he says simply. "What should we do with the bodies?"

"Take them to the medical unit," Claire replies coolly, her eyes still glassy. "We'll incinerate them with the other dead."

Liz stands, followed by the others as they emerge from their mental fog.

"I'm sorry if that was shocking," Seth says plainly, his eyes unapologetic. Jarrod nods brusquely, and Mathilda bites her lip as silent tears spill over her lids. Claire has no words, but absent-mindedly reaches up to pat Seth on the shoulder.

"You did what you had to do," Harry adds gruffly, scrubbing his eyes. "Hopefully this is all behind us now."

"I hope so," Seth agrees, "but we have to stay vigilant. Get some rest, and we'll convene in the morning."

Liz hears him exhale deeply as he turns his attention to his tablet, leaning heavy on the desk as he types the commands and provides the authentication to unlock Level 1. The thick metal panels recede back into the ceiling, and the other Council members disperse without a word. Ellis collects the remaining security officers from the conference room, and they carry the two lifeless bodies to the lift.

"Don't go yet," Seth says in a loud whisper, reaching for Liz's hand as if she might leave without him. "Are you tired? I'm not ready to go to sleep yet." *He's afraid of the dreams,* Liz thinks, catching a glimpse of something wild in his eyes.

"What do you have in mind?" she asks.

***

Seth warns Liz before the lift doors open onto Level 7. "It's a mess, but we'll clean it up." It seems to Liz that the entire ship is a mess, but at least here they can find refuge in the trees. She steps onto the soft green grass, taking in as much as she can see in the thin silvery light that simulates nighttime. The light shimmers off the silver adornments of Seth's uniform and gleams eerily on his polished boots. He looks like an apparition from a bygone era, standing tall amid the destruction. The grass is strewn with branches and leaves, some of which have already been collected into piles for chopping and shredding.

Seth takes Liz's hand as they begin to pick their way through brush and branches, edges sharper and shadows deeper in the dim, frosted light. They head toward the apple trees, but Liz is in no hurry as she surveys the damage. They walk silently until they find the first row of apple trees, stepping carefully around the hard, green fruit now scattered the ground.

Seth ducks as she pulls him beneath the canopy of a taller tree.

"Now we're alone," she says, studying the contours of his face in the thin, dappled light.

"I'm a ruthless killer," he whispers. "Aren't you afraid?"

"And yet, I'm the one who lured you in here. Maybe you are the one who should be afraid."

"True," he says, pulling her close, warm hand flat on her lower back. She presses her face against the side of his chest, exhaling deeply. The silver filigree on his jacket is cool, and she can hear his heart beating steady. She stands there for a minute then pulls away to sit on the musky ground, brushing tiny apples and leaves aside and inviting him to settle next to her on the soft green grass.

"It's heavy, isn't it?" he asks softly. Liz doesn't need to see his face to know he's talking about the people he killed, about the weight of knowing that he extinguished all they were and all they could possibly have been.

"Yes," she replies. "It's the cost of surviving, bearing the burden of what you did."

"Nine people, Z." His voice starts to choke, but his heart beats steadily. "I executed two today, and I killed six during the insurrection. I'm almost to double digits."

"It doesn't help to count them," she says, lowering her eyes.

"I think I see now why you blame yourself. For Sam," he says. "I don't feel like I killed nine people. I feel like I killed eighty-four."

"And I see why you tell me it's not my fault," she counters, raising her head to meet his eyes. "It's not your fault either."

"Maybe I could have done something differently," he says wistfully. "Maybe there was a way to avoid this."

"Maybe," she replies, "but it might have all turned out the same, or it might have been worse. There's no way to know now. You can either drive yourself crazy with the possibilities, or you can move on. But if you fall apart, so will all of this. The crew will follow you, but you have to lead them."

"Z?" His voice sounds weak. "Are we jake? I don't want you to … think of me differently now. I don't want you to be afraid of me."

"Afraid of you?" She laughs. "Evidently, I'm some kind of New Generation royalty! I should be asking you."

"True," he says, chuckling, "but you can't be responsible for what your brother does. I know you better than that."

"It doesn't feel real," she says. "I'm not sure if it feels like a dream or a nightmare. Is he really still alive?"

"Let's make it a dream," he says, turning to face her, brushing his fingers across her cheek. His touch is lightning, setting her skin on fire with a brilliance that can't be anything but right. She can feel his heart thump faster in his chest as she leans up to meet him, pressing her lips to his for a kiss that has been years in the making.

"You're beautiful," she tells him, caressing his cheek as their lips part.

"You stole my line," he whispers, eyes soft.

"I mean it, Seth. You're beautiful. You had a choice to be strong or be weak, and you chose to be strong. I'm sorry it came down to killing people, but you did what you had to do."

"I don't feel very strong right now," he says softly. "I feel weak, and I don't want to be a burden to you."

"Please, Seth, lean on me when you need to. I need you to need me, because—I need you, too."

"Z," he says, standing up from the ground and pulling her up behind him, "I'll need you until the day I die. And then after that, I'm pretty sure I'll still need you." He winks at her, grinning recklessly as he ducks his head to exit the canopy. Liz feels her insides melt as she follows him back into the silver light, which seems brighter than before.

"Seth, do you know that I love you?" she whispers. He pauses for a moment, squeezing her tightly.

"I do now," he says, voice thick. "And I love you, Elizah Goeff."

She walks under the protection of his arm, feeling the warmth of his body through his jacket. When the ground becomes too littered with debris for them to walk side by side, he takes her hand and they pick through the branches wordlessly. They make their way back to the tool barn, back to the place where Liz killed the young man with the New Generation credential. She pushes the memory away, not wanting to associate this place with death—or with her brother.

"You look amazing in your uniform," she says, taking in the sight of Seth one more time.

"This old thing?" he teases, brushing a stray leaf off the bottom of his jacket.

"It looks a bit stifling, though," she says, eyes burning hot into his in the silver light. "It looks a bit … warm. Maybe we should get you out of it."

He leans down to kiss her, then sweeps her off her feet, carrying her toward the lift. He sets her down gently as she presses the button. "I can't wait," he says, his hot breath in her ear sending a chill down her spine.

CHAPTER 15

JACKSON

***

The Council meeting is somber, the members quiet and apparently deep in thought. Liz assumes the weight of the prior day's executions still burdens them, although the present discussion is almost equally troublesome. The ship is hurtling toward deep space, and it's unclear how they are going to get home.

Sure, the ship is self-sufficient in many ways—they can grow their own food and manage the air and natural resources, but traveling so far away from Earth was never their plan. And they aren't prepared to do it. Thruster fuel, navigation tools, and parts for mechanical and structural repairs to the ship are limited. The ship isn't designed for the rigors of deep space travel. The farther away they get, the longer it will take them to get home and the greater the risk that critical parts will wear out or fail with no way to replace them.

***

After the 9G acceleration, Mathilda's only directive was navigating the asteroid belt beyond Mars' orbit. And given the speed of the ship, managing course corrections to avoid any known obstacles that might breach the hull in a collision was no small feat. But clearing the asteroid belt was only the first problem they had to solve, and by some measures, the least complicated. Now that they're past that danger, Mathilda needs to determine where they are going and what they should expect to encounter.

Now in the Council meeting, Seth looks at her expectantly as he waits for her to speak, to provide the update he requested. She struggles to compose herself, sitting with her face buried in her hands, breathing deeply. Everyone waits until she raises her head, brushing the tears out of her bloodshot and swollen eyes. She fits the telltale glasses on her face and breathes in deeply. Her hair is disheveled, and her clothes rumpled.

"I'm sorry," she says quietly, voice still wavering. "It's been a long few days. We've cleared the asteroid belt, and there aren't any major known obstructions we need to worry about now. The immediate danger is gone, but for all practical purposes, so is our solar system. The remaining planets are on the far side of their orbits, so we have no chance of intersecting with any of them." She falls silent, gaze softening.

"Options?" Seth prods gently. Liz studies the slight woman through the crushing weight of the silence. Mathilda is quiet and unassuming, with a gentle and compassionate character. She is usually a pillar of silent strength and reason, but now she looks frazzled and broken, frenetic. Liz knows that some of her team members died in the insurrection, and one of them had a New Generation credential. Has Mathilda ever been so close to this much danger? Has she ever known such betrayal? *Maybe not,* Liz reasons, *or maybe this this is simply how she's dealing with seeing two people shot in the head.*

Mathilda's eyes brim with tears again as she looks at Seth.

"We have infinite options, and they are all nothing!" she exclaims. "Literally, there is nothing, and it spans every conceivable way except the only way we can't actually go—backwards! Even at our current rate of speed, and if we happened to be heading in the right direction, we won't encounter any stars, planets, or other gravitational bodies for decades. It's called space because it's mostly empty!"

Mathilda's face returns to her hands, and Jarrod takes over, his voice calm. "I think what Mathilda is trying to say is that from an astronomical perspective, there isn't an option that's obviously better than the others. At this point, it's really more about our speed and the capabilities of the drive."

All eyes focus on him as he continues. "We have two problems—speed and direction, and the more urgent problem is our speed. Most of our navigation strategies involve using planets or stars to manage our speed and control our direction. Without any gravitational bodies, those strategies are now irrelevant.

"Even if we could turn around, we'd be going too fast to navigate our solar system—much less stop when we got back to Earth. We can't use the thrusters to slow down; we don't have that much fuel. Our best option at the moment is to identify other options."

"We can't reverse the antimatter drive?" Seth asks.

"Not really," Jarrod replies. "It only produces thrust in one direction." Seth nods silently, searching the other faces in the room for dissension.

"So, let's keep going," he says. "Keep working, and we'll check in again tomorrow."

Mathilda scuttles out quickly, shuffling off toward her quarters with her eyes glued to the floor. Seth watches her go but doesn't follow. Liz sits down in the chair next to him as the rest of the Council leaves.

"Seth," she says quietly, "I want to tell Albert Wyndham what happened to his brother in Minneapolis. He's asking me questions, and I think he deserves to know."

Seth looks up from his tablet, eyes wary. "We need to be careful with him, Z. I don't know if it's his grief or just the way he is, but he's becoming a troublemaker."

"How so?" she asks, wondering what she doesn't know.

"Can we talk about it later?" Seth asks with a deep exhale.

"Sure." She knows he has more pressing matters that require his attention.

***

It isn't hard for Liz to catch up with Harry as he shuffles to the lift. She smiles at him as she slows her gait to match his.

"I appreciate the help, but are you sure this is what you want to do?" he asks as they step onto the lift. Liz presses the button for Level 7.

"It's a win-win, Harry," she replies. "You need the help cleaning up the orchard, and I need to stay busy. Besides, I miss the trees."

"Well, there's certainly plenty to do," Harry muses. "But you know I can't promise you won't get questions about the hearings—or your brother. Although, I suppose the sight of your pistol, as well as that death blade you call a knife, will probably deter the sane people from inquiring."

Liz smiles at him. She already knows how she will respond to any questions about her brother. *As far as I know, he's dead, and the man on the broadcast was an imposter.* Maybe if she says it enough times, she can believe it, too. She'll take the rest as it comes.

"So, what's my assignment for today?" she asks, thinking back to the damage report she saw on Seth's desk this morning. Even three days after the rapid acceleration, it's daunting. Mechanical crews have been working around the clock, but as of this morning, the number of systems failing is still greater than the number of systems working—gravity, air purification, and water reclamation, to name a few. Luckily, the ship was designed with layers of redundancy, backup systems for backup systems that are dispersed across all of the levels. It's a lot to maintain, but the redundancy saved them—at least for now.

But it isn't just the mechanical systems in need of repair. The land and livestock suffered as well. Most of the pastures and field crops survived, but the orchards on Levels 7 and 8 sustained varying levels of damage to the trees. Almost a third of the livestock were injured or killed, most of the bees have died, and the status of the hummingbirds and butterflies is still largely unknown.

Ordinarily, the animals are managed much as they would be on the surface—they are bred judiciously and live normal lifespans. But presently, Claire's cloning labs are running in full force, repopulating cows and goats and pigs from the vast repository of DNA frozen in her lab.

"Tabitha Smith is down a few people, so I assigned you to her team," Harry replies, drawing Liz back to the conversation.

"I don't think I know her," Liz muses, sifting through her memories but coming up with nothing. Willow wasn't wrong when she told Liz she lost touch with the crew, but Liz is intent on changing that. It's the only way she can help Seth, and she wants to help him now more than ever. She thinks back to the night before, to his bare skin pressed on hers, tips of his fingers trickling down her back. She feels a ripple of pleasure and forces herself back to the present.

"Will Dabato works on her team," Harry replies. "When you find him, you'll be in the right place."

Liz nods as the lift doors open, striding purposefully onto the level to look for Will. She doesn't have to go far; he is gathered with a team at the tool barn, listening to a petite brunette woman give them assignments. Her clear, melodic voice cuts through the air. "I need one team of four at the chipper-shredder station, and the rest of you will divide into two teams to collect the debris for shredding. Any limbs thicker than three inches should be chopped and stacked to dry. Collect the crushed fruit separately in baskets for the pigs and goats.

"We have two tractors and trailers to use, and I expect the rows to be neat and tidy when you're done. Cut off any branches still hanging, but be delicate with the trees. They've been through just as much as we have. And before you ask, I don't yet know if we're going to have to restart the growing cycle. Our food stores are still being assessed, and decisions have not been made. Any other questions?" Tabitha's sharp brown eyes scan the group and rest on Liz.

"Liz Goeff," she says, unenthused, as everyone turns to look at her. "I heard you might help us today."

"You must be Tabitha Smith," Liz replies, hoping her smile is warm. The woman nods but offers no greeting in return. "I've worked on this level before," Liz adds, "and I hear you can use the help."

Tabitha lets out a deep sigh. "What would you like to do?" she asks as the rest of the group takes the cue and begins to divide into teams.

"Assign me where you need me," Liz replies quickly, watching Will leave with three other people toward the chipper-shredder station. "I can do any job."

"Is that utility belt going to be a hazard?" Tabitha's eyebrows raise as she motions to Liz's holstered pistol.

"No," Liz replies simply.

Tabitha glances around, taking stock of the three people who remain. "Well, it appears you'll be collecting branches and gathering crushed fruit." Liz nods and quickly joins her group inside the tool barn. A man she doesn't know climbs on top of a small tractor and starts the engine. His face falls when he sees Liz.

"Do you want to drive?" he asks reluctantly.

Liz is determined to be no different than anyone else on the team. "I'll walk behind with the others. Here, let me hitch your trailer." His face lightens a little. She pushes the pin through the hitch, securing it on the bottom before she stands up and waves him on. After grabbing a few empty baskets for the crushed fruit and a pair of gloves, she trots off to catch up with the group.

Liz works silently, pretending she doesn't hear the occasional whispers of the three other people around her. She digs deep into her memories, smiling as she thinks back to the playful banter that used to accompany her shifts in the orchard. She remembers those days fondly, but they feel foreign to her now, like she is peeking into the life of a different girl. In some ways she is.

Never again will she be the orphaned child who hoped to find her brother and who refused to speak of how her mother died. Never again will her life be that simple. Now she is a member of the Council, known by many more people on the ship than she knows in return, and the brother she knew is lost to her forever, replaced by a dubiously notorious figure who, in a single broadcast, has changed the way everyone on the ship regards her.

And her mother? Liz pauses for a moment, closing her eyes to consider the woman who gave her life, the woman who still haunts her with a single act of desperation that only took minutes to complete. She feels the familiar pain creep into her awareness, the regret that she's lost something she can never get back. But even that pain seems different now—less personal, somehow.

Could Liz have saved her mother? Possibly. But Jackson could have saved her as well. *Or she could have saved herself,* Liz thinks, toying with the idea, perhaps for the first time, that her mother's death may not have been her fault.

She loads an armful of branches onto the trailer, stacking them as neatly as she can and then turning to help the woman behind her with her own bundle. As the man slowly pulls away to drive the branches to the chipper-shredder, Liz assesses the progress they've made cleaning up the row of apple trees. Once again, order is restored. The trees, although thinner, look healthy and alive. The space between, carpeted by soft green grass, is free of fallen branches and the crushed, green fruit that will never have a chance to ripen. Baskets line one side of the path, ready for collection, full of the discarded possibilities that might have one day been apples.

When the tractor creeps past her once more, Liz falls into step behind, loading the baskets onto the empty trailer as they make a final pass down the aisle. It's nearly time for lunch. She glances at the man who has been driving the electric machine since the morning. He has only spoken to her in passing, never telling her his name, but his face is content, full of a peaceful joy Liz assumes has to do with the machine he operates.

They are fun to drive, she admits, chuckling as she realizes he assumed she would pull rank on him this morning and take the job for herself. She ambles along as he drives toward one of two huge service lifts, designed for animals and large machinery, that will transport them down to Level 17 where they will deliver the remains of the apples to the pigs.

The lift moves slowly through the body of the ship, much more sluggish than the ones that carry people, but she is in no hurry. Her stomach growls as she follows the tractor off the lift onto Level 17, reminding her that despite everything that has changed in her world, she still occupies a body that requires feeding.

She hears and smells the pigs before she sees them, recognizing a familiar face as the writhing beasts come into sight. It's Ruben, one of The Fifty-Two that fought with her in the stairwell. He doesn't speak, but Liz is beginning to understand his movements and gestures. She laughs when he smiles and holds his nose.

"Yes," she says, as the rest of her team studies them with interest, "the pigs are very … earthy. Can you bear it?" He rolls his eyes, sighing deeply and flicking his wrist as he smiles once more, as if to say, "I've got this." She bids him farewell and goes to help her other team members carry the baskets into the feed barn. They return to the tractor, hopping onto the trailer and riding in silence as the man pulls them along, back to the tool barn on Level 7.

Liz isn't required to keep a time log because she isn't officially assigned to the level. So while everyone else stands in line to clock out for lunch, she heads straight to the nearest bathroom to clean up. Paging Seth on her wristband communicator, she waits for him to acknowledge her as she washes her hands and her face. The water is cool and sanctifying, rinsing away not only the dirt and sweat of the morning but also a touch of the grief and anger that stains her hands and her soul.

"Are you hungry?" she asks Seth when he responds to her page.

"Very," he replies, "but I can't get away."

"You're in luck then," she says playfully. "I happen to know someone who might be willing to bring lunch to your office."

She thought things might be awkward with Seth today, but they aren't. In fact, it all seems completely natural, other than the way her heart flutters when she thinks about the previous night, the way the silver on Seth's uniform gleamed in the night's light, the way he smiled when he told her, *I'll need you until the day I die.* Her steps seem lighter and her breathing easier as she makes her way to the lift, unburdened—at least for now—by the foul anger and bitterness that seems to live on the edge of her awareness. She has no doubt that everyone on the ship has a mountain of challenges ahead of them, including her. But today is a new day, and Liz is determined to hold on to the possibility of it with both hands.

Seth has little time to eat and none to spend with her, but Liz sits there anyway while he works through a series of reports, reports that detail repairs, inventory, personnel, and medical incidents. Then he takes a call from his mother.

"I'm worried about Mathilda," Claire says, voice resonating on speaker while Seth takes a large bite of lasagna. "She's a wreck, but she refuses to come to the medical unit for treatment." *Imagine that,* Liz thinks, remembering Zag's truth serum and her own medically induced coma.

Seth swallows quickly, eyes bulging slightly as the large bite works its way down his throat. He gulps a sip of water before responding, "I told her to rest, but she said there was too much to do. She found more star charts in our archives, and she's running calculations to plot a course home."

"She's the only one who can do that?" Claire asks.

"It certainly seems that way," Seth replies, eyeing the remainder of his lasagna wistfully.

"Look," Claire says, "it's up to you, but this is serious. I went to check on her in her office, and she had the door locked. When I insisted that she let me in, she drew her pistol on me. Are you sure it was a good idea to give one to her?"

Seth sighs deeply.

"I'll deal with it," he says, terminating the call. He pushes his lasagna around on the plate with his fork, but then he dives in again, shoveling another large bite in his mouth. Liz smiles—nothing seems to interfere with his appetite. They sit in silence a few moments more, eating until Seth's tablet starts to buzz. He groans.

"Mathilda," he says, looking up at Liz with apprehensive eyes. She kisses him on the head and bids him farewell, whisking both of their plates away as she leaves his office to return to the orchard.

***

When her shift ends on Level 7, Liz enters the lift and considers which button to push. She plans to meet up with Seth later; they seem to have so many things to catch up on, but he will be busy for several more hours. There's time to visit Level 20. She wants to see it again, the place that Harry agreed to make a garden for The Fifty-Two's nightly story time.

Ruth assures Liz that story time is fine in the cafeteria after the dinner rush. In fact, having it in such a visible location seems to encourage more of the crew to join in. But the cafeteria is a cold, institutional place. Story time belongs somewhere warm and alive, somewhere that embodies the earth that the tradition remembers.

Liz can't imagine a better home for story time than Level 20. When she first came to the Green Grow 3, it was where the rice grew. But as conflict with the New Generation increased and the number of crew and surface runs diminished, the level became harder to maintain. Being close to the center of the ship, it was one of the largest levels, and it was the first Captain MacAbee ordered abandoned. The paddies were drained, and grass and trees planted in their stead. Now the only thing Level 20 produces is oxygen for the ship.

The level is abandoned but not forbidden, and so members of the crew still go there sometimes. Liz doesn't presume to know why others go—she only knows why she does it. She goes there to be alone, to wander and wonder if this is how the earth used to be. She rarely sees anyone else there when she visits, but over time, she's noticed new plants turning up. Not the ones from Claire's lab, but ones that Liz suspects the crew grew, smuggled onto the ship from a lovingly preserved seed or cutting—roses, lilacs, tulips, and orchids.

The lift doors open and she steps out, deeply inhaling the warm, musky air. When Jackson hacked the broadcast system, Harry was here, briefing a small group of people on the project that would have commenced in earnest the following day. Now the garden is delayed, overtaken by the need to repair the ship and manage the food supply. Delayed, but not forgotten—Liz will make sure of that.

She sees a makeshift table that Harry must have created, made from two sawhorses and a few planks of wood. The pieces are strewn on the ground, large rolled papers resting precariously on top. Liz rights the sawhorses, resets the planks, and carefully unrolls the landscaping plans, securing each end with a rock. Her eyes take in the plans as her mind imagines how beautiful it will be.

Mom would have loved this, she thinks, quickly scanning a list of plants Harry titled RELOCATE. Those must be the ones the crew already planted on the level. She sees a second list called NEW and assumes those are the ones he requested from Claire's lab—wisteria, hydrangeas, and lilies.

What is a hydrangea? she wonders, knowing that her mother would have known. Mom would have appreciated this in ways Liz can't begin to understand. She barely remembers things like gardens and cities, but her mother had a lifetime of memories to remind her every day of all that had been lost. Her mother started off with a home, a husband, two children, a garden, and a good and comfortable life. She'd been able to hold on to so very little of that.

I never thought of it that way, Liz realizes. *She held on until she couldn't.* She remembers her mother's words—*I can't make it any further, it's your time now*—and she feels the familiar sadness. But this time, instead of guilt, it comes with a question. *What was Jackson doing the day she died?* Everything about Liz's life changed the instant their mother crossed the threshold from life into death, but what about her brother? Did his heart know? Did he have any idea that the world was less than it had been moments before? *As far as I know, my brother is dead, and the man on the broadcast was an imposter,* Liz recites, turning her attention away from the past toward the future.

Ruth will love this, she muses, studying the plans for the winding gravel path that will lead to a wooden footbridge, across a small pond with a series of waterfalls. She sees markings for a cluster of arbors with a handwritten note—WISTERIA. It all culminates in a clearing inside the trees, set with concentric circles of wooden benches. *Is that a fire pit in the middle?* she wonders, glad that such a thing is possible now that they knew more about managing oxygen in space. It feels good to imagine what this place will become, so much better than being angry or sad.

She makes her way back to the lift, stopping on Level 4 to pick up a bag of clean laundry before returning to her new quarters. She feels happy as she begins to unpack the clean clothes, placing the items in their proper locations. But then she freezes as she feels something hard in her laundry bag, something wrapped in a pillowcase tucked between a blue tunic and a pair of gray leggings. Carefully, she unwraps an electronic tablet. It resembles the many other tablets on the ship, but Liz can see that it's been modified. It's thicker than a standard one, its back made of metal, and there is a strange coiled tube connected to one side. A piece of paper with a handwritten note is carefully placed on top of the screen.

LIZZIE, WE NEED TO TALK. WATCH THE VIDEO ON THE TABLET TO FIND OUT HOW TO CONTACT ME. LOVE, JACKSON

Sweet shit sauce.

***

Seth sits across from Liz at the dining table in her quarters, both of them looking at the tablet like it might explode.

"It was in your laundry?" he asks again.

"Yes," Liz replies, "with this note."

"Does it look like his writing?" Seth asks.

Liz pauses for a moment to consider this. "I wouldn't know."

Seth appraises her intensely, blue eyes aflame as he turns the situation over in his mind. She doesn't have to ask what he's thinking. *We still have spies. How do we still have spies?* They checked all of the crew for New Generation credentials. Did they miss someone? Or are there spies without credentials? Of course, it wouldn't require an army to infiltrate the ship's laundry, but nonetheless Liz realizes their newfound sense of safety is an illusion.

"Let's watch the video," he suggests doggedly. Liz's eyes widen.

"Are you sure?" she asks. "What if it explodes or something? Shouldn't someone examine it?"

"Who? The Council? Jarrod? Mathilda? They have enough on their shoulders right now. Besides …" Seth's voice tapers off. Liz already knows what he doesn't articulate—Jackson knows things only the Council knows. Somehow, the Council has been compromised.

Liz moves around the table, sitting beside Seth as she carefully presses the power button, holding her breath as if that will somehow protect her. She hears the familiar whir as it boots up, but instead of the typical home screen menu, a video automatically begins to buffer. Before Liz can tell herself to exhale, that strangely familiar face fills the screen. Jackson.

Seeing him isn't as jarring as last time, but it is still surreal. She notices the scar again, the white ropy vine that frames the left side of his face. His eyes drill into her, rugged and worn but still the muted blue she remembers. The light is dim, wherever he is. His head and shoulders fill most of the screen, but Liz can see part of a lamp in the corner of the frame, an old lamp that stands on the floor. Its shade is a patchwork of colored glass, glowing from the light of a strange bulb in the middle. She can see the worn fabric of an armchair behind him, the wings of the chair framing his head, and tall stacks of books flanking either side.

"Lizzie, I've missed you," he starts. "No doubt, my prior broadcast may have been a little shocking. I had hoped to talk to you first, but unfortunately, circumstances didn't allow that to happen. I hear you are well and thriving, and I'm glad. I am so very proud of everything you've become." He offers her half a smile, revealing straight, handsome teeth that make Liz gasp. The raiding parties were full of rotten and missing teeth—why are his different? She clutches Seth's hand, eyes glued to the screen as Jackson continues.

"Lizzie, I'm sorry I didn't find you more quickly. By the time I made it back to our house, it was empty. I saw … remains inside, and I assume our mother is dead. I meant to come back sooner. I tried, but—look, I've never forgotten you." He casually reaches into the stack of books to his right, pulling one from the middle with ease. He opens the cover and removes a piece of paper, leaning in toward the camera and holding it up for her to see.

Liz feels all the air leave her body as she recognizes herself in the faded photo. She sees her mother—her healthy, vibrant, laughing mother, sitting under the old cottonwood tree behind their house, settled on a blanket that appears to be spread for a family picnic. With one arm she holds a small, plump Liz on her lap. Her other arm is outstretched, reaching toward Jackson, who is running toward her with the obvious glee of an innocent child. Liz quickly blinks the tears from her eyes, burning the image into her brain. Much too soon, Jackson pulls it away, carefully placing it back into the book before he continues speaking.

"I hear you carry my old survival knife," he continues, the hint of mirth in his voice incongruous with his scarred face. "Undoubtedly, I am the only person in the New Generation who is glad you have it, but I hope it has served you well. I made the leather sheath for Mom, you know. I hoped it would make it easier for her to carry on her body, even though she wasn't keen on having a weapon." Liz freezes, not wanting to believe that her knife belonged to Jackson; it's all she has left of her mother. *But you well know it wasn't hers,* she chides. She's always known her mother got it from somewhere.

"Lizzie," he continues, "we have so much to catch up on. But we also have pressing business. Your Council and the *captain* need to come to terms with the New Generation." Liz doesn't like how he spits the word, as if it were foul.

"I can offer terms. I can help you get home. I can help you make a difference again. But I won't negotiate with anyone else—it has to be you. This tablet has been specially designed, with cutting-edge technology that will allow us to communicate in nearly real-time, even though you're already millions of miles away. It's so very important that you call me, Lizzie. It's the only way I can keep you safe." His face softens, but only for a second before his gaze turns hard again.

"I still have people on your ship," he continues. "I have technology that you don't have. And even though you're no doubt out of the solar system by now, I still have the ability to destroy the Green Grow 3. When you are ready to talk, use the application on the home screen to call me. But, please don't wait too long. If anything Seth Harris says is true, he will support you in this. Peace benefits all of us. I'm counting on you, sis. I hope to hear from you soon. I love you always."

A second later, the video window closes, leaving a home screen on the tablet with one application—CALL JACKSON.

"Bushwa," Liz whispers, incredulous. "This can't be real." She turns to Seth, whose eyes are wide as saucers.

"Z, how does he know all of this?" His voice is a choked whisper.

"Fresh hell, Seth, I don't know!" She stands and turns away from the tablet. She doesn't want to see it or touch it anymore. But Liz doesn't question the truth of what Jackson said about the spies or destroying the ship. If she has learned anything over the last week, it's that the New Generation has capabilities beyond anything she could have imagined.

"Seth, what are we going to do?" she asks, turning in time to see him rake his fingers through his sleek dark hair. When his eyes meet hers, they are wild.

"I think—" His voice falters. "I think we're going to have to see what he wants. Then we can decide what to do."

"Talk to him? Seth, I can't! I just can't." Liz's chest constricts. She can't breathe. Her vision blurs with hot tears as she begins to gasp for air. Seth rushes to her side, rubbing his hand in gentle circles on her back as he leads her to the sofa.

"Breathe, Z." He cradles her head against his chest. Liz doesn't try to fight the tears that come in sobbing waves. She has no capacity for anything other than crying now. She wipes her nose on her sleeve and looks up at him, face pleading.

"How could he not know where I was?" she cries. "I looked for him, Seth. For a long time. I posted fliers on the same depot billboards that he used to advertise his monthly recruitment meetings! How could he not know?"

"I don't know, Z." Seth strokes her hair, resting his chin on her head.

"We can't trust him!" she insists.

"Of course we can't trust him. We can't trust anybody now."

Liz pulls away, a wave of anger and confusion crashing over her. "Seth, what are you asking me to do? How can you ask me to do this?"

"Liz." He holds her shoulders tightly, forcing her to look at him. "I'm not asking you to do anything. We know we need peace with the New Generation, and at this point we can't rely on the Green Grow Executive Board—if it even still exists. If he will only speak with you, then what choice do we have? I would happily do this for you, but I don't think Jackson will let me. I promise not to leave your side. Whatever it takes, until the end."

***

"Are you sure you want to do this now?" Seth asks, looking at Liz sidelong. When he suggested they call Jackson, he imagined they'd do it in the morning, after their minds had time to absorb this and after a night's sleep. He certainly didn't imagine that Liz would take five minutes to compose herself and insist on doing it immediately.

Liz narrows her eyes and turns her freshly washed face to glare at him squarely.

"I am not going to dread this any longer than I have to," she hisses, turning her fiery gaze back toward the tablet. "If you want to do this, we're doing it now."

Seth doesn't reply. Instead, he gently caresses the clenched fist she presses into her thigh. She lets her fingers relax, and they wait in silence as the tablet rhythmically flashes the same status again and again—*connecting*. Liz studies her reflection in the otherwise blank screen, steeling herself with the most impassive expression she can manage. *He doesn't deserve to see you upset,* she thinks, still unbelieving that after all this time, she is calling her brother. The screen freezes and then flashes, giving Liz only a moment to prepare for the face that follows.

Jackson seems to be sitting in the same chair as before, but the angle of his camera is different. Liz can still see the lamp and one stack of books, but this time she can also see a makeshift bookcase—a series of wooden planks separated by clusters of bricks. The shelves overflow with books, pressed together in rows and stacks with no regard for shape or size.

For a moment he beams, flashing her a charming smile. His teeth still confound her, and she gets the impression he doesn't smile often. His weathered face bears deep wrinkles—between his eyes and across his brow, but none in those familiar places that testify to smiles or laughter. His exuberance falters as Liz maintains her most unreadable expression, Seth sitting at her side.

"Lizzie," he begins, barely missing a beat, "it is so very good to see you. I knew you would be beautiful, but I never could have imagined how much you look like our mother. How are you?"

Liz measures her response carefully as Jackson waits, his expression patient and expecting. "I'm well," she says, "although I'm still having some trouble processing all of this. Why did you choose to contact me after all these years?" She waits quietly for a response.

Jackson opens his mouth to speak and then closes it again. For just a breath she sees the face of the boy who was once her brother, looking a bit hurt and deciding what to do next.

"Lizzie, can't we speak alone?" he finally asks cautiously. Her mother's voice rings in her mind, drowning out her own thoughts. *Trust no one,* it says, as Jackson continues, "I have so many things to tell you. So many things to show you. I know you're angry at me, but please—"

"Angry?" Liz interrupts, incredulous. "Why would I be angry? I don't know who you are. You can't be my brother. My brother wouldn't have abandoned his mother and his sister. If my brother was alive, he would have come back. Like he promised. He didn't come back, so he must be dead."

"Yes," Jackson agrees solemnly, "I can't expect you to forgive me—not yet. It's just that … There was so much to do, and the time went by so fast. By the time I got back, you were gone."

Liz waves her hand, cutting him off. *He doesn't deserve the satisfaction of knowing how much he hurt you,* she decides as she narrows her eyes. "I'm not interested in lies or excuses," she says pointedly. His mouth tightens, and he nods slowly.

"You are right," he says, "and I shall offer none. But I am your brother. Look, Lizzie. Look at this." He turns to the bookcase and carefully slides out a small volume from the top shelf. "I read this one when I think of you. *The Velveteen Rabbit.* Do you remember? I used to read it to you." He regards the book solemnly, delicately raising it toward the camera as if it is sacred. Liz scrutinizes the faded cover until it comes to her—*the shabby toy rabbit with no feet.*

The rest of the memories come like a tsunami: Jackson reading to her at night by candlelight or, if they were lucky, a battery-operated lamp. The two of them with their mother, eating a simple dinner. Jackson smiling at her as their mother braided her hair, humming. Liz can hear the lullaby again, the haunting tune that her mother would hum, and now she remembers that it was Jackson who would sing the words.

Hush-a-bye, don't you cry. Go to sleep, my little baby.

Suddenly, Liz doubles over in her chair, world spinning as she gasps with pain.

When you wake, you shall have all the pretty little horses.

She doesn't want to remember this now.

Blacks and grays, dapples and bays, all the pretty little horses.

She flies out of her chair, needing nothing more than to be out of Jackson's sight as she leans heavily on the table behind the tablet.

"Lizzie, are you okay?" Jackson cries out.

"She needs a minute," Seth barks as he comes around to her, behind the camera to hold her while she cries.

"Leave her alone," Jackson commands, voice unsettled as he addresses the empty seat where Liz was sitting moments before.

"Unlike you," Seth replies in his coldest voice, "I will never do that."

"I'm okay," Liz gasps softly in his ear. "Go sit down. I'll be right there." She breathes in deeply, until her lungs can hold no more, and then pushes the air out of her nose until the room begins to spin.

Jackson's voice cuts the air like a knife. "And you must be the *boyfriend.*"

"I'm sure you well know who I am," Seth says coldly, narrowed eyes steely as he retakes his seat.

"I won't negotiate with you," Jackson spits.

"You've made that clear," Seth hisses in retort. "And I won't leave her alone with you. I am the captain of this vessel, and I will be present at all negotiations."

"You are a spoiled, pompous child," Jackson declares. "I do not recognize your authority."

Seth replies evenly through gritted teeth. "Your endorsement is of no concern to me."

"Enough!" Liz growls, as she sits down rigidly in front of the camera once more. "Let's cut to the chase. What are you offering, Jackson? And what do you want in return?"

Liz watches the emotion drain from her brother's scarred face. When he speaks again, his voice is quiet. "I know how you can make more fuel for your thrusters—enough fuel to slow the ship. I know which way you should go, where you should turn around, and how you should come back. I know this because I have access to star charts, satellites, and telescopes that you don't have. That's what I have to offer you presently, and this is what I want in return. You have medical technology I want, and I want access to your head bioengineer, Claire Harris, for the purposes of consulting on crop enhancements. We're growing food hydroponically underground, but it's not enough to feed everyone. I need to increase our productivity to keep my people from starving until you get back."

"That's it?" Liz asks bluntly.

"For now," he says. "We have plenty of time to haggle over what happens when you get home."

Liz cocks an eyebrow, looking sidelong at Seth. He squeezes her hand.

"We'll talk to Claire, and I'll call you tomorrow," Liz agrees.

"Okay," Jackson replies, quickly adding, "Goodnight, Lizzie."

She ends the call before he can say anything else.

CHAPTER 16

MATHILDA

***

AUGUST 22, 2059 – FRIDAY

The Council sits in stunned silence as Seth studies the faces of the members, waiting for them to absorb what he just told them before continuing.

"Peace negotiations with Jackson Goeff?" Harry repeats, unbelieving.

"I know," Seth replies, "but it's what we wanted, isn't it?"

Liz doesn't want to think about Jackson anymore, so she turns her gaze left to study Mathilda, who sits next to her. The woman appears more composed than yesterday, but Liz suspects this is because Seth ordered her to report to medical for treatment. Who knows what Claire dosed her with? Liz is sure it made her sleep, but even now Mathilda's eyelids look heavy, her face slack and drained, her hair and clothes disheveled. She appears to be listening just as intently as everyone else to Seth's account of the communication with Jackson, but her face lacks expression.

She simply sits in her chair, doodling on a paper notepad Liz has never seen her carry before. Mathilda appears to be drawing a flower. Or is it a bird?

"It sounds like most of what he wants is in my shop," Claire says, pulling Liz back to the conversation.

"Well," Jarrod adds, "Zag already gave him the specs for the antimatter drive, and who knows what else had already been leaked from my team?"

"We need to know exactly what medical technology he thinks we have, but I don't see the harm in giving him what he wants," Claire continues. "If the technology and information we have can save lives, it seems like the right thing to share it."

"Mathilda," Seth asks, casually looking at the distraught woman slouched in her chair, "did you learn anything from the star charts you found in the archives?"

"We've got nothing beyond our own solar system," she says, looking up from her paper with still-droopy eyes, liquid through her heavily rimmed glasses. "I suspect Jackson probably found the old NASA deep space telescope data. It was widely available, but the files would be huge—not a priority for the space farm servers since we never intended to leave orbit."

"So those records are lost to us now?" Seth asks. "Haven't you been trying to connect with old surface systems to get this information since we cleared the asteroid belt?"

"Yes, I've tried and failed repeatedly," she says calmly, gazing back down to her paper. "If Jackson has the old NASA records, he might be able to give us critical information."

"And what about the thruster fuel?" Jarrod asks. "Claire, do you think it's even possible to manufacture onboard?"

"It's a chemical propellant, right?" she asks, as Jarrod nods. "We've never considered it before, but I don't see why it wouldn't be possible. We might be able to figure out a viable formula and production method without Jackson, but it would take time to explore."

"Time we don't have," Jarrod adds, shaking his head.

"So what do we have to lose?" Harry asks somberly, fixing his faze on Seth.

"I don't know," Seth says, sounding distracted. "Is it really this straightforward?"

Heavy silence blankets the room as everyone considers Seth's question—everyone except Mathilda, who appears once more engrossed in her doodling. Liz considers her again. *Is she really this fragile?* No one who is brave enough to pull a pistol on Dr. Claire Harris can possibly be this fragile. Could Mathilda actually shoot someone? Liz can't imagine it, thinking back to the woman's devastated face at the executions. She looked so traumatized.

Has she experienced death before? Liz wonders, realizing that she knows very little about Mathilda's past. In fact, all she knows for sure is that Mathilda seems highly intelligent and exceedingly kind, thorough and thoughtful with her work. *But why did she ask for more time to check her calculations? And why was she asking so many questions about the drive's security system?* Suddenly, an even more important question plays upon her mind. *Where was she during the insurrection?* Liz realizes she doesn't know.

Mathilda seems to lose interest in her indiscernible flower-bird and begins to doodle a word. *Hubble?* Liz watches her trace the letters absently, almost forlornly. Liz doesn't know what a hubble is, nor does she care. *Her handwriting …*

Liz flies up from her chair, startling everyone in the room. Without a word, she spins Mathilda around, grabbing her head firmly as she searches her bewildered face. *One … Two … Three …* Mathilda's eyes grow wide as she clenches her fists, but it isn't enough to hide the blue light emanating from her palm. Liz releases her, taking a step back and appraising her ruefully as Claire gasps and Harry exclaims, "What the hell?"

Mathilda's face flashes, first with uncertainty and then with fear, as she grabs for her pistol. Liz yanks it away, sending it skittering down the table toward Seth as she grabs Mathilda forcefully, pushing her face-first onto the conference table.

"Her handwriting," Liz gasps. "Look at it, Seth. It's the same as the note on the tablet." Seth stands frozen, expression wavering between shock and disbelief. He draws his own pistol and levels it at Mathilda.

"This can go one of two ways," he says, eyes stony and voice cold as steel. "Are you going to play nice?"

"Yes," she gulps, face pressed hard against the table. "Let me sit down, and I'll tell you whatever you want to know."

***

"You should be shot, right here and now!" Jarrod exclaims, words choked and face purple. He rises from his chair and starts to pace, pulling his hair and mumbling to himself. Seth looks bewildered but continues to stand firm, his pistol aimed squarely at Mathilda.

"Oh for fuck's sake," Mathilda retorts in a disgusted, self-righteous tone, "if I wanted any of you harmed or for the New Generation to overtake the ship, it would have happened months ago." She sits slouched in her chair, looking conquered but undefeated.

"Sit down, Jarrod!" Seth barks. "None of us are going anywhere until I get some answers." He looks back at Mathilda, pistol still leveled at her.

"So, what do you want?" Liz demands, perched on the edge of the table and ready to fly at Mathilda again if she attempts to rise. "Why do you have the credential?

"It's like Willow told you," Mathilda says gently. "They give them to everyone who comes to an informational meeting. I attended one before Captain MacAbee disappeared. And why wouldn't I get one if I thought it would keep me safe from the raiding parties?"

"But you never mentioned it to anyone," Liz presses. "Not even when Claire found the credential on Zag. And you've clearly been in communication with Jackson. I know it was you who slipped the tablet and note into my laundry."

"It's not a crime to talk to people," Mathilda replies, indignant. "And yes, Jackson gave me instructions to modify the tablet. It wasn't easy, you know. I'm not an engineer. But I also wanted you to have a way to talk to your brother, Liz. He's your family, and if you would just give him a chance ..." Her voice fades under the weight of Liz's chilling stare.

"You make it sound so innocent," Seth says flatly. "And yet, it's not. Jackson has information only known to the Council—information that, no doubt, you gave him. These meetings are secret by my order. Orders you violated by telling him things like when we were planning to depart and where we are now. And not only did you give him this information, but you tried to help him by delaying our departure, presumably to give him time to find a way to stop us. At the very least, you are insubordinate, and that's only what we know so far. I suspect the deeper we dig here, the more we will find."

"Insubordinate?" Mathilda retorts, indignance catching flame as she sits straighter in her chair. "With all due respect, Captain, are we here to do what you tell us, or are we here to try and improve the condition of the human race?" Liz feels a strange sensation in her stomach—a mix of nausea, disbelief, and fear that she can't quite label. Thoughts begin to spin in her head as Mathilda continues in a shrill voice, wild eyes filled with tears. "You know, you should be thanking me. You claim to want to make peace with the New Generation, and now that might be possible!"

"Thanking you?" Jarrod bleats, face flushing a deep red that borders purple. "Shoot her, Seth! Right here. Right now."

"Enough!" the captain barks, exhaling deeply and lowering his pistol. "We need to be smarter than that, Jarrod. I'm sure we can make better use of Mathilda if she is alive."

Fear floods Mathilda's doe eyes.

"What are you going to do to me?" she asks, voice choked.

"For now, I am taking you into custody," Seth replies. "Harry, I need two of your most trustworthy security officers to guard her at all times. I don't want her in the brig—news will travel too fast. Jarrod, find any quarters on Level 2 that weren't previously Mathilda's and make sure they are swept for any electronic devices she might use to communicate. The rest of Level 2 will be sealed. Mathilda, you will be confined to your assigned quarters and under guard until further notice. You will have contact with no one except the Council."

"But my work—" she gasps.

"It's done," Seth commands. "We will break for thirty minutes to make this happen, and then I expect to see the rest of you back here in this room. We still have business to conduct."

***

Two hours later, Liz rubs her bleary eyes as she rides the lift down to the cafeteria on Level 4. The rest of the morning was spent discussing the upcoming call to Jackson and what to do with Mathilda. Liz is still surprised by the intensity with which Jarrod insisted she be executed, especially after all the time he's spent working with Mathilda. *Maybe that's the reason he feels so strongly,* Liz muses, imagining that his own sense of betrayal must cut at least as deeply as Ellen Ryan's betrayal cut her.

For now, Seth is confining Mathilda to a room on the otherwise abandoned Level 2. They can't be certain at this point that she played a critical role in the insurrection, and whatever information she compromised was not nearly as much as she could have. Besides, as Claire pointed out, keeping Mathilda alive might be the only way to get and effectively use information from Jackson from the old NASA deep space probes. Jarrod seems to be the only one who wants her dead at the moment. Even Liz, who doesn't know how to feel about Mathilda's betrayal, knows that she doesn't want to see more executions.

Nonetheless, Mathilda lost it when Ellis and Charlie came to escort her to Level 2. She cried and sobbed, and they each had to grab an arm as she started to collapse, pulling her down the hallway with her feet dragging behind her. Liz can think of far worse fates than being confined to quarters, but even this punishment seemed to bring Mathilda's world collapsing down around her. Her work seems to be her lifeline, along with whatever communication she was having with Jackson.

The lift stops on Level 3, and the door opens to reveal Albert Wyndham's face. Liz isn't prepared to see him, and a fresh surge of pain washes over her as she remembers Mathilda's insinuation that Sam lost his life for no reason. Is she right? She stands alone with him on the lift as the doors close again.

"Liz," Albert greets her curtly.

"Albert," she replies, looking up at him. He refuses to meet her gaze, instead looking straight ahead toward the lift doors. "I haven't forgotten about you," she continues. "I asked the captain for permission to brief you, and he's considering it."

"Of course you haven't forgotten me, Liz," he says coldly. "I'm still here. Sam is one you're forgetting."

Albert's words hit Liz like a closed fist. Before she can contemplate a reply, the lift doors open again, and he stalks out ahead of her.

***

"What did you do to Mathilda?" Jackson demands, as soon as the call connects that evening. Was he expecting a call from her today that didn't come, or did another spy tell him something? *No, he must have been expecting communication,* Liz thinks. *Otherwise he would know more about what happened to her.*

"She is detained," Seth says flatly, sitting on Liz's left while Claire sits to her right. "I assume you know why."

"Do not harm her," Jackson commands.

"She's fine," Liz interjects, "but she won't be calling you anytime soon. We've cut off her communication."

"Lizzie," he says more softly, "please make sure nothing happens to her. She's a brilliant woman, and we can't afford to lose any more people."

"We're all sick of the killing, Jackson," Liz replies, disgusted and impatient. "She'll be treated fairly." Jackson opens his mouth as if to speak and then closes it again, remaining silent.

Liz can feel Seth's eyes burning into the side of her face as he gently squeezes her hand, urging her to move on. She returns her focus to the screen. "Jackson, we have Dr. Claire Harris with us to discuss your request about medical technology. What, specifically, are you asking for?"

The hint of emotion that previously blossomed on Jackson's face promptly withers back into an impassive stare. He begins to rattle off a list of technologies that Claire seems to understand. Liz fixes her eyes on the screen, but she's not paying attention. She can feel the intensity of Claire's focus beside her. The heat from Seth's body radiates on her other side, his hand still resting gently on hers. Jackson's words begin to run together in a low hum as Liz's own questions begin to echo more loudly in her mind.

How did he become a captain in the New Generation?

Did he ever wonder where I was?

What happened to his face?

The questions tumble in her mind until only one remains.

When did my brother turn into a monster?

"Do you have access to a genetics lab?" Claire asks dubiously, as Liz forces her attention to the conversation at hand. "I can tell you how to enhance the hydroponic crops, but it may be of little value if you can't access the proper equipment."

"Yes," Jackson replies earnestly. "I discovered a reasonably intact lab nearby, at a satellite location of an old university. I've had additional equipment brought in from the East Coast from an old government facility."

"The East Coast?" Liz interjects. "You've established transportation lines?"

Jackson smiles. "We're working on it, but yes. We are making progress. I updated your tablet with a drop box where we can share data files and information, and I'll send you a report to get us started." *How does he do this?* Liz wants to scream. There seem to be no limits to what Jackson can do. *And yet, he still needs our help,* she reminds herself.

"Is that how you plan to transmit the star charts and the thruster fuel specifications?" Liz asks, determined to bring them back on point.

"Yes," Jackson says, his face darkening, "but Mathilda is the only person who will be able to make sense of the star chart data. I'd prefer to communicate with her directly."

Liz doesn't bother getting a read from Seth on this one. "We can't promise that," she replies briskly.

"Lizzie," he replies patiently, "do you want to get home or not?"

"And do you want Claire's help or not?" she yells in response. "Foul mother of hell, Jackson! Would you allow us to speak to a known spy in your high command?"

"Of course not," he replies, "but that's not the situation, is it?"

"Besides," Liz adds, calming herself, "who said we're coming home? We haven't promised that. All we've promised is an exchange of information." Jackson's mouth falls open, face confounded. Liz continues, voice icy. "I'm sure you think you're in charge here, Jackson. And I know all about your smooth promises to the people you've recruited, about how all you want to do is keep them safe and make the world a better place. But I know the truth. I've seen your raiding parties. I saw one less than two weeks ago at the Denver depot. I've heard the stories of the women who escaped from the New Generation. So let's not pretend that you're the hero here, or that you're somehow saving us. And let's not pretend that you're the only person capable of blowing this ship. I'd just as soon blow it myself than witness the carnage I know would follow if you found a way onboard."

The silence stretches as Liz's words settle on Jackson. "Very well," he finally replies, eyes downcast. "Just know, Mathilda is indispensable. But, if you say she's well, then I believe you. I'll transmit the star chart data first. You can have Mathilda validate it—I know for a fact that she is *very* interested in coming home."

"Goodnight, Jackson," Liz replies, surprising herself as she hears her own words. She ends the call and turns to Seth and Claire.

"Well now," Claire replies, "you certainly know how to hold your ground, don't you?" The three of them laugh, a too-loud, nervous chuckle, full of pent-up anxiety and frustration. "I'll have to figure out how to package the information he wants, but I'm glad we're doing this. It feels like we might finally be doing something for the human species, instead of just ourselves."

"What are we going to do about Mathilda?" Liz asks, looking at Seth. "I think we all know she's indispensable."

"Well, we certainly aren't going to execute her," Seth replies. "We can update the rest of the Council in the morning, but I think we're going to have to work with her. And to do that, she's going to require access to our systems. As much as I hate to say it, I think we're going to have to trust her a little."

"Is there really no one else who can interpret the star chart data?" Claire asks.

"I suspect there is not," Seth replies. "And even if there were, how could we trust anyone on her team? She chose them all."

Claire sighs heavily as Liz checks the time. *Story time,* she thinks, feeling a surge of lightness at the thought of seeing Ruth again. She desperately needs the refuge and belonging she finds with The Fifty-Two, and she needs it now.

***

Neither Seth nor Claire is interested in story time, and so Liz goes alone. She enters the cafeteria to the sound of Ellis's guitar and stomping feet. Story time must be over already. They often close with music, it seems, dancing and singing, but Liz is sad at having missed the rest. Ellis concludes his tune, and the crowd claps and cheers. Liz sees many of The Fifty-Two as well as several of the other crew members she remembers from Level 7. Ruth rises as Ellis smiles and takes a small bow, finding a seat with his guitar.

"And now for the main event!" Ruth calls out jubilantly. "I'm pleased to present our own production of the Three Little Pigs." Ruth's eyes lock with Liz's as she turns to sit, smiling and waving her forward. Liz eagerly makes her way to Ruth, pulling up an empty chair to sit next to her.

"I thought I missed it," Liz whispers.

"Oh no," Ruth replies softly, "our actors just needed a few more minutes to get ready. This will be fun."

Indeed, Liz has never seen a play before. She vaguely remembers the story from a book of fairy tales her mom used to teach her to read.

Ruben quickly rushes onto the scene, planting an empty chair in the middle as he smiles and waves to everyone before rushing off. Melissa enters the makeshift stage from the side, hobbling dramatically like an old injured woman as she sits in the chair. Three children scurry in behind her, exhorting joyous snorts and oinking sounds. Liz feels the smile creep on her face and her heart lighten.

"My little piggies!" Melissa cries, in a shrill voice. "It is time for each of you to leave my house and make your fortune. You must each build a house of your own, and make your way in the world." The three little piggies snort and jump.

"But Mom," one replies, "why can't we live here with you?"

"Because, my precious piggies, you are almost grown and it is time for you to live in your own houses!"

"Okay!" a second piggy says jubilantly. "Let's go build our houses." They scurry off the stage, and Ruben once again pops in to collect the empty chair. Zachary makes his debut as the wolf a short time later. Liz smiles so hard her face hurts, and she laughs so hard that tears fall from her eyes. Has she ever been this happy before? She can't remember.

She thinks back to the nights cuddled in bed with Jackson reading to her—her older brother, who seemed even more magical back then than the stories he read. Liz scours her memory for the details, details that are practically new since she blocked them out so long ago. How much has she forced herself to forget? She doesn't know. She can still feel the cool air coming through her bedroom window, when the weather was warm and clear enough to allow for open windows. She remembers a faded quilt on her narrow bed, and a pillow with a clean pillowcase that felt soft on her face. And then getting lost in the stories, lost in the moment, with no worries about the future, or the past, or even the present. No worries. Somehow, even though they had so little, she remembers life being very good in those moments.

Liz hears Zachary yowl dramatically as her attention focuses again on the play. It seems he received a stern poke in the rear when he pretended to climb through the window of the piggy's house, and he ran off holding his bottom, trying to play the part of the wounded wolf but laughing between yowls.

Moments later he reappears, crying out, "And they all lived happily ever after!" He takes turns bowing with all his fellow actors who receive quite a bit of applause and cheering.

"Oh my," Liz wheezes, trying to regain her composure. "I needed that."

"That's why we do this, dear," Ruth replies. "We all need it."

The group starts to break up a short time later, although several linger to chat. Liz isn't ready to leave yet. She doesn't feel the need to talk but knows she might have to in order to keep Ruth there a little longer. She just needs to be near her—*to feel the sunshine she radiates to my soul.*

Ruth seems to sense her need and sits there quietly with her for a few minutes longer before speaking.

"I'd say it's been an interesting few days, but that wouldn't quite do it justice," Ruth starts. "I would imagine your life has been even more interesting."

The old woman places her knobby hand on Liz's knee. "I'm sure there's a lot you can't tell me, but how are you doing, dear?"

"I still can't believe my brother is alive, nor that he's a senior member of the New Generation. I can't decide which is worse—thinking he's dead, or knowing what he's become."

"True," Ruth starts slowly, "but can you really say for sure that you know what he's become? Sometimes the truth is more complicated than it seems." Liz isn't sure what to make of her comment, but sits silently trying to think about it for a moment.

"Had you ever seen one of those credentials before?" Liz asks, thinking about the blue light emanating from Mathilda's palm.

"No. When I saw the young man in the orchard, I thought I might have been having hallucinating. But then I realized other people saw it too. You seemed unfazed, though."

Liz shakes her head, thinking back to the day that her brother hijacked the broadcast system.

"We discovered one earlier that morning," Liz says quietly. "So it wasn't quite as shocking to me, although it's still hard to believe. How is something like that possible?"

"I've been wondering the same thing myself," Ruth replies. "It certainly casts the New Generation in a different light, doesn't it?"

"What do you mean?"

"Well, there must be more to them than the raiding parties we've all seen and experienced. There must be more to them than that if they are not only capable but interested in making things that advanced."

"What do you think it all means?" Liz asks, curious about the old woman's perspective.

Ruth considers this question thoughtfully, long enough that Liz isn't sure she will respond. But eventually she does, voice tentative.

"I think it's a good time for all of us to take a step back and make sure we know what we're working toward and how we plan to get there. I think—" Ruth pauses. "It's really for Captain Harris and the Council to decide. You've brought us this far, my dear, and I know you'll help everyone see the right path, whatever it is." Liz leaves the cafeteria feeling heavy, wishing Ruth could have said something simpler.

CHAPTER 17

ALBERT WYNDAM

****

AUGUST 23, 2059 – SATURDAY

Liz studies Mathilda as she and Seth sit in her temporary Level 2 quarters. The woman seems nervous.

"Jackson tells me you're indispensable," Seth starts, his face expressionless. Mathilda doesn't respond. She only studies her hands.

"Look Mathilda," Seth starts again. "Regardless of what Jackson says or does, I well know that you are essential. It pains me that you've made yourself that way for the purpose of manipulating us, but I recognize the truth in what you said before—if you wanted to undermine the Council or the ship, you could have done so. It's going to take all of us to get out of this mess.

"I cannot express how angry and disappointed I am in you. No matter how you choose to frame it, you have betrayed all of our trust. You could have helped when you didn't, and you compromised our security. No matter how you spin it, you are partially responsible for every life that was lost in the insurrection. But, we have to work together to survive this. So, I am releasing you into your own custody."

Mathilda looks up, surprised, as Seth continues.

"Don't take this as a vote of confidence, Mathilda. I simply realize that you have the capacity to subvert whatever restrictions I place upon you unless you are in complete isolation. So, I'm going to save us some time. You will report to the Council meetings each day, but you will be dismissed when your updates are done. And Claire will implant a tracking device in you so I know where you are at all times.

"I also insist that I or Liz be present at any discussion you have with Jackson Goeff. I will certainly not give you free reign to talk to him. Liz is the designated representative in all negotiations with him. While I realize that you may still have the ability to rig your own communication device, know that I will have you under scrutiny—some of which I'm sharing with you now and some of which I'm not—and if you are caught communicating with him privately … If I even suspect you are communicating with him privately, all of your privileges will be revoked and you will be moved to the brig. No one is truly irreplaceable, not even you."

"Agreed," Mathilda says quietly, apparently resigned to her fate. "All I ever wanted was the best for everyone."

"And yet," Seth challenges her, "you assumed that you could decide what was best for everyone and act accordingly. Not even I do that as captain, even though I have unilateral authority to do so on this ship. You know better than that, Mathilda. This could have all gone down very differently, and eighty-four people might still be alive had you come clean sooner and helped us find another way."

Seth rises from his chair. "I've got other business to attend to. Liz can bring you up to speed on what has happened and what you need to do."

Mathilda looks relieved when he closes the door.

"Do you need a break?" Liz asks. "Or should we dive in?"

"Well," Mathilda considers, the lenses of her glasses smeared, "I haven't bathed in days, and I'm still hungover from whatever Claire dosed me with when Seth forced me to go to medical. But why not? Let's dig in."

"Why don't we go to your office?" Liz suggests. Mathilda nods and then stands, looking as if she is navigating a dark dream.

They leave the Level 2 quarters, and Liz notices Mathilda's slight frame shudder as the door closes behind them. The security officers that previously guarded her door are gone. They are alone in the corridor, walking slowly toward the lift as Liz strikes up a conversation.

"You said that you went to one of the New Generation meetings," she starts. Mathilda's gait becomes stiff. "Did you meet my brother there?"

"Yes," she replies tentatively, looking over toward Liz with a curious expression.

"What's he like?" Liz asks quietly, refusing to meet Mathilda's gaze.

"Well—" Mathilda's eyes go soft as she retreats to some distant place in her mind. "He's tall. And very handsome, although I'm sure you know that. He has a dashing smile. He's kind and gentle and extremely intelligent."

"Kind and gentle? That's a bit hard to believe."

"Oh, no doubt he is strong enough to do what needs to be done, but Liz—he's a man of vision. Whatever he does, it's for the good of humanity." Mathilda's face starts to glow and her body becomes more animated.

Sweet shit sauce, she's infatuated with him.

"Men like him," Mathilda continue, "are going to change our future. He's changing the New Generation, from an organization that destroys civilization to one that will build a new one."

"But Mathilda," Liz interrupts, feeling confused, "don't you know how ruthless they are? Women are treated like slaves, like property. I've heard it firsthand from Gabriella—one of The Fifty-Two. When the New Generation found out she was pregnant, they tried to come take her away, to somewhere she'd never return from."

"Jackson has talked about that," Mathilda says wistfully. "Liz, women aren't slaves. They're protected. I'm sure some men treat their wives better than others, but the thing about the babies … Babies are cherished! Jackson tells me pregnant women are taken to a special underground complex, where they receive all the medical care and nutrition they need. And then when their babies are born, they have the option to stay with their children and raise them as part of the community underground. The women don't want to leave! Do you know the chances of successfully delivering a baby on the surface? There's not enough food, and the chances are much greater that the babies will be born with birth defects or serious illnesses. It's not what you think."

"Mathilda, why would you believe all this?" Liz asks, incredulous. "It's a dream. Have you ever seen a raiding party? Have you seen what they do? They're not building a civilization, they're still tearing it down. And if they're so benevolent, why didn't someone ask to negotiate with us? They seem to know so much about everything we do. Why simply gather information to plan a violent insurrection instead of make themselves known and come to terms?"

"Seriously, Liz? And how would Seth have responded to that? How would the Council? You of all people know how self-interested the leaders of this ship can be." Mathilda cuts herself off abruptly. Liz is certain she didn't intend to be so forthcoming. *Are we really the bad guys here?* Liz wonders, trying the idea on for size and deciding she doesn't like how it fits, not at all.

"So why did you stay? I'm sure even after Captain MacAbee left, you could have found a way to the surface if that's what you wanted."

"This is where I could make the biggest difference," she says simply. "And don't get me wrong, Liz, I believe in what we're doing."

"Really?" Liz asks, incredulous. "So we're not the bad guys, and the New Generation aren't the bad guys. Is anyone wrong in your world?"

"Does anyone need to be?" Mathilda asks, inquisitively.

"Well, there must be some reason we're killing each other. There's a reason eighty-two people died on this ship. There's a reason people are starving and being hunted on the surface. There's some cause of all of this."

"Perhaps," Mathilda muses, "or maybe we all need to take some ownership."

This takes Liz off guard. She wants to refute Mathilda, to expound on the ridiculousness of her perspective, but she remains silent. Maybe there is some truth to this. She thinks back to Sam Wyndham, back to her own mother.

The truth can be complicated. And Liz is sure that even the New Generation raiding parties think they're on the right side of the problem. They speak no more as they make their way to Mathilda's office.

***

Liz has never been to the office before, and she immediately wonders if it was a mistake coming here. As the door slides closed behind them, the space becomes stiflingly small, although Liz knows that the office isn't small at all; it's just full. She sees several monitors and large computers. And paper. Stacks and stacks of paper. It flows over Mathilda's desk like an avalanche, precariously perched to break loose once again and smother any poor soul caught in its path.

Beyond the desk is another table, also completely covered in stacks. Mathilda moves them easily, gracefully even, to locations on the floor as she invites Liz to sit in the only seat not filled with piles of paper. Liz feels a chill flow down her spine, and she tries to suppress a shudder. She notices a whooshing noise as she sits, and it makes her jump. It sounds like water gurgling.

"You get used to it," Mathilda says playfully. Liz looks at her, startled. "The water. You look like you hear the water."

"Yes, I thought that sounded like water."

"There's a water processing station on the other side of that wall." She motions carelessly. "Lots of water moving through pipes. You get used to it after a while." She looks thoughtful for a moment, then continues. "I actually find it quite soothing."

She's quirky, Liz thinks, *like a little mouse in her paper-crowded nest, right next to a burbling brook.*

Liz suggested they met in Mathilda's office so that she could look for communication devices the woman might be using to communicate with Jackson. The tablets seem complicated to rig—there has to be some other way that people communicate with him. There were simply too many people doing it to rely on a system like she had. But now Liz realizes that she could never find anything in here, certainly not hidden contraband.

Liz unwraps the tablet she uses to communicate with Jackson. She still uses the same pillowcase she found it in to contain the modified device and the strange antennae. Mathilda watches her carefully set it up on the table.

"Jackson set up a drop box, and there are data files in here you need," she says. "He says there are star charts to plot a course back."

"Well, let's see what he's sent us!" Mathilda sounds excited as she reaches for the tablet, but then she draws back and cautiously adds, "Can I take the tablet? I need to connect it to my larger computer to download the files." Liz nods, and Mathilda gently takes the tablet, the glee once more returning to her face. Liz sits and watches as she connects the tablet and clicks buttons. She hears the most subtle whirring of the computers between the whooshing sounds of the water. Liz decides she can't wait to get out of the office. She doesn't like this place.

"Where did they get all this technology?" Liz asks as Mathilda waits for her computers to churn. "The tablet, the chips. Where do they come from?"

Mathilda studies her. "I don't know," she finally replies. Liz considers this.

"Would you tell me if you did know?"

"I'm not sure why you'd ask me anyway," Mathilda replies, avoiding the question. "All you need to do is ask Jackson. I'm sure he'll tell you whatever you want to know."

Liz ponders this as she waits for Mathilda to finish with the modified tablet. *Willow said the same thing,* she remembers. *Ask your brother—I'm sure he would tell you.* How can these people speak of him so casually? Like he wasn't someone who went missing for years, abandoning her and their mother, and then reappearing at the worst possible time in the worst possible way? It is insulting, and it is infuriating. Liz can feel her confusion start to melt into anger. She knows she needs to get out of here.

People like Mathilda have her second-guessing everything, and why? Mathilda has so little experience with the New Generation, basically whatever Jackson tells her. *He brainwashes them,* Liz decides, knowing that she needs to maintain her wits. *Everything was going fine until they started raiding the depots and pillaging survivors. They don't get to come in now and look like the good guys. They don't get to make us the enemy.*

***

By the time Liz makes it to the cafeteria for lunch, it seems more like bedtime than lunchtime, and most of the lunch rush has already passed. She considers her options as she assesses the food that remains and settles on a cheese sandwich and an orange.

She notices Albert Wyndham sitting at a table on the near edge of the dining room. Unsure what to do and lacking the energy to ward off more of his icy glances, she pretends not to notice him and sits at an empty table at the other end of the room. But Albert comes over and sits down next to her as she chews the first bite of her sandwich. *Foul mother of hell.* She has no choice but to deal with him now.

"I'll follow up with the captain this afternoon," she says without bothering to greet him. "I haven't forgotten you or Sam. Unfortunately, I need the captain's approval to tell you everything." She looks up at him, startled to see that the anger that usually besets his face is gone.

"I appreciate that, Liz," he says softly. "But I'm not here to ask you about that. I've seen and heard things that bother me. I know Sam was a patriot, and I know he trusted you. I'll never forgive you for letting him die, but I know Sam would want me to tell someone what I've found. It could be important. And at least I could spare someone else the heartache of losing someone. If we can fix this in time, that is."

Liz's senses heighten as she loses interest in her sandwich. "Fix what, Albert?" Her eyes narrow.

"I'm scared, Liz," he says, as his voice becomes more frantic. Liz realizes that he does, in fact, look quite scared. "I don't know who all is involved, but there are still spies on the ship, you know?"

Liz does know. But how does Albert? She nods, leaning in toward him as she waits for him to continue. When he speaks again, his voice is a whisper.

"I found something. I don't know how to explain it, but it might be important. Can I show you? It's on Level 8. Will you come with me? I don't know how much time we have left."

Liz thinks for a moment about what to do. She could call Seth, but it might be nothing. Besides, Albert seems to be willing to make peace with her. He came to her because Sam trusted her. Maybe she can redeem herself in his eyes.

"Let's go then," she says, wrapping the remains of her sandwich and slipping it, along with the small orange, into a large pocket on the front of her tunic.

"Do you need to be anywhere soon?" Albert says cautiously. "This might take a few minutes."

"I have as long as it takes, Albert," Liz assures him as they walk to the lift.

"They have code words, you know," he whispers as they walk into the dense, tropical air of Level 8. Liz is certain the level was damaged like the others during the acceleration, but the level looks as lush as she remembered it.

"At first I thought I was misunderstanding, or reading into things," he continues as he ushers her into a row of orange trees, "but the words were completely out of context. Like 'hash brown casserole' when there was none in the cafeteria that day. Or 'did you see the red humming-bird' when we were working in the goat pens. Then I noticed them handing things to each other, sly-like. I followed a couple of them yesterday, quietly enough that they didn't notice me. And that's when I discovered this."

Liz notices they are heading toward one of the big service lifts. *It would make sense to hide something here,* she realizes. *There aren't any cameras.* They pass through the rows of oranges, into rows of bushy lemon trees. Liz loves the smell of the lemons.

"Wait," Albert says, urging her to crouch down as he makes himself as small as possible. She does the same, hearing two voices on the other side of the glossy foliage. It's a man and a woman, laughing and exchanging what sounds like casual conversation. Liz strains her ears, listening for anything out of context, but she can't make out what they're saying. After a few minutes, they pass.

"No one is supposed to be working on this level this afternoon," Albert whispers. "We better be careful." Liz nods, trying to keep track of where they are going, but she isn't nearly as familiar with this level as she is with Level 7. "We're almost there," he says quietly, motioning her ahead of him.

They round the end of the row and come into a clearing near the service lift. She sees a small tractor parked by the lift, with a cart hitched to the back. The cart is draped with a cover. Liz freezes, eyes furiously scanning to see if anyone else is around.

"Is this it?" she whispers to Albert. She turns to look at him, just in time to see a large wooden dowel swinging through the air, Albert's face a focused fury of rage. She hears a whoosh of air and feels a sharp thud on her head. Her eyes flutter closed and then open again as she feels the soft green grass rise up to meet her body.

Liz's eyes register Albert's boots planted firmly in front of her face as his strong hand grabs her arm, pulling her body up from the ground. She knows she is in trouble. *You can't let him put you in the cart,* she commands herself, instincts returning through the haze that envelopes her senses. *Stay out of the cart,* she orders her body, as he begins to hoist her up and over the edge.

Liz regains enough of her senses to realize how much trouble she's in, and her heart begins to thump wildly, pumping surges of adrenaline to every fiber of her body. She flies to action, landing a solid kick to Albert's knee. He cries out and stumbles toward the ground. Liz throws another kick but misses as he rolls right, quickly recovering his balance. She falters as she glimpses his face, the face that holds the only remaining trace of her friend Sam.

"Albert, stop!" she pleads, reaching for her knife as he grabs the wooden dowel out of the cart. She ducks as he swings for her head. *I don't want to hurt him,* she realizes, momentarily paralyzed with her knife in hand before she lands a second kick to his chest.

"You don't have to do this," she begs, tossing the knife from her right hand to her left as she tries to call Seth on her wristband communicator. She could easily lunge and sink her knife into his belly, or slash an artery on his thigh. Yet, she can't. For the first time in her life, she cannot defend herself. She cannot see the face of her enemy. All she can see is the living remnant of Sam, and how much she has hurt him.

Albert stumbles but recovers quickly, crouching and barreling into her like a battering ram before she can page Seth. His strong hands lock onto her wrists, and her knife lands in the grass with a muted thump as he smashes her body against the side of the cart.

She hears the breath leave her body with a soft *woof,* unable to inhale as she heaves herself forward, shoving him far enough away to bring her knee up hard into his crotch. *Breathe,* she commands herself as he briefly falls away from her. Her breathing reflex returns just as she lands another kick to his knee. Albert begins to fall with a muffled cry, but dodges her next blow, connecting his balled fist squarely with her ear. It's a hard hit, and she falls back, stumbling and fighting the wave of dizziness that threatens to unbalance her. Before she can move, Albert's fist crashes into her stomach. Her muscles contract but not soon enough, and she crumples onto the ground.

Liz tries to roll to her side, but Albert is on her in a flash, cracking her head with the wooden dowel. She teeters into unconsciousness, her vision filled with stars as she feels her body betray her, easily bending to his will as she loses all bearings. He quickly hoists her up then tosses her into the cart, binding her legs, hands, and mouth with a sticky tape. She feels something wet on her belly and realizes it's the smashed remains of the orange she put in her pocket. Then she uses her remaining energy to stifle the urge to vomit. *You'll choke on it and die,* she thinks as the world fades to black.

***

Liz begins to find her way to consciousness, driven by a nagging thought on the edge of her awareness that she needs to wake up. It's important to wake up now, but she can't remember why. Does she really want to leave the sightless, soundless eternity of this quiet, dark abyss?

Her left eye flutters open, the rest of her body remaining still. She sees pin pricks of dull, throbbing, pulsing light. The rest of the world is a blurry haze. She tries to move and is greeted with a wall of pain in the back of her head. The pulsing makes her nauseous. She cracks open her right eye, evaluating the situation.

She can't see the cart or the tractor. She can tell she's sitting upright, but she can't move. She can feel something against her arms and legs, rope or tape perhaps, but her hands and feet are numb. She's tied to something. A chair? A tree?

Her first instinct is to stay very still, to not attract attention to herself or let anyone know she is conscious. She opens her eyes a bit wider and sees a shape, muttering as it paces back and forth in front of her—Albert. She remembers him attacking her in the Level 8 orchard, but where are they now?

"I see you're finally awake," Albert mutters, still pacing.

"Albert, why did you do this?"

"I want answers," he growls. "I want to know what really happened to my brother. And I want him to have justice."

Liz can hear the weariness in her own voice as she speaks. "Nothing I can say will bring him back."

"Don't you think I know that?" A crimson wave crashes over his face as he grabs his hair, still pacing. He strides toward her, leaning ominously over her body as he glares into her eyes. "I want the truth. I *need* to know."

"Albert," she begins softly, "I still need the captain's permission to …"

The man plants a right hook squarely on her jaw, and the dim light fades to black.

Liz fights her way to awareness again, trying to survey her surroundings before Albert knows she's awake. She is tied to a tree. Can she break the rope? Wriggle free? No, she doesn't have the strength for that.

On the edge of her vision, she thinks she sees a dim outline of the tractor. Albert must have taken her on the service lift to a different level, an abandoned one. But which? There are twenty abandoned growing levels, and each one is huge. Liz can see the shadow of trees, but that doesn't help. Most of the levels have trees, and without knowing what kind, all she can deduce is that she and Albert are well hidden.

I can't assume anyone will find me, she realizes, feeling the spot on her left wrist, naked without the communicator Albert took from her. *No doubt he took my gun and knife too,* she thinks ruefully, knowing that they must be close by but that even if she gets loose, she can't afford to lose time searching for them. They might be in the cart, or on the tractor, or hidden somewhere in the trees. *Fresh hell, he might even have them on his person.*

She broadens her awareness again, and she hears a new sound—the subtle lapping of water. There is only one abandoned level with a reservoir. They're on Level 13.

"I know you're awake." Albert's voice is low and even. He looks at her with a vacant stare. "I didn't get to tell him goodbye, you know. I finished my shift and went back to our bunk and saw a note he left for me. It said he was chosen for a day-long security drill with Liz Goeff, and he might not be back for dinner. I could tell he wrote it in a hurry."

Liz lets him lapse into silence, unsure what else to do. Her mind is racing through countless scenarios, trying to find some advantage or some way out of this. Suddenly, his eyes jerk back to rest on her.

"You didn't deserve to have his last few minutes. You didn't deserve to hear his final words. You, of all people. Those words should have been mine—those minutes belonged to me," he hisses.

He's right, Liz thinks, knowing that if Sam had last words, they were forever lost. She saw him lying on the warehouse floor in a pool of blood, but by the time she got to him, he was dead.

"What happened to him?" Albert pleads with her, leaning in close to her face, eyes full of desperation.

"We were betrayed, Albert," she whispers, feeling his grief flow through her. "I tried to save Sam, but I was too late. I … Albert, this isn't the way!"

He slaps her, open-handed. It stings but isn't hard enough to knock her unconscious.

"Bushwa! Stop lying to me!"

"Albert," Liz says evenly, feeling her insides starting to burn, "don't you know I would have gladly traded places with him?"

"Then why didn't you?" he demands. "Why wasn't it you instead of him?"

"Because that's just not the way it happened," she spews back at him. "I'm not your enemy. Now let me go before you cross a line you can't uncross!"

"No, Liz!" Albert roars. "Here's how this works. I ask the questions, and you answer them. That's it!"

She thinks he might hit her again as he rushes her, but instead he stops short, clenching his fist in a rage he struggles to control.

"You killed my brother on a surface mission and then a week later bring up fifty-two unknown survivors. You knew they were spies, and you knew my brother wouldn't stand for it! So, you stole his life. You stole my brother. You stole my future. You stole everything about this world that makes sense," he says fiercely.

"Your brother was my friend," Liz says sadly, realizing that in this moment, no amount of truth will stay Albert's rage.

The man's face contorts as he screams with anguish, "I want the truth! When did people on this ship stop caring about the truth? When did people stop caring about justice?"

Liz doesn't know how to answer this, but it seems Albert doesn't expect her to. He paces in front of her, back and forth, clutching his head in his hands.

"I certainly have to give you credit for your elaborate story to get me here," Liz says bitterly, mind unable to process any more possible scenarios for escape. "You knew just what to say to lure me in, didn't you?"

"Story?" Albert looks at her with amusement, squatting in front of her. "No, Liz, I didn't have to make up any story. Why would I even try? The truth is far stranger than anything I could imagine."

"So then what did you find? What did you intend to show me?" she demands.

"Well, sure, that part was made up. But the code words, passing items, all that stuff is true. This can't be new information to you, Liz. You brought some of these people on board."

"No, I rescued fifty-two survivors. They aren't spies."

Albert studies her, then breaks out into a maniacal laugh. "You actually believe that, don't you?"

Liz has no response. She's angry he's laughing at her, but she is also confused and bewildered.

"What have you seen, Albert?" she demands. "What do you know?"

He laughs until tears roll down his face, and then his laughter becomes sobs—horrible wailing, cries as a waterfall of tears cascades down his contorted face. He stands up and turns his back to her, hands pulling at his hair. She can hear him sucking breath into his body, trying to quell the tears.

He spins around to face her again, face filled with anger. "I don't believe you!" he screams, briskly stepping toward her. She thinks he might kick her, so she tries to brace herself, but instead he plants his fist in the trunk of the tree. She feels the whole tree shudder, and small pieces of bark land in her hair. "Of course you knew about this. You killed my brother to protect the New Generation!"

Even in her compromised position, this makes Liz furious. She screams without restraint, "The New Generation took everything I had! They took my home. They starved my mother. They took my brother. And I thought they killed him too, but now I find out it's worse than that. They've turned him into a monster! Sam knew how much I hated them. Sam knew how much I lost! So don't claim to know your brother so well and accuse me of being a traitor in the same breath." She looks at him defiantly, waiting for whatever price she will have to pay for her outburst.

Albert studies her for a moment longer before his face crumples, shoulders slumped. "You really don't know why he died, do you?" he says softly.

"I do know why he died," she says firmly, no longer concerned about the formality of Seth releasing information. "He died because Ellen Ryan betrayed us. She was a spy, and when we went down to the surface she tried to contact the Minneapolis New Generation. She killed Sam and then tried to kill me so that they could hijack the shuttle." She feels her own face crack and hot tears begin to erupt.

"You're right about some things," she says, voice thick with tears. "It is my fault Sam died. I chose him for the mission, and Ellen too, because I thought they were both incorruptible. But I was wrong. It is my fault. It was my mission, my responsibility.

"If I could trade places with him, I would have done it already. The best justice for Sam is to keep going, Albert. That's what he would want you to do—continue believing in the Green Grow mission."

"I don't believe in anything anymore," he says softly as he turns his back to her and walks to the cart. When he returns, he holds her pistol tentatively in his hands. It's awkward in his grip.

Everything Liz is thinking and feeling drains from her body. She has no options here. No way to defend herself, unless she can talk him down.

"Albert," she whispers, "what are you doing? This isn't who you are. This isn't what Sam would want."

"Sam is dead," Albert says deadpan. "He's not here to want anything anymore." He aims the gun at her, eyes sad. "You know, I can't figure you out. All this time I've watched and learned just how bizarre everything is on this ship. First, I thought you were a traitor, then I thought you were being used. Now, I can't tell. Are you the beguiler or the beguiled, Liz? Do you even know?"

Liz opens her mouth to respond, but no words come. He starts crying again as he continues to speak.

"I'll tell you what I know. No one on this ship cares about my brother. No one cares about justice. Not you, not Captain Harris, and certainly not Harry Goodworth." His voice gets louder, growing with angry momentum. "You're all too immersed in your petty drama and infighting to remember what matters here. My brother mattered. Justice matters. He should still be alive, and he's not. And there's one thing both you and I agree on, Liz Goeff—it's your fault."

He levels the gun at her. Liz's eyes take in the scene, and she feels her heart beat faster. Beyond that, she feels nothing. She watches as Albert's hand begins to tremble, and he lowers the gun.

"You know," he continues, "I tried to get people to listen. I thought Harry might help me; he's always been fair and level headed. But as soon as I mention your name, it all changes. You have them all entranced, Liz. No doubt we all know how you keep the captain enamored with you, but it doesn't even stop there. Harry. The other pickers. The people who worked with you before. They all think you're some kind of goddess.

"Do you know Harry actually reprimanded me for asking questions about you? He told me that I needed to be careful about spreading unfounded rumors about you and contributing to the crew's panic after your brother tried to take over the ship. Your brother, for fuck's sake! Yet still, no one questions you.

"Do you know after all of that, he actually had the nerve to tell me that he was sorry about Sam's death? That I needed to be patient? I don't need to be patient, Liz. I can't. The only thing at the end of the waiting is everyone forgetting Sam. No one cares what happened to him. There's no place for his memory here anymore! The only justice he will get is what I give him."

Liz's eyes grow wide. "No, Albert. You'll be executed. Don't you think there's been enough killing?"

Albert's face flushes purple. "There's been more than enough killing, Liz! It should've stopped before Sam died. We were supposed to be safe. We made it to the Green Grow 3. The danger was supposed to be behind us!"

"Albert, I know." Liz feels hot tears flow down her face. "But none of us were really safe. We weren't going to be safe until we got out of the New Generation's killing range. That's what Sam was doing with me in Minneapolis—getting the antimatter for the drive we needed to leave orbit."

"Bushwa!" Albert cries. "Don't try to make this something that it's not. There's no reason for his death. No one cares. Nothing matters. He's too good for this place anyway. And without him, none of this makes sense for me."

He levels the pistol, aiming at her head. She refuses to look away. There is nothing more for her to say, but she won't give him the satisfaction of breaking eye contact. His hand starts to tremble again, and he screams in anguish as he lowers the gun again.

"This is too good for you. You don't deserve a quick end," he says as he turns away, stomping back to the cart. She hears him toss the pistol onto the metal. She can see his chest heaving. She can feel her heart breaking. His muffled sobs reach her, and then she hears him mumbling, but she can't make out the words. He turns toward her again, and this time he holds her knife. Her stomach lurches, seeing someone else hold it. No one touches her knife.

"Is this what you used to kill him?" he asks.

"No," Liz says flatly, noticing how awkwardly he grips the knife. "If I killed Sam, it was with bad judgment, but I've used that knife to kill plenty of other people."

"Yes, this is more just," he says, eyes dark as he strides toward her, bending only slightly to press the tip into her neck. She can feel the sharpness of it, and then a small dribble down her skin. She always keeps it razor-sharp, so this won't take long—even if he doesn't know what he is doing. Liz sees his eyes widen.

"You see the blood, don't you?" she says. "That's just a tiny bit. Don't worry, there's so much more to come. I cut Ellen's throat, there in Minneapolis—after she killed Sam. Her blood spewed out of her body like a raging river,

Albert. All of her life force. All of her wisdom and experience, it just flowed out until she was no more. Prepare yourself, Albert. Killing people is bloody business."

His eyes look uncertain as she continues, "I know Sam wasn't a killer. He was brave and strong, but he wasn't a killer. And I'm thankful he never had to carry the burden of taking someone's life, Albert. It's heavy. Oh so heavy. You don't look like a killer either. Is that what you want to become? The very thing you say you hate? Don't you think there are enough killers here, Albert?"

She is done reasoning with him. She expects to feel the blade plunge deeper. She expects some pain, and then hopefully that sense of disconnected numbness she's seen creep over the faces of the others she's killed. But she won't let him pretend it's something it's not.

Her eyes jump back to the cart as she hears her wristband communicator buzz against the metal of the cart's floor. Seth is paging her. What will he do when she doesn't respond?

She feels the tip of the knife fall away as Albert jumps back.

"What's that?" he demands.

"Captain Harris is paging me. And when I don't respond, he'll come looking for me. It won't take long, Albert. He can track me. So, untie me and let me respond to him. Please Albert. Let's put the killing behind us. No one needs to know what happened here."

"No!" His eyes are frantic. "I won't let you brush Sam's death under the rug! He deserves justice!"

"The best justice is to live, Albert. And to serve. Help us get home. Help us keep the ship safe."

"That's not justice!" he wails. "That's not justice at all. He deserves more. He deserves … He …" Albert's face falls.

Liz suddenly feels frantic, wanting to know what he is thinking.

"Albert! Talk to me!"

"There's no justice to be had for him, is there? No one will do anything to make this right. And even if they try, nothing *can* make it right. I can't go on like this, Liz." His eyes grow wide, filled with tears as he clutches the knife. "None of this makes sense anymore. There's no place for me here. I can't sell myself out like all of you have done."

"Albert, I'll help you get through this! We all will."

"No. No. No." Albert's eyes look far away. "I can't. I just can't. He's coming, isn't he?" His voice quiets to a whisper. "Captain Harris is coming, isn't he?"

"Yes, but there's still time, Albert. Untie me. We can fix this."

He looks at her. She thinks he might be considering her offer. He might untie her. She hopes he will. She couldn't save Sam, but maybe she can save Albert. Then she sees panic wash over his face.

"No, Albert! Stay with me!" Liz pulls against the rope, and feels her arms stretch tight around the tree. His eyes lock with hers for a moment, looking uncertain and full of pain. Then he looks down at her knife, wraps both hands firmly around the rubberized tactical handle she knows so very well, and with a final cry, plunges the blade right underneath his sternum, up toward his heart.

Liz hears her wrist band communicator buzz again. She screams, pushing her back against the tree, writhing against the ropes as she tries to get free. She hears one shoulder pop but feels no pain. All she can sense is Albert's life force slowly draining from his body. He looks up at her briefly before he slumps forward, head bowing close to the handle of the knife as he rests on his knees.

"Hold on, Albert!" Liz screams. "Seth will find us. You have to hold on!"

He looks up at her again and smiles before his head falls for the final time. She's seen it enough to know that he's gone. Liz sits there crying, feeling like her heart might explode in her chest. She doesn't know how much time passes. Her wristband communicator buzzes again, but there's nothing she can do except wait until Seth finds her.

She wishes she could hold Albert's hand. His lifeless body seems so very forlorn and alone, collapsed on the ground only a few feet from her. The man was right—she lost sight of Sam's death. It seemed like so many more important things were happening, with Jackson and Mathilda.

Another casualty of the New Generation? she wonders. But no, she only has herself to blame for this. She could have made the time for Albert. She could have talked to him without Seth's approval. No doubt, she's committed far more disobedient acts. She looks at the man's body again and cries, hot tears raging down her face as if they've been building for years. Maybe they have.

"I'm here, Albert," she says, "and I'm sorry."

She hopes Sam is there to meet him on the other side, wherever it is that he went in death. She hopes he finds the peace he wanted.

"I'll be better in the future, Albert. I'll do better. I'll make the time to listen."

With nothing left to say, heart still aching, Liz does the only thing she can think to do. She begins to hum, and then to sing.

"Hush-a-bye, don't you cry. Go to sleep, my little baby. When you wake, you shall have, all the pretty little horses. Blacks and grays, dapples and bays—all the pretty little horses."

By the time Seth finds her and cuts her free from her bindings, she is so hoarse she can barely whisper the words of the lullaby, but she still sings. He scoops her up into her arms, babbling words she doesn't bother to try to understand, as he carries her to the medical unit.

CHAPTER 18

ALPHA

***

"Don't let her put me in another coma," Liz whispers to Seth, her voice still hoarse and ragged. Claire's eyes grow wide as she approaches Liz, attempting to look innocent.

"You've suffered another concussion," she concludes after taking a scan of her head. "And you dislocated your shoulder. You need to rest and wear this brace." Claire points to the thin sleeve that stretches firmly around her shoulder and straps across her chest. Liz nods in acknowledgment. Honestly, she is ready for some rest, and the brace is barely noticeable.

"You also cracked three ribs," Claire continues, her voice turning sour, "and if you trust me enough to put you in the bone mender for a few minutes, we can take care of those now."

"Agreed," Liz says flatly, completely uninterested in the status of Claire's pride right now.

"You should leave the bandages on your wrists for another day or so, and unfortunately there's not much I can do for the bruises and contusions on your face. They will definitely look worse before they look better, but I can give you cold packs to treat the swelling."

Liz looks at her bandaged wrists, suddenly washed in memories of her mother cutting her own wrists. She squeezes her eyes shut, knowing the memories will still come. Seth stays by her side as she lies on the table to allow the bone mender to heal her ribs.

"Holy bearcats, Z," he murmurs as his mother leaves the room to retrieve the cold packs while the machine pulsates its signature little red lights. "He could have killed you."

"No, Seth," Liz says ruefully. "He couldn't have. He's not a killer." *Wasn't,* she reminds herself. *He wasn't a killer.*

"I failed him," she continues. "We failed him."

Seth tries to interrupt her but she refuses to allow it.

"Seth, we failed him. It's no wonder our crew is so divided. Everyone who has betrayed us talks about how welcoming the New Generation was to them. How they feel like they're part of something important. But what did we do for Albert? What did I do? I couldn't even be bothered to talk to him, to comfort him when his whole world flipped on its head. If we can't do better than that by our own crew, then what is all this for?"

Seth studies her intently, finding no response.

✳✳✳

Liz stares at the increasingly familiar *connecting* message on the screen of the tablet, but this time she sits in front of the device alone. She doesn't plan to make a habit of this, but just this time, she will speak to Jackson without Seth by her side. Finally, his increasingly familiar face fills the screen, first impassive and then filled with bewildered concern.

"Lizzie, what happened to your face! Are you okay?"

"I'm fine," she says, feeling no emotion about her bruises and contusions. "A score needed settling, but it's over now."

"A score?" he asks, incredulous. "Is this how you settle scores on the Green Grow 3?"

"You should see the other guy," Liz replies bitterly.

"Oh? What does he look like?"

"He's dead," she says flatly.

Jackson looks shocked and bewildered, but he finally nods his head in agreement. "Very well, then. It seems your world is just as brutal as the one you think I live in, isn't it?"

"Maybe," she replies with indifference, not interesting in discussing the merits of their respective experiences. "Look, I told Seth I wanted to speak to you alone tonight because I need information. And Jackson, I need you to be honest with me. We need to set aside whatever differences we have and figure out how we are going to work together. I'm tired of this war. I'm tired of the casualties. And I'm tired of being confused about who is right and who is wrong. Tell me, Jackson, can we have an honest conversation?"

His eyes widen as he answers earnestly, "Of course."

"Tell me about the New Generation," she says urgently. Jackson's eyes widen more.

"Of course. What do you want to know?"

"I want to know everything. I want to know why I hate the New Generation so much, and yet you've still been able to turn people."

"Well, Lizzie, that's not a simple discussion," he says soberly. "But I will tell you what I can."

***

"I should start at the beginning," Jackson says thoughtfully, "but which one? There have been many beginnings and many ends. That's important for you to know, Lizzie. Things have changed so much over time.

"I'll admit that you aren't entirely wrong about the New Generation, although I'm only willing to tell you this because I truly want to be honest with you. I was shocked when I first joined up. It was hard in the beginning for me to find my place—to find my way. But I knew I had to stay. I knew I had to conquer the organization from the inside out, because the triumph of the New Generation was inevitable."

"Inevitable?" Liz asks.

"Oh, yes. On the surface, the war is over."

"So there aren't any peace talks?"

Jackson considers his words, and after a silence, continues.

"The world is a big place, Lizzie. The battles that we fight are ours and ours alone. We are but one piece on the chess board, alone in our square but surrounded by so many others."

"Speak plainly, Jackson," Liz admonishes.

"We have to unite, Lizzie, or we will all be conquered," he explains. "While you and yours have been hiding in space, our situation on the surface has gotten even more precarious. To the south, Mexico has closed the border. Anyone who tries to go beyond the flood basalt is turned back. To the north, the situation is more dire even than we face here. The Canadians are coming, and they aren't coming peacefully. And meanwhile, what remained of the Green Grow Executive Board fled. Haven't you wondered what happened to the Green Grow 2, Lizzie?"

"Of course," she says. "We've all wondered. Ever since Captain MacAbee went to the peace summit, we've been cut off from the Board and the Green Grow 2." She is certain this isn't new information for him. It simply can't be.

"I was there in Detroit, for the summit," Jackson says without ceremony. Liz feels her stomach drop. *What is he going to tell her next? Can she believe him?* "The Executive Board was weak, Lizzie. They were nothing more than pampered, spoiled children trying to get the best deal for themselves. They never intended to work with us. And no doubt, it would have been challenging. Green Grow was a corporation. The New Generation is more like a set of related tribes—I am influential in the Western region, but not so much in the Midwest or the East. When I arrived in Detroit, the negotiations had already gone straight to hell. The Midwest captain was firing on a shuttle, I believe the one piloted by Captain MacAbee. The remaining members of the Executive Board used the diversion to take off in the other shuttle, and I believe they continue to hide on the Green Grow 2."

"No, that can't be true," Liz says. "We would detect them orbiting the earth."

"Maybe. If they were orbiting the earth, but I don't think they are. I have an idea of where they are hiding, but it's only speculation. I've intercepted a few radio transmissions that indicate they're attempting to negotiate terms with India and China."

"India and China? But why?"

"Because they don't really care about saving anyone but themselves, Lizzie. Those places aren't struggling the way we're struggling. They can still grow food on the surface. They aren't killing each other or starving. They aren't as dangerous. So, instead of focusing exclusively on producing food, the Board can focus on other priorities— the science of space, engineering, medicine."

"So why don't they contact us?" Liz presses.

"Best I can tell, they've left you there to distract people like me, until they can secure a better deal for themselves with a country equipped to protect them."

"So what happened to Captain MacAbee?"

"I don't know," Jackson says solemnly. "His shuttle took a hit, and he went down somewhere over the Great Lakes. We looked for a while, but it took too many resources."

Liz finds it hard to believe they would simply give up looking for a shuttle. She speaks tentatively, "When I was in Minneapolis, Ellen Ryan tried to contact the New Generation there. She killed the other man on our team, Sam Wyndham, and then she tried to kill me. The New Generation wanted the shuttle."

Jackson's face darkens. "She didn't understand the nature of the organization as well as she should have. She must have thought there would be a way for our Western faction to work with the Midwest faction. Even had she been successful, they would have killed her too."

"Bushwa, Jackson! If you had the chance to hijack a shuttle, you would have taken it just as fast as those people did."

Jackson laughs. "Well of course I would, Lizzie! But I wouldn't kill you. In fact, there's a standing order across the Western region that you are not to be harmed. It certainly hasn't made me popular among my subordinates, but you are my family—I am your brother. I will always protect you as much as I can."

His face grows serious again as he continues. "But yes, I would do anything short of that to get a shuttle. We all want the ship, Lizzie—all of the New Generation. The difference between us is what we want to do with it."

"What do you mean?" she asks.

"Well, I'd restart the food supply," he says eagerly. "And I'd set up a research station on it to study the earth. I'm a scientist, Lizzie, not a leader. But leading people, well, it's been necessary. So many things have been necessary— things I'm not proud of.

"We're in trouble here, Lizzie. Birth rates are declining, and cancer seems to be growing in prevalence. The atmosphere is continuing to change in ways we don't understand, and I don't know if humanity can survive it. The Green Grow 3 could be a lifeline for our whole species."

"And the others? What would they do with the ship?" she inquires.

"Lizzie, the other factions of the New Generation are …" Jackson searches for the right word. "Fundamentalists, I suppose. Some of them actually want to destroy the ship, as a show of strength to quash any more questions about who is in charge. Others want to turn the Green Grow 3 into a weapon."

"A weapon?" This is too much to believe.

"Yes, a weapon," he confirms. "To conquer other parts of the world and take what they have. I'm sure it sounds strange," he admits, "but at the end of it all, Lizzie, people are animals, and many of them are still ruled by baser instincts—by fear. They see the disasters not as something to be overcome but as punishment that requires atonement, punishment for living too freely."

"It's important for you to know, Lizzie, that people like Willow Brown and Mathilda didn't sign up for the New Generation, per se. They signed up for a dream—my dream. And if we can't make that dream come true, Lizzie, we will leave nothing but hell for those who come after us."

"And yet," Liz replies, "the Green Grow 3 is flying farther and farther away. Even if we want to help, we are limited in what we can do."

"Yes," he agrees. "On the face, it seems very unfortunate. But, there are still ways we can help each other. I can hold on here for a while, and a while longer if we can grow more food and develop better medicine. Those improvements will give me enough leverage to maintain and perhaps even expand my circle of influence. And who knows what opportunity this may provide? We must always stay vigilant for opportunities."

Liz finds herself nodding. She finds herself hoping, and maybe even believing—just a little bit. *He's really charismatic, isn't he?* Liz begins to understand how people get swept up in his message.

"I need to go, Jackson," she says after a thoughtful moment.

"Can we speak again, Lizzie? Just you and me?" he asks, looking hopeful.

"We'll take it as it comes," she says, not wanting to commit to anything. "But in the meantime, Mathilda is fine, and Claire is putting together the information we agreed to send you."

Jackson's face sours. "Good, I'm glad the *captain* didn't execute her."

Liz studies him a moment.

"What is your problem with Seth?" she asks.

Jackson looks startled. "Don't you see how weak he is?"

"No," she says, "I don't."

Jackson looks at her, contemplating what to say, and sighs deeply.

"Goodnight, Lizzie. I hope you rest well and heal soon."

Liz terminates the call and then powers down the tablet, carefully placing it back into the pillowcase she still uses to house the strange antenna as well as the modified device. She takes a deep breath before seeking out Seth's bright blue eyes, right across the table where he's been sitting for the entire conversation.

"What do you think?" he asks. Liz simply shakes her head, trying to process everything Jackson told her.

"It's a lot to take in," she says, "but I'm not sure why he would lie. It would be a lot to fabricate."

"Indeed," Seth replies, "but now we know what he has that we don't—a dream."

Liz feels the bruises on her face begin to pulse. She goes to the bathroom to splash water on it. When she emerges, Seth stands waiting to fold her in his arms. He gently kisses her forehead, then her nose and then her lips.

"We have time to figure this out," he whispers in her ear.

"Stay with me tonight?" she asks. She couldn't feel more grotesque, with all the swelling in her face and body, but she needs him nonetheless. No matter what her brother says, she knows now that Seth will always be her refuge, her soft place to fall, her protector and her hiding place. And tonight, she needs to hide.

***

Elsewhere on Level 1, Mathilda Greenberg sits in her office, poring over sheets of numbers from the data file Jackson had sent. Her eyes gleam as she carefully counts, making notes on a scratch pad. Of course, she's already processed the primary message: their turnaround point. And it is exciting. Jackson labeled it Omega.

She likes the name—it signifies the end point of their journey out—but it's not the name that has her excited. The information about Omega's solar system is far more interesting, although by the time this data started flowing into the Hubble telescope, humanity had bigger problems to solve at home.

Omega itself is a rocky planet, just the right distance away from the star it orbits. Initial readings suggest it has a breathable atmosphere. Could it have water? Could it be habitable? Can they really get there? It's so far away. Jackson seems to want them to speed up—a lot. He said he will give them ways to slow down, and Mathilda believes this as surely as she believes the air around her will continue to fill her lungs.

The information about Omega is very exciting, but even more exciting is the Walkabout 2—a deep space probe already in the depths of space between them and the planet that Jackson reprogrammed to move into its orbit. Mathilda has to do the math about how long it will take to get there, but it will still be at least slightly ahead of the Green Grow 3. And those are the obvious parts of his message.

What Mathilda is most excited about is the hidden messages. She can't wait to see what Jackson has in store for her next. And so, she sits there gleefully astonished as it starts to come together in her mind. Is this really possible? She wants to call Jackson, but she doubts he will answer. He generally seems to be busy when she tries to call him, but she knows how much she matters to him. He simply has other things to tend to.

CHAPTER 19

OMEGA

***

The scientist sits alone in his secret lab, one final time. He needs no further tests on the transporter, and so he has Alex engaged in other matters. He tidies his notes, downloads the files from his computer onto a portable drive, and takes one final look before he closes and locks the door behind him. The game has changed now, but that's okay. Changing situations—whether by chance or intention—create a whole new set of opportunities to explore. It's a glorious challenge, and he feels hopeful once more.

He still needs the transporter, just not right now. The Green Grow 3 is hurtling through space, and he needs the ship to slow down, for its coordinates to be comfortably predictable. As bold as he is, he's not willing to risk his own life on the extreme precision required to predict the location of a vessel moving so fast.

In the meantime, he has many other things to do. Mathilda is keeping him busy. She's usually such a bright, articulate woman, but she's not at her best now. She's distraught and distracted, a bit needy and clingy. He accommodates her the best he can, although it's wearisome at times. He thinks of her as indispensable, but perhaps he should reconsider that. *Indispensable* is such a severe word anyway—judgmental and permanent. He knows he still needs her, for now. But perhaps even that will change in the future. In fact, he knows it will.

He quietly navigates his quarters, pausing for a moment to study the sleeping woman nestled in his bed. Shelby. Mathilda doesn't know about Shelby, and he knows that Mathilda will not abide when she finds out. Shelby will be a nasty surprise for sure, but even though he's allowed Mathilda to believe he has feelings for her, he doesn't. She has no right to expect anything from him. She sees what she wants to see, and he makes no promises.

At the same time, he knows he doesn't need Shelby either, not really. He could go on without her, but he doesn't want to. Just as energy never dies, neither does love. He wants to curl up next to her in the bed, to feel the warmth of her body and smell her hair. But he won't disturb her yet. He still has business to tend to. So, he finds his tablet and settles into the farthest corner of the room, a small nook where the light won't disturb his sleeping love. He sees that Mathilda sent him more messages, but she will have to wait.

It's time to make a call. And so, he secures his tablet to a portable stand, types in some numbers, and waits. He can be patient, at least for a little while. He calls up the image he so often uses to calm his mind – the woman and the baby. His mother has a beautiful, symmetrical face, and his little sister overflows with life. Of course, his mother is gone, and he feels no sorrow about that. He has no need of someone so weak. But his sister—she still overflows with life, a ferocious, beautiful life of which he is so proud. She is strong, and she is worthy. He knows her path hasn't been easy, but thinking of how she's blossomed makes him smile.

Brushing the image affectionately out of his mind, he opens his eyes, just in time to see a worn, wrinkled face fill the screen.

"Jackson Goeff," the old woman says evenly, her brown eyes soft but scrutinizing.

"Ruth," he replies warmly. "I'm so glad we've connected. There is business that needs doing, and I can't do it without you."

"I sincerely doubt that," she says, "but please tell me more."

Jackson is not pleased, but he maintains a neutral expression.

"Seth Harris is still alive," he says flatly.

"Indeed," Ruth replies, face impassive.

"Kill him, and we will be even."

"We're already even, Jackson. You gave me a suggestion to go to the depot and a head start to get there before you slaughtered us all. I connected you to the ship's servers to disable the propulsion drive. I'm sorry it didn't work out like you hoped, but our deal is done."

"I saved your lives." Jackson's meaning is clear.

"No dear, your sister did that. Not just the children, as you imagined, but all of us. She stepped outside the depot gate and cast her lot with us, picking off your men until we were all safe. We are Liz's fifty-two now, and I won't betray her like that."

"Her?" Jackson cocks an eyebrow.

"She loves Seth Harris, and I won't be the one to take him away from her."

"She told you that?" Jackson is indignant.

"She doesn't need to, Jackson. Some things can be known without telling."

He considers this.

"Will you work against me?" he asks.

Ruth isn't expecting this. She appraises him thoughtfully before replying.

"No."

He nods.

"I can accept that."

"Good."

"I may have further need of you," Jackson admonishes.

Ruth sighs, "I'm an old woman, Jackson, and I'm too tired for shenanigans. If you want something from me, make it plain."

"Fair enough," he says. "We'll talk when I arrive."

"Oh? When are you coming?"

"I don't yet know precisely," he admits.

Ruth nods. "Then I'll see you when you get here."

"Goodnight, Ruth." Jackson ends the call before she can reply, but she doesn't mind. She wraps the tablet carefully in a spare tunic, deciding she can wait until the morning to give it back to Will. She tucks herself into the narrow bed of her new quarters, which is profoundly more comfortable than the quarantine cot or any other bed she can remember. The room itself is plain, but it will do for now.

"Are we finally done with him?" Ellis asks from the other narrow bed across the room. His blue eyes pierce her weary face.

"The better question," she replies, "is whether he's done with us."

Time will tell, but it's not tonight's problem. She closes her eyes and waits for sleep to find her.

ACKNOWLEDGEMENTS

It may not require a village to write a book, but it sure does help. I am grateful to everyone who helped me along the way, and indeed it has been a long journey. I'd like to extend special thanks to a few extraordinary people who helped me get this far—those who walked next to me, pushed from behind, pulled from ahead, and sometimes carried me until I could take my own steps yet again. To Max Regan at Hollowdeck Press, thank you for mentoring, encouraging, and inspiring me—for patiently holding my hand as I took my first steps in this new world called the writing industry. To Jennifer Rees, the developmental editor who told me the truth, thank you for always fitting me into your schedule, for telling me where I'm strong as well as where I'm weak, and most importantly, for believing in me. To Dylan Garity, thank you for keeping me on track when I was inclined to jar my readers, and for all of your brilliant editorial contributions—especially the fact checking. To Dane Low, thank you for a cover design that inspired me to stay the course, to do the work I needed to do to make the story worthy of such a great cover. To Laura Flavin, none of this would have been possible without your tutelage and friendly support—thank you for helping me navigate the publishing waters. To Maggie Babb and the Firedrake Writers, thank you for opening your arms and your community to me, for holding space to laugh, cry, celebrate, despair, and most importantly, to write. Finally, if you've read this far, thank you. I look forward to sharing many more adventures together.

ABOUT THE AUTHOR

C.J. Hall is a former civil servant who now indulges her passion for writing full time. She lives quietly in the woods, with her slightly neurotic canine companion named Crash, where she writes passionately, reads avidly, and tends the land with care. *Evolving Elizah: Initiatum* is her debut novel. For more information, visit www.CJ-Hall.com